Spring Fling

Spring Fling

A Novel

Annie England Noblin

AVON

An Imprint of HarperCollins*Publishers*

SPRING FLING. Copyright © 2025 by Annie England Noblin. All rights reserved. Printed in the United States of America. No part of this book may be used or reproduced in any manner whatsoever without written permission except in the case of brief quotations embodied in critical articles and reviews. For information, address HarperCollins Publishers, 195 Broadway, New York, NY 10007.

HarperCollins books may be purchased for educational, business, or sales promotional use. For information, please email the Special Markets Department at SPsales@harpercollins.com.

Avon, Avon & logo, and Avon Books & logo are registered trademarks of HarperCollins Publishers in the United States of America and other countries.

FIRST EDITION

Interior text design by Diahann Sturge-Campbell
Fishing boat art © Serafima Antipova/Shutterstock

Library of Congress Cataloging-in-Publication Data

Names: Noblin, Annie England, author.

Title: Spring fling : a novel / Annie England Noblin.

Description: First edition. | New York, NY : Avon, 2025.

Identifiers: LCCN 2024010277 | ISBN 9780063222281 (paperback) | ISBN 9780063222298 (ebook)

Subjects: LCGFT: Romance fiction. | Novels

Classification: LCC PS3614.O27 S67 2025 | DDC 813/.6—dc23/eng/20240307

LC record available at https://lccn.loc.gov/2024010277

ISBN 978-0-06-322228-1

ISBN: 978-0-06-342758-7 (hardcover)

25 26 27 28 29 LBC 5 4 3 2 1

For my parents, Gregg and Paula:
high school sweethearts since 1973

Spring Fling

Mylie fumbled with her graduation cap, threading her fingers through the blue-and-white tassel. Now that the ceremony was over, people were streaming in and out of the high school gym, arm in arm, happy and smiling, on their way to graduation parties and other festivities. Mylie had a couple to get to herself, but she wanted to talk to *him* first.

When he saw her, sitting on the picnic table, he grinned and walked over. He was so tall that his gown was just short enough to be noticeable, and his mass of dark curls spilled out of his cap like ink.

"Hey," he said, hopping up on the table to sit next to her. "I looked for you inside."

"It was crowded," Mylie replied, looking up at him. His glasses were crooked on his nose.

"How do you think I did on my speech?"

"You know it was great, Ben," Mylie replied. "Everything you do is great."

He bumped his shoulder into hers and said, "You all right?"

"I'm fine."

"You don't seem fine," Ben replied. "Besides, you told me once that when a woman says she's fine, she's really not."

"I did say that, didn't I?" Mylie asked, grinning despite herself.

"You did," Ben said. "So, tell me what's wrong."

"Do you really have to leave?" she blurted. "Why can't you at least spend the summer here?"

"We're moving tomorrow, Myles," Ben said. "There's nothing I can do."

"You're an adult," Mylie said. "You can do whatever you want."

"I'm going to college in Chicago," Ben continued. "And I need to help get Mom and Grandpa settled before that. Besides, what would I do here for the next three months?"

Mylie shrugged. "What we always do."

"Mylie," Ben said, his voice gentle. "You know I have to go."

"But you're my best friend."

"And you're *my* best friend."

"So, stay!"

Ben sighed. "I have to get out of here, Mylie. You know I've never fit in. Not the way you do. Clay Creek isn't my future."

Mylie knew that. She'd known that since the sixth grade. But it didn't make it any easier, not when he was leaving her behind and not when she was losing her best friend to a college that might as well be on another planet.

"Please don't be mad at me, Myles," Ben said, taking her hand in his. "We'll still talk. It won't be that bad, I promise. And we've got the party tonight. That will be fun."

"When will you be back?" Mylie asked. She was trying not to cry, but it was hard.

"I don't know," Ben said. "We aren't selling Grandpa's house right now, but I don't know of any reason why we . . ."

"Would need to come back?" Mylie finished. She yanked her hand away from him.

"That's not what I meant," Ben said.

Mylie glared at him. "Yes, it is."

"Mylie . . ."

"It's okay," Mylie said at last. "I know you have to go. It's just . . . I'm going to miss you."

"I'm going to miss you, too," Ben said, leaning in to wrap her in a giant hug. For a moment, Mylie thought he was going to do more than just hug her, but he pulled away, pushing his glasses farther up onto his nose.

"I'll see you at the party, then," Ben said. "I've got to go. My mom *still* hasn't gotten enough pictures."

Mylie wiped her eyes, clearing the streaks of mascara running down her cheeks with the back of her hand as Ben walked away. She wanted to tell him so badly how she felt. But she knew that the night of their graduation wasn't the time. It was never the time, especially since she knew that Ben was leaving, had always planned on leaving, no matter what.

For now, there was nothing she could do but watch him walk away from her, from here, and from everything Mylie always knew they could have been.

"Hey! Hey, Mylie!"

Mylie looked up to see her friend Jodi walking toward her, waving her graduation cap in the air. "Hey," Mylie said.

"I've been looking for you everywhere," Jodi said. "My mom wants pictures, and I'm pretty sure Ben's mom does, too."

"I'm pictured out," Mylie replied.

Jodi squinted at her in the waning sunlight. "Did you tell him?"

Mylie shook her head.

"Why not?" Jodi asked. "You said it wouldn't matter now, anyway, since he's leaving. Might as well tell him, remember?"

"I know what I said," Mylie replied. "But it was easier to say than actually do."

"I get it," Jodi said, looping her arm through Mylie's. "But I still think you need to tell him. I think he feels the same way you do."

"Then he should have said something," Mylie said.

"Fine," Jodi replied, rolling her eyes. "Do what you want."

"What I want is to not be having this conversation," Mylie muttered.

"You're right," Jodi said. "We need to go and get ready for the party, anyway."

"I don't know if I want to go," Mylie said.

"Oh, you're going." Jodi half-dragged Mylie back toward the crowd. "You're going to stop sulking and go to this party. It's our *graduation*, Mylie!"

"Okay," Mylie replied. "Okay, you're right. Let's go. But I'm telling your mother no more pictures."

"Good luck," Jodi said, laughing. "My mother has infinite space on her digital camera."

"I'm not throwing my cap again," Mylie said. "Your mom can't make me."

"I'll let you take that up with her," Jodi replied. "Now, come on. Put a smile on that pretty face of yours. Tonight is our night!"

Chapter 1

Mylie really didn't want to fire him. In fact, firing Robbie Price was literally the last thing on planet Earth she wanted to do. She'd been avoiding it for nearly a week, until this morning, when her best friend, Jodi, reminded her that she had to pay Robbie for every day she put it off.

Most of the time, Mylie liked being the boss, liked owning her own business. She'd worked hard for it, after all. Since she was fourteen, she'd been working toward it, spending her free time running her Granny Violet's bait and tackle truck at the lake, learning how to make lures, marketing her product. Now, all these years later, she had an entire warehouse full of employees crafting handmade tackle that went out to people all over the state of Arkansas and beyond. They'd even sent packages to Europe and South America. She employed one third of the townspeople in the small resort town of Clay Creek, Arkansas. Despite that, she tried to keep out of local politics *and* local gossip. It wasn't easy, though, with someone always asking for a favor . . . which was exactly how she'd gotten herself talked into hiring Robbie in the first place.

His granny was friends with her granny, and despite the fact that Robbie had been in prison up until six months ago, it had somehow been *Mylie's* problem that he was living with the aforementioned granny and eating up all her retirement savings. As if she'd somehow forced him to steal copper wiring from a subdivision being built outside of town and "forget" to pay child support for the last decade.

Robbie Price was two years older than Mylie, and she'd always tried to avoid him, even in elementary school. She guessed he'd been this way for a long time, but she'd always figured, at least when they were kids, that it wasn't his fault. Like her, his father had taken off long before Robbie got a chance to know it. The difference was that while Mylie had her granny to help raise and guide her, Robbie's mother sold illegal moonshine and had a rap sheet nearly as long as her son's. As they'd gotten older, Mylie and Robbie took very different paths in life. His drinking was a well-known issue, and she should have trusted her gut. Sobriety hadn't lasted long, and drinking on the job wasn't something Mylie could tolerate, even if a small part of her felt bad for him.

Hook, Line, & Sinker was a successful business, she'd busted her ass to get here, and she'd be damned if she was going to let the likes of Robbie Price compromise the integrity of all she'd done.

"You're gonna let me make up this lunch time I'm missin', right?" Robbie asked, heaving himself down into the chair in front of Mylie's desk.

Mylie winced. "Well," she began. "After today, you'll have plenty of time for lunch."

"Am I gettin' a raise?"

The laugh bubbled out of Mylie's throat before she could stop it. It was nerves, clearly, because that was what she did when she was nervous. But it was also the absolute ridiculousness of Robbie's comment. A raise? A raise for a man she'd hired out of pity and now had to fire for stealing and being drunk on the job more days than he was sober.

"Robbie," Mylie said, clearing her throat. "You know we have cameras in the warehouse, right?"

He shifted a little in the chair, but he didn't break eye contact. "What of it?"

"Great, then you also know that we generally have a direct count of how many lures we make in a day, right?" Mylie continued. "You know that we'd notice if, say, fifty of them went missing over a week's time?"

"What are you gettin' at?" Robbie asked.

He just kept looking at her, staring right at her, even though they both knew what was coming. Well, if he could do it, so could she, Mylie supposed. She pulled herself up as high in her chair as she could and said, "Robbie, I know you've been stealing lures. I know you're drinking on your lunch break and coming back drunk as a skunk, which is probably why you think you can get away with stealing so much merchandise, but you can't. You just can't."

"Now, listen," Robbie said, starting to stand up.

"I have to fire you," Mylie continued, afraid if she stopped, she might lose her will. "But I'm not going to report you to the sheriff. And I'm going to give you two weeks' severance pay."

Robbie sat back down. "I'd take a month."

Mylie squinted at him. Now she was starting to get angry. "You haven't been here but three weeks. I think two weeks' severance is more than generous, especially considering I also know you've been selling those lures on the down-low for a profit."

"This is bullshit," Robbie spat.

"I'm pretty sure what's bullshit is using my granny to guilt me into giving you a job in the first place when you've been fired from nearly every place in town," Mylie shot back. "I'm only offering you the option of not getting arrested because I know it would embarrass your granny."

"Charges wouldn't stick." Robbie sniffed.

Mylie could smell the corn liquor on his breath from where he sat. "Robbie," she said, softening her tone. "I could help you, you know. If you were interested in rehab. I know a couple of guys up in Rockbridge who run a facility . . ."

"I don't need your help," Robbie replied, narrowing his eyes at her. "You think you're such hot shit around here, that everybody has to listen to you."

"I don't think that at all," Mylie countered. "I'm just trying to let you know that you have options, you know? Then when you're sober, maybe you could come back here and we could talk."

"Don't pretend like you give a shit," Robbie said. "You ain't the Mother Teresa of Clay Creek."

"Everything okay in here?" Jodi stuck her head in through the office door. "I can call Paul to walk Robbie out if you need me to."

Robbie turned around and glared at Jodi. "Fuck you, Jodi."

"Well, fuck you back, Robbie," Jodi replied. "Now, it's time for you to go."

Robbie stood up for the final time, looking back and forth between the two women, clearly deciding what his next move should be. All three of them knew that Old Paul the security guard couldn't escort a possum off the property, but by now, it was the principle of the matter.

Was he going to leave or was he going to cause a scene?

He was going to cause a scene.

Robbie picked up an entire box of lures that was sitting on the shelf to his right, and dumped them out all over the floor, scattering them. He took the time to look Mylie right in the eye before crushing one of them underneath his muddy boot.

Mylie shot up out of her seat. "Robbie Price, if you don't get your ass out of this shop right now, I'm going to call the sheriff."

She slid her eyes to Jodi and shook her head slightly at her friend. The last thing either of them needed was for Jodi to jump on him like a spider monkey, which was exactly what Jodi's face was telling Mylie she was thinking about doing.

"Somebody ought to take you down a peg," Robbie said, grinding onto the lure beneath his foot. "This ain't over," he said, stomping out of the office, nearly knocking the door off of its hinges.

Jodi collapsed against the doorway. "Jeeeesus," she whispered. "I really did think we might have to kill him."

"I told you yesterday we couldn't kill him," Mylie replied, finally allowing herself to relax. "But yeah, it was close."

"You never should have hired him," Jodi said.

"I know that," Mylie replied. She reached into her desk drawer and pulled out a hair tie, desperate to get her thick mass of blond hair off her sweaty neck. "But Granny asked me to do it for her as a favor. What was I supposed to say?"

"All of that because you fired him?" Jodi asked. "He's been fired from every place in town. It's not like this is new and different for him."

Mylie sighed. "I offered to help," she said. "You know, get him into a rehab facility and all of that. I thought maybe . . ."

"Oh, Mylie," Jodi replied. "You should have known better."

"I know," Mylie said. "But I felt bad for him, you know?"

"He hates that more than anything," Jodi continued. "Now that he thinks he's been insulted; this won't be the last time we hear from him."

Mylie knew he'd be bad-mouthing her all over town before the day was over, and she'd have to avoid the grocery store for a week at least. She also knew that when Robbie said something wasn't over, he meant it.

"Do you want to call the sheriff?" Jodi asked.

Mylie shook her head. "I'll talk to him," she said. "Let him know the situation."

"You're the boss," Jodi replied, bending down to help Mylie pick up the lures. "Good thing these were all defective."

Mylie plucked a lure from her hair. "At least there weren't any hooks in them."

"That, too," Jodi agreed. "So, you meeting that guy from Tinder tonight? You better get on home if that's your plan. You look like you need to spend some time getting ready."

"Thanks a lot," Mylie grumbled, finishing up with the lures. "Can you close up for the weekend if I leave?"

"Just go," Jodi said, swatting Mylie on the ass as she sidled past her. "And don't forget to send me your location in case he murders you and drops you into the lake!"

Chapter 2

Mylie's favorite part of the day was driving home from work, especially during the springtime. She was too tired and cranky in the morning to appreciate the beauty of the Ozark Mountains, but at night, when everything was quiet and the day was wearing off, Mylie felt like someone had created this entire expanse of earth just for her. In a few weeks, the tourists would be coming in droves. They'd be gearing up for the big Spring Fling fishing tournament next month. Hook, Line, & Sinker played a huge role in the festivities. They were one of the biggest sponsors of the tournament, and they even had an all-women's team this year to compete.

Nearly all of the businesses in town sponsored the tournament in one way or another. The Cracked Egg, the best restaurant in town, did the most. Her friend Melissa, whose family owned the place, had already pledged to make this year the best year yet.

There was a lot to think about, but not right now. Right now, it was just a few days into May, and everyone was still shaking off the chill of winter. The mornings were cool, but the afternoons were warm, and Mylie loved it. Spring was in the air, and right now, she had time to enjoy the calm.

Right now, it was quiet.

Some nights on her drive home, Mylie would take the long way. Which really meant she drove along the road behind her house, with the scenic lake views that led right past another house she didn't visit anymore.

That was primarily because nobody had lived there in a long time. Once in a while, it would be rented out for the summer, but mostly, it stayed empty. Mylie didn't like to be reminded of its emptiness, but occasionally, she was able to drive past and not think about the former occupants too much.

Tonight was not one of those nights.

As she rounded the corner and the house came into view, she noticed a large sign in the front yard. She knew that sign because there were similar signs all over Clay Creek. It was a real estate sign from Courtney Williams, the best (and most annoying) Realtor in town.

The house was for sale.

Mylie felt a hitch in her throat. She hadn't expected this. Why would they be selling after all this time? Ten years was a long time to keep a house empty to suddenly sell it. For some reason, the fact that she didn't know this was going to happen, that she'd just driven up on the sign pushed down into the grass outside the house, made her furious.

She didn't have much time to think about it, though, because her sister, Cassie, was out in the front yard waiting for her when Mylie finally pulled into the driveway. Her sister was fourteen, and literally everything was a catastrophe. Today was sure to be no different. In her hands, she held the remains of what looked like a T-shirt, tears streaming down her face.

"Look what Granny's stupid dog did to my favorite T-shirt!" She said before Mylie had even gotten out of the car.

Mylie could have sworn she saw that exact same T-shirt in the rag pile the day before, but she didn't say that. Instead, she said, "You mean the dog *you* brought home from the Walmart parking lot in Little Rock?"

This just made Cassie cry harder.

"It's okay," Mylie said, taking what was left of the shirt. "We can get you another one."

"You can't!" Cassie wailed, her ponytail whipping back and forth as she shook her head. "It's a Twenty One Pilots *concert shirt.*"

"I bet we can find one online."

"It won't be the same!"

It took every ounce of strength Mylie had not to roll her eyes. "You didn't even go to that concert, Cass."

"Ryan brought it back to me!" Cassie replied. "That's why it's so special!"

Mylie looked down at the shirt. "Let me see what I can do."

She shooed her sister inside. Surely Granny had something in her sewing table Mylie could use to fix . . . whatever this was. Mylie wasn't sure why Cassie hadn't taken the shirt to Granny. She was probably out on the back porch smoking a cigarette. Granny's movements weren't much of a mystery, especially on Friday nights.

"Where's Granny?" Mylie asked, when she didn't see her sitting out on the back porch. "Is everything okay?"

"She's out there," Cassie said, wiping her face. "She's down toward the lake with Morris. I walked in on them whispering about something, and Granny told me it was adult business and to go away."

"I wonder if it has anything to do with the old Lawrence place going up for sale," Mylie said more to herself than to Cassie.

Cassie shrugged. "Can you fix it?"

"I don't know," Mylie said honestly. "How do you feel about making this shirt a crop top?"

Technically speaking, Mylie and Cassie were half-sisters, but that wasn't a term they used for each other. Cassie's father lived in Little Rock, and she saw him a few times a year when it was convenient for him. Their mother had never been married to Cassie's father, and in fact, he hadn't even known Cassie existed until she was nearly a year old. Mylie still remembered the fear she felt when Cassie's father came to Clay Creek for a visit, and Mylie spent the entire time watching him with an eagle eye, afraid he was going to take Cassie away from them. Looking back, she realized that had been a ridiculous thing to worry about. Cassie's father was a bassist for a metal cover band. He wasn't equipped to raise a child.

Of course, Mylie's mother hadn't been, either, and her own father had been dead for as long as she could remember.

For the last twelve years, it had been just Mylie, Cassie, and Granny, which was the way they liked it.

When Cassie refused to let Mylie cut her shirt, Mylie sighed and said, "Okay, well, I'm going to need more time than I have right now. I've got a date tonight."

"I wanted to wear it over to Allie's," Cassie said, her eyes welling up all over again.

"You can wear something of mine," Mylie offered. Normally, Mylie would never offer to let Cassie anywhere near her closet. Cassie had a habit of dropping food and all manner of things onto her clothing, but tonight she could see that it was either offer up her own clothes or spend the whole evening fixing a shirt that was bound for the church rummage sale when Cassie and Ryan inevitably broke up.

Cassie perked up. "Can I pick whatever I want?"

"Within reason," Mylie replied. "I can't let you leave looking like a hooker."

"Why not?" Cassie quipped. "*You* leave the house looking like a hooker all the time."

"That's because I'm an adult."

"Fine," Cassie grumbled. "But I want to borrow those cute sandals you bought last week."

"I haven't even gotten to wear them," Mylie protested, and then, seeing the look on Cassie's face, she relented. "Fine. But please don't ruin them."

Mylie threw the destroyed T-shirt down on her bed and opened her closet to look for something to wear for her date that night. She didn't date often, not when she had so much responsibility at work and at home. But occasionally it was nice to get out, have a date with an attractive man, spend the night with him, and then never call him again. Which is why she only dated men who lived at least an hour away from her. The drive was inconvenient, yes, but it made everything else uncomplicated.

Eventually, she settled on a pair of jeans and a white blouse that made her skin glow. It also didn't hurt that the top made her boobs look fantastic. Granny called it the "generous bosom of the Mason family tree."

Mylie would never have admitted it to anyone, not even her best friend, Jodi, who she'd known since kindergarten, but Mylie liked being appreciated by men. When she looked in the mirror, the first thing she noticed was her blond hair, which she knew was just average—you couldn't throw a rock in Clay Creek without hitting someone with blond hair. But her eyes were the color of the lake. Not the deep and murky brown of the depths, but blue with a hint of green, like when the sun reflected on the water just right in the summertime.

Those eyes were her father's, but the rest of her was all her mother. Her easily tanned skin, the freckles across the bridge of her nose, and hips that were wide enough for any man to get a firm grip. And once they'd gotten a grip, they usually had a hard time letting go. Those hips, Mylie was proud to say, had been the source of more than one bar fight.

Cassie was shoving her feet into Mylie's sandals when she said, "That looks okay, but I think you need to add something."

"Like what?" Mylie asked, turning to her sister.

"Hmm." Cassie abandoned the sandals and went to Mylie's jewelry box. She took out a small gold chain. "Here," she said. "Try this."

Mylie admired herself in the mirror. She had been missing something. "Wow," she said to Cassie. "You're pretty good at this."

"I am the only person in this house who has a boyfriend," Cassie reminded her sister. "I know a thing or two."

"Now, that's not fair," Mylie replied. "Granny has Morris."

At that, the sisters dissolved into giggles. Morris was Granny's "special friend." They'd met years ago when Morris was Mylie's high school history teacher. Granny pretended not to know him in public, but everyone in town knew that Granny and Morris were an item. He wasn't usually over before dinner on a Friday night, though. Before she left, Mylie needed to go and see what that adult business they'd been discussing was all about.

"Ryan's not coming over tonight, right?" Mylie asked once they'd stopped laughing. "You said earlier you were going to Allie's."

"Ryan's out of town with his dad," Cassie replied.

"Because you know the rule, right?" Mylie continued. "No boys at the house . . ."

"Without you or Granny home," Cassie finished, rolling her eyes. "I know, I know."

Mylie squinted at Cassie. She believed her sister, but she didn't trust Ryan. He was a little shit. "Okay, but . . ."

"I'm going to Allie's," Cassie said. "I promise. And both of her parents are going to be home."

"All right," Mylie conceded. "If you need me, just call me. I can be home in forty-five minutes."

"Only if you want to get arrested," Cassie replied. "Rockbridge is sixty miles away."

"Just call me!" Mylie called over her shoulder.

She went outside and peered over the deck to the lake, where she saw Granny and Morris sitting in rocking chairs on the dock. It was an old dock, and it needed repair. Mylie hated it that Granny insisted on plopping down into a chair as it rotted beneath her, but nobody could tell Granny anything. If she wanted to do it, she was going to do it.

"Hey," Mylie said as she neared them. "What are you two doing out here?"

Morris twisted around in his chair to greet her. "Hey, Mylie Girl. Wow, you look like you're headed somewhere fancy."

This prompted Granny to turn around and squint at Mylie. "Hot date tonight?"

"Just dinner in Rockbridge," Mylie said, waving them off. "Cassie said she was going to Allie's tonight."

"She told me," Granny replied. "That's why I'm down here instead of slaving away in that kitchen in this heat."

Mylie looked from Morris to Granny. "Well," she said at last. "What was the adult conversation you two wouldn't have in front of Cassie?"

Morris and Granny shared a look.

"Does it have anything to do with the FOR SALE sign in front of the Lawrence place?" Mylie continued. "Because if it does, it's fine. It's absolutely . . ."

"He's coming back," Granny said, cutting her off.

Mylie's words stuck in her throat. She knew the answer, but she had to ask. "Who?"

Granny's usual demanding countenance softened, and she replied, "Benjamin."

Mylie wished there were more than two chairs on the dock. Just then, she wouldn't have cared if the damn thing collapsed and took her with it. She cleared her throat. "When did you find this out?"

Granny stopped to light a cigarette, took a long drag, and blew the smoke out onto the water. "That idiot Realtor," she said. "She tried to put the sign in *our* yard. She about had a come apart when she saw me on the front porch."

Their houses—the Lawrence house and the Mason house did look nearly identical, and they were basically next door to each other. They'd been built by the same contractor back in the 1950s. Granny bought their house in the 1980s before Mylie was born, but the other house had been owned by the Lawrences since it was built. That's why Mylie had always assumed they'd never sell, even though what was left of the Lawrences had moved to Chicago nearly ten years ago.

Ben.

Ben was what was left of the Lawrences. His grandfather and mother were both gone now is what Mylie had heard through the grapevine in town. Still, nobody assumed he'd sell, and it had been at least two years ago when they'd gotten that news. Emily Lawrence had always said that the house would stay in the family. Of course, Emily was no longer in charge of the Lawrence legacy.

Mylie knew there was one more question she needed to ask, but she couldn't bring herself to ask it. Finally, Granny took pity on her and offered, "Courtney said sometime next week."

Mylie rolled her eyes. Courtney was the worst. She was always parading around town like she knew everything. Mylie supposed in some ways, she did. She always found out when someone was going broke—house in foreclosure. She knew when people were getting divorced—family house for sale. In fact, some people in town had begun hiring out-of-town Realtors just so that Courtney wouldn't blab their business all over town.

"I guess Courtney has told the whole town," Mylie said.

"I warned her against it," Granny replied. "I reminded her just how many sales that big mouth of hers cost."

"He doesn't need to come back to town to sell the house," Mylie countered. "Does he?"

Granny shook her head. "No, I reckon not."

Mylie took a breath and straightened her shoulders. "It doesn't matter," she said finally. "I've got to go. I'm going to be late for my date."

And with that, Mylie Mason turned on her heel and walked away, hoping like hell that by the time she reached Rockbridge, her emotions would catch up to her words.

Chapter 3

Benjamin Lawrence turned right onto the little two-lane highway toward Clay Creek, his mood worsening with every mile.

It's just a few weeks, he said to himself.

That was the mantra he'd been repeating since the second he'd gotten that phone call from that Realtor, reminding him that there were still things in the house that might be, in her words, "important to the family."

Reminding him of the promise he'd made to his dead mother.

He was the family now, and he'd nearly told the woman to sell everything; he didn't care about what was in there, but deep down, he knew that wasn't the truth. He'd promised his mother before she died that he'd go back at least once and spend some time there. She'd known he wouldn't keep the house, so this was her compromise, her way of blessing the inevitable.

He couldn't break that promise to her now.

But going back to Clay Creek? Well, it wasn't exactly on the list of things he wanted to do . . . ever. He'd put it off for two years. Every time the Realtor called, he said he wasn't ready, but the truth was, once he agreed to sell, he knew that also meant he had to go back.

It wasn't that he hated Clay Creek. In truth, he hadn't. But he'd also never wanted to move there—hadn't wanted to leave his friends in Chicago. He'd promised himself that when he had the chance, he'd go back. He'd go to college and start a career in a town with more than 5,000 people. It was a promise he'd kept.

Mylie had been his first friend in Clay Creek. She wasn't his only friend—he'd been friends with several other kids in town, but none of them had been like Mylie. Ben tried not to close his eyes and think about her as he drove. Ten years was a long time, but he could still see her face in his mind, hear her laugh, and if he really concentrated, sometimes he swore he could still smell that perfume she always wore. In fact, occasionally, a woman would pass him in Chicago wearing that same scent, and he'd have to fight the urge to turn around and follow her just in case she was, in fact, Mylie.

He didn't follow anyone, of course, because that would have been creepy. It was the same reason he refused to look Mylie up on any social media, refused to let her know he was returning to Clay Creek just in case she still lived there. He doubted very much that she ever even thought about him. It would have been weird to tell her, to expect that she would care, not after all this time.

Ben straightened in his seat. Besides, none of that mattered. He wasn't the same person he'd been back then. He'd just finished his PhD and had a job offer from a prestigious university, which was exactly why he was selling. He needed the money for the move.

He was finally where he wanted to be in his life. He was on the verge of being a respected member in the field of economics. He had plenty of friends. He dated plenty of women, which had been a welcome perk to his late-as-hell physical evolution his sophomore year in college. He was a goddamn adult, for fuck's sake. Why was he dreading this so much?

Ben tried to relax, rolling his neck and loosening his death grip on the steering wheel. This wasn't going to be anything at all. The town might still be the same, but he wasn't.

This wasn't a trip back to his past. It was an obligation, another job he had to complete, and once he was done, he'd leave Clay Creek in his rearview for the last time and never look back.

He pulled into the gas station just outside of town to fill up and grab a few snacks. This late, most places would already be closed. He remembered that much from his time in Clay Creek. When he'd first moved here, that had been one of the hardest things to get used to—the way everything pretty much shut down after eight p.m. In Chicago, that just wasn't the way the city operated. It wasn't, he'd learned later, the way any city operated. But small towns were different, especially in Arkansas.

The woman behind the counter looked up from her phone when Ben entered. He tried to give her a friendly smile, but she eyed him with suspicion as he made his way around the stacks of junk food, grabbing enough to get him through the night.

"Help ya find something?" she asked, standing up and leaning over the counter to watch him. "Don't get too many people out this way after dark."

Ben eyed the coffeepot, trying to decide just how long that coffee had been sitting there. "I'm okay," he said. "Just grabbing a few things before heading into town."

"Mmmhmm," the woman replied. "That coffee ain't fresh."

"I'll just take these, then," Ben said, unloading his armful of snacks.

The woman picked up a package of powdered sugar doughnuts. "You local?"

"Not really," Ben replied.

The woman narrowed her eyes at him. "You look familiar, but I can't place ya."

Ben sighed. He hadn't prepared himself for these kinds of questions yet. He figured he'd at least have the night to decompress before he had to explain himself. "I used to live here," he said, "about a decade ago."

"What brings you back to town?"

"Just visiting," Ben replied, hoping this was the end of the conversation. All he wanted to do was rip into that package of doughnuts.

"You still got people here?" she asked.

"Not anymore," Ben said.

She grunted and continued to scan. Ben felt maybe a little bad about not being more forthcoming, but honestly, he was out of practice with small-town small talk. He was no longer used to people asking who he was or where he was going or who he was related to. Most of the time, he was able to go into a gas station without saying a word to anyone.

"Wait," the woman said as she bagged his snacks. "I know you. You're Emily's boy. Shit, you've grown up real nice. *Real nice*."

Ben cleared his throat. "Um, thank you."

"Sure thing, sugar. You have a great night."

Ben nodded to her and took his bag. He wondered if he'd even make it into Clay Creek before the whole town knew he was back.

Chapter 4

Mylie sat in the parking lot of Papa Pig's, the BBQ restaurant where she was supposed to meet . . . she checked her phone . . . *Seth* for dinner. They'd been chatting for a couple of days and there'd been a phone call the night before to ask her out on a date. Mylie wasn't afraid to go in and meet him. She'd checked him out the same way she did everyone else—on social media. They had a few mutual friends, and they'd all said he was a good guy. Recently divorced with a two-year-old. He seemed like a completely normal, nice man.

Still, she didn't want to go inside. She didn't want to sit down at a sticky table and make small talk until one of them decided it was time to leave with or without the other. Most of the time this awkward dance was fun; it was an escape. But tonight, she couldn't keep from thinking about her grandmother's words, *He's coming back.*

So what? Mylie told herself. *So what if he's coming back?* She hadn't concerned herself with Ben Lawrence for a long time. They'd been friends, best friends, since the sixth grade when Ben moved into town with his mother after his father died. Ben's grandfather, the town's only doctor at the time, was a sweet man who adored Granny. Ben was a lot like his grandfather, only quieter, and he and Mylie had hit it off *almost* immediately.

But then he'd left, and that had been that. There were a few phone calls and emails from college, but they'd lost touch. Mylie had responsibilities at home, working to get her business off the ground and helping Granny care for Cassie, and Ben . . . well, he'd started a new life. There just wasn't room for their childhood friendship, even if she'd always thought that eventually it would be something more.

Beside her, Mylie watched a couple get out of their minivan and haul two small children out, the oldest child chattering a mile a minute while her patient father listened. Mylie smiled. She remembered those days with Cassie, although the only other person there to listen to her had been Granny. People always assumed Cassie belonged to Mylie and that she was some unwed, teen mom. It didn't bother her for the most part, but sometimes when she watched scenes like this, she wondered if she'd ever have a family that didn't make people stare at her.

She often had to remind herself that she was, in fact, an accomplished, successful woman. It should be enough that most aspects of her life were great. Mylie didn't *need* a relationship, but that didn't mean she didn't *want* one.

She got out of her truck and went inside, glancing around the crowded dining area for anyone who looked remotely familiar. After a few seconds, a sandy-haired man in a Kansas City Chiefs T-shirt waved at her, smiling.

Seth is pretty cute, Mylie thought as she made her way toward him.

"Hi," he said, extending his hand to greet her. "I'm Seth, and you must be Mylie."

Mylie smiled. "Yes. Hi."

"I'm glad you suggested this place," Seth said as they sat. "I've only lived here a few months, and I've been wanting to try it."

"Oh, that's right," Mylie replied. "And what brought you here again? I'm sorry, I forgot."

Seth gave her an easy grin. "Landscaping. My brother has a business here, and I moved a few months ago to help him out."

The waitress appeared with menus, and asked them for their drink orders.

"You want a beer or something?" Seth asked.

Mylie shook her head. "I better not. I have to drive all the way back to Clay Creek tonight," she said. "I'll just take a sweet tea."

She could see the disappointment in Seth's eyes when she revealed she'd be going home tonight. Mylie wished she could tell him that it didn't have anything to do with him. Ordinarily, she would have waited until later in the date to make that decision. But tonight, she'd made the decision before she even went inside the restaurant. She had too much on her mind to smile and flirt her way into someone else's bed when all she wanted to do was throw herself down face-first onto her own bed and scream into a pillow.

"So, have you ever been married?" Seth was asking her.

"What?" Mylie asked. "Oh, no, I've never been married."

"Not even close?" Seth asked.

"No," Mylie replied. She was used to these kinds of questions. A woman didn't get to be twenty-eight in the rural Arkansas Ozarks without being asked a few times why she wasn't married, why she had never been married, and if she ever wanted to get married.

"And no kids?"

"Nope."

"Do you like kids?" Seth asked. "You know I've got a two-year-old. Her name's Serenity. Want to see a picture?"

"I do like kids," Mylie said. She leaned forward in her chair to look at Seth's phone, where a chubby-cheeked toddler smiled, holding a puppy. "She's adorable."

"She lives in Little Rock with my ex-wife," Seth continued. "But I get her every other weekend."

"I'm sure you miss her," Mylie said, trying to be sympathetic.

"I've got her next weekend," Seth said.

Mylie understood the unspoken words—he'd been hoping that *this* weekend, he'd get something else. She was about to change the subject when her phone dinged from inside her purse. Then it dinged again. And again. And again.

"I'm sorry," Mylie said. "I better check that."

She pulled her phone out and saw several messages from Cassie.

Had a fight with Allie.

Coming home.

I'm so mad.

I hate her.

That was all the invitation Mylie needed to make her excuses.

"I'm so sorry, Seth," she said. "I've got an emergency back at home."

Seth scrunched his eyebrows together as if he didn't believe her, but said, "Is everything okay?"

"I think so," Mylie said. "But I have to go. I'm just so sorry."

She went to put money down on the table, but Seth waved her off. "I've got it," he said. "So, you'll call me?"

"Of course," Mylie lied. "I'll call you!"

Seth followed her outside. "Hey!" he said, jogging after her. "Are you sure you aren't just trying to get out of the date? Because you can tell me if that's the case. I'm a really nice guy, I swear."

It was Mylie's belief that most men who *said* they were nice guys weren't *actually* nice guys at all, but she did her best to smile at him when she replied, "No, I'm not making it up. I really do have to go."

"I've had women do this before," Seth continued. "It's okay if you aren't attracted to me or something."

Mylie suppressed her urge to sigh. "I'm not making it up."

"So, I'll give you a call," Seth said, backing up a step. "Okay?"

"Great," Mylie replied. She unlocked her car and got inside. Seth watched her from the parking lot. She knew neither of them would call each other. In fact, she would bet that he was going to go back inside that restaurant and unmatch her right then and there. She couldn't really blame him.

BY THE TIME Mylie got home with a sympathy pizza from Cassie's favorite place in Rockbridge, it was already dark. She'd also stopped and gotten Cassie a Route 44 Cherry Limeade from Sonic, her favorite, along with a frozen Limeade for herself that she entirely planned on pouring some gin into that she had stashed away in the freezer.

It was a Gin and Sonic kind of night.

Cassie looked up from her phone when Mylie walked through the door, her eyes red-rimmed from crying. Their dog, Stanley, was cuddled up next to her, the shredded shirt incident from earlier clearly forgotten.

They'd had Stanley since he was just six weeks old. He was a beautiful blue pit bull that Cassie's father bought for fifty dollars in a Walmart parking lot when she was visiting him in Little Rock. Now, he was a big, blockheaded sweetheart, but back then, he'd been the runt of the litter, and Cassie told Granny and Mylie that she couldn't just leave him there. They'd been inseparable ever since.

"What happened?" Mylie set the pizza box down on the kitchen counter. "Where's Granny?"

"She's still outside with Morris," Cassie said with a sniff. "I don't even think they know I'm home."

"That's probably for the best," Mylie replied. "Unless you want to hear Morris tell you about his bunions."

"I definitely don't want that," Cassie said, a hint of a smile on her face.

"So," Mylie said, sitting down next to her sister. "What's going on?"

"It was stupid," Cassie admitted. "Ryan sent me a snap while I was over at Allie's, and she got all mad saying all I cared about was my boyfriend. I wasn't trying to ignore her, I swear."

"But were you?" Mylie asked. "Was it just one snap?"

"It was about ten," Cassie said, looking sheepish. "But I was listening to her, too!"

Mylie sighed. "I know Ryan is like, totally, hot . . ."

Cassie reached out and smacked her sister's arm.

Mylie laughed and continued. "But you need to pay attention to your friends sometimes, too. Especially when Allie invited *you* to her house. Not you and your phone and Ryan."

"She's just jealous," Cassie muttered.

"Maybe," Mylie replied. "Or maybe she misses her friend. Not everybody wants to have a boyfriend, but everybody wants to have friends. And it doesn't seem like you were being a very good one tonight."

Cassie looked up at Mylie. "You're supposed to be on my side."

"I am on your side," Mylie said. "I'm always on your side. Which means I have to be honest with you every once in a while."

"I know," Cassie replied. "I know. I guess I should apologize."

"I think she'd probably appreciate that," Mylie said. "But only if you really mean it."

"Can I invite her over to spend the night tomorrow night?" Cassie asked.

Mylie grinned. "I don't see why not," she said. "As long as Granny doesn't mind."

"As long as Granny doesn't mind what?" came a voice from the back door.

"Allie at our house tomorrow," Cassie answered.

"I don't mind a bit, dear one," Granny said, sitting down on the couch so that Cassie was squished in the middle. "That girl is sweet as pie."

That was as high a compliment as a person could get from Granny. Violet Mason, the matriarch of the Mason family, didn't like just anyone. In fact, she actively *disliked* most people. At sixty-eight years old, she'd spent most of her life taking zero bullshit from anyone, and that included her beloved granddaughters. Most people thought with a name like Granny, which she insisted anybody younger than she was call her, that Violet would be a demure, white-haired senior citizen who spent her days knitting and fiddling with the television remote.

But that couldn't have been further from the truth. While most kids had a Nana or a Memaw to cuddle them and bring baked goods to the school fundraiser, Mylie and Cassie had Granny, who had fire-red hair and lipstick to match, could drink any man under the table, wore skintight hot pants, and would curse at the elementary school secretary when she wasn't allowed to smoke in the gymnasium during Christmas performances.

Not everybody in town loved Granny, but they sure as shit respected her. Granny just had a way of making people believe she was someone to be respected. Mylie admired that more than just about anything else about her grandmother.

Granny was an institution in Clay Creek, and even though they liked to complain occasionally, Mylie and Cassie wouldn't have it any other way.

Cassie picked up the pizza and the Sonic cup and said, "I'm taking this to my room."

"Don't you squish that pepperoni into the carpet!" Granny called after her.

"I guess I don't get any pizza," Mylie grumbled.

"I can do you one better than pizza," Granny said. "You use the rest of that gin in the freezer?" She pointed to Mylie's Sonic cup.

Mylie shook her head. "No," she said, taking a long sip through the straw. "There's a little bit left."

"Thank the lord Jesus," Granny replied, getting up and padding toward the kitchen. "You know I can't drink around Morris."

"You would go for a teetotaling Pentecostal deacon, wouldn't you?" Mylie asked.

Granny pulled down a glass from the cabinet and turned to face her granddaughter. "Well, girls," she said, winking at them. "You know damn well they're the most fun."

Mylie laughed. "So you keep telling me."

"How come you're home so early, kiddo?" Granny asked. "I thought you had a date."

"I did," Mylie said.

"That bad, huh?" Granny replied.

"It wasn't that bad," Mylie replied. "I just wasn't in the right headspace for it tonight."

Granny raised an eyebrow and said, "You're still thinking about the house, aren't you?"

"Not the house, exactly," Mylie admitted. "I'm just wondering about Ben. You know we haven't spoken in *years*."

"I know," Granny replied.

"I don't even know what I'll say to him," Mylie said.

"Hello would be a good start," Granny said with a grin.

Mylie laughed. "The last time we talked was the spring break of his sophomore year in college," she said. "He was going to Florida with his friends, and I was so jealous."

"What's Florida got that we don't have?" Granny asked.

"The ocean," Mylie said. "White sand."

Granny rolled her eyes. "Well, I reckon you two will get caught up and it'll be just like old times."

"Maybe," Mylie said.

"I always knew he'd be back," Granny said.

"You did?" Mylie asked.

Granny nodded. "I just didn't know how long it would take."

"Why does he need to come back to sell the house?" Mylie asked. "Why can't he do that from Chicago or wherever it is that he lives now?"

"I'm sure he has his reasons," Granny said.

"I'm sure he does," Mylie agreed. "Do you think he'll look the same? I tried to Google him once a couple of years ago, but he doesn't come up on any social media searches, except for a few mentions from his college. But there weren't any pictures."

Granny shrugged. "I feel like you ought to have permission before you *Google* somebody."

"I Google everyone," Mylie replied.

"So I've heard."

"Granny!" Mylie said with a laugh.

"Sorry," Granny said, wiping at her eyes. "I couldn't help it." She patted Mylie on the shoulder. "It's time for this old gal to hit the hay."

"Good night, Granny," Mylie said.

"Good night, my darling," Granny replied, kissing the top of Mylie's head as she stood. "See you in the morning."

Mylie watched as Granny sauntered down the hallway and off to her bedroom. She leaned back into the sofa and let out a sigh. It was going to be weird to see Ben again after all these years. Losing touch with him had been gradual, and she didn't blame either of them for it. Life just . . . happened. She couldn't even remember who had been the last to make an effort.

She picked up her phone and scrolled idly through it. She checked Cassie's Instagram, the secret one Granny didn't know about, just to make sure her little sister hadn't posted anything that needed to be deleted. Overall, Cassie was a good kid. But she was also a teenager, and being a teenager on social media was perilous. Mylie was glad that she'd never had it when she was in high school. Some of her friends had, but it wasn't as common as it was now. It made her cringe to think about all the trouble she—and Ben— would have gotten into if their lives had been posted all over the internet when they were teens.

Ben.

God, it had been so long. What did he look like now? Who was he? Was he the same old Ben? Mylie set her phone down on the coffee table. She guessed she'd find out soon enough. In a few days, if Granny was right, and she nearly always was.

Mylie looked down at Stanley, who'd been snoozing at her feet and said, "Come on, dude. Let's go to bed."

Chapter 5

Mylie lay in bed and stared up at the fading glow of the little plastic stars she tacked to her ceiling in junior high. She didn't understand how they could have any glow left after being stuck up there for so many years. Sometimes they fell off in the middle of the night and hit her in the head with their pointy ends. Still, she refused to remove them. They helped her fall asleep.

Most nights.

She remembered the day she put those stars up. Ben had helped her. She hadn't been able to find the stepstool that Granny kept in the kitchen, and even standing on her bed, Mylie had been too short to reach the ceiling. Ben, however, tall and lanky as he was, had no trouble reaching up and sticking the stars.

Later that night, they'd laid down on her bed, pressed together, and stared up at the stars. One had fallen down and nicked Ben's forehead.

The memory made Mylie smile.

She willed the gin and the stars to lull her to sleep, but all the gin had done was make her have to pee. When she stripped the cover off her bed and sat up, Stanley began to growl.

"Hush," Mylie said to him. "I told you to go sleep with Cassie."

Stanley didn't hush. Instead, his growling got louder. Mylie was just about to scold him again when she heard a noise outside. It sounded like scraping against the door. Not a knock exactly but something brushing up against the door over and over.

"Shhh," she said to Stanley.

Mylie walked over to her window. She looked down and saw nothing but darkness. She'd turned the light on the front porch off before bed—she didn't want to be able to look out her window and see Ben's house—even though they usually left it on.

She wished she hadn't been so dramatic, because now the scraping sound, or rather whoever or whatever was *doing the scraping,* sounded like they wanted into the house.

"Mylie?"

Mylie turned to see a sleepy Cassie standing in her doorway.

"Why is Stanley growling?"

As if in response, Stanley growled, hopping off the bed and trotting to the window before beginning his alert bark usually reserved for squirrels and mailmen.

Mylie squinted, trying to see what was causing Stanley to freak. It was too dark for squirrels *or* mailmen.

"Is somebody here?" Cassie asked, getting up to stand with Mylie.

"I don't know," Mylie whispered.

"Who would be here now?" Cassie continued. "It's after midnight."

"*I don't know.*"

"Think we ought to call the sheriff?"

Mylie leaned closer to the window. She thought she could see the outline of a figure pacing the porch steps. Were they trying to get inside? She couldn't tell.

"Should we call the sheriff?" Cassie asked again, her voice more urgent.

"If someone is trying to break in," Mylie replied. "Sheriff Oakes won't make it in time. He's on the other side of town."

"Good point," Cassie said, nodding.

Mylie tiptoed away from the window and to the doorway where Cassie was standing. "Go to Granny's room," she said. "Wake her up and tell her to go ahead and call the sheriff. I'm going downstairs."

"You're going to get murdered!" Cassie said, her voice rising with each word. "Don't go down there!"

"I'm not going to get murdered," Mylie replied, although she wasn't entirely sure of that herself. Getting murdered in her own home wasn't on her bingo card for this year.

"Be careful," Cassie said.

"Stay with Granny," Mylie instructed her sister. "Do not come downstairs."

Unlike most people in Clay Creek, the Mason women were not big hunters. They had approximately one gun, an old shotgun that was a leftover relic of her grandfather's, a man who'd died before she was born and whose pictures lined the nightstand of Granny's room. As far as Mylie knew, the gun didn't even work.

But it might scare someone.

She slipped downstairs without turning on any of the lights and felt her way through the hallway closet, where she'd last seen the gun laid up against an old coatrack. She felt its cool weight in her hands, tried to remember how to hold it. She doubted very much that she would be able to intimidate anyone into leaving if she didn't even know how to hold a stupid shotgun. Granny could shoot with the best of them. Mylie, as it turned out, was terrible with guns. She could hold her own with a fishing pole, but that wasn't going to scare anyone off, and this late at night, all the way outside city limits, nobody messed around on your front porch without letting you know first.

Maybe this was a bad idea. Through the window, she could see a figure hovering, although it was too dark to tell who it was. At first, it sounded like they were jiggling the handle, but now it looked, and sounded, as if they were putting their full weight on the door to try and force it open.

Mylie moved closer to the front door, and she could hear what was for sure a human and not an animal. She heard distinct footsteps, what sounded like a key being forced into the lock, and then mumbling that she couldn't make out. Stanley continued his barking and growling, pawing at the door.

Did someone other than Morris have a key to the house? Maybe he'd forgotten something and was coming back for it. That couldn't be it. There was nothing Morris could have left that would require a midnight trip back to the house. He'd just wait until the next day.

Mylie held her breath, clutched the shotgun with one hand, and then reached out to flip the switch to the porch, bathing it with light. She could make out a form on the porch, and it looked male—decidedly *not* like Morris. She'd never wished to see Morris's face so badly in her entire life.

The only thing she could do was try to scare whoever it was off the porch and back to wherever they came from. She readied the broken shotgun and began to speak.

Chapter 6

Ben fumbled with the keys to the house and cursed under his breath. He couldn't see anything. He should turn on the flashlight on his phone. But it was late, and he didn't want to bother anyone who was already in bed, or who might be, as he knew from experience in this little town, watching him.

Getting to the house had been pure muscle memory. He hadn't even had to plug the address into his phone. One minute he'd been on the highway, and the next he was parking in front of the house where he'd spent many of his formative years. When he tried the third key and couldn't get it in the lock, he started to think maybe he should have gotten a hotel for the night.

Was that a dog barking? Was there a feral dog in his house?

He started to turn around, and that's when the light on the porch buzzed on, leaving him so startled he froze where he stood.

"You've got three seconds to tell me what you're doing here" came a voice from inside the house. "Then I'm going to start shooting."

Ben blinked furiously, trying to adjust his eyes to the light. He could see the front door was cracked just a little, and the barrel of a shotgun was nearly in his face.

"Don't shoot," he said instinctively. "I'm just trying to find my keys."

"Just get in your car and go," the voice continued. "Get on out of here, and there won't be any trouble."

Had he heard that voice before? Ben squinted and tilted his head to the side in a futile attempt to see. "I own this house," he said. Which was technically a lie, but it was true enough.

"No, you don't."

"Yes, I do."

"Nope."

Now he was starting to get frustrated. And confused. Why was someone in the house? As far as he knew, it hadn't had a renter since the previous summer. Wouldn't the Realtor have told him if she'd rented it for the season? Then again, he hadn't seen the FOR SALE sign in the front yard when he pulled up, and Courtney told him she'd placed it that day when he told her he was making the trip earlier than expected.

Oh. No.

Realization dawned too late. He was at the wrong house.

And if he was at the wrong house, a house that could easily be mistaken for *his* house, then that meant . . .

"Ben?"

The door cracked open an inch wider.

"Ben, is that you?"

In the distance, he heard sirens. Great. This was just great.

"Uh, hi?" He said, sounding just as ridiculous as he felt. "Mylie?"

"Oh my God. It *is* you!"

The door flung open, and Mylie was standing there barefoot, holding a shotgun, and wearing the flimsiest excuse for a night-gown he'd ever seen.

"I uh, I got the wrong house," he said, finding his voice.

She stared at him, not moving, not even blinking.

"Do you maybe want to put the gun down?" he asked. "I'd prefer not to get shot."

"Fuck, I'm sorry," Mylie said. She shut the door and then opened it back up again without the gun. "I thought you were trying to break in."

"I mean, I kind of was," Ben replied. He tried and failed to keep his eyes from scanning her body as she stood there. God, how long had it been? Ten years? He'd missed out on *this* for ten years? She looked like Mylie and yet, not like Mylie. A woman stared back at him.

The sirens grew louder, and Mylie winced. "Shit, Granny called the sheriff. I forgot."

Ben couldn't help but grin to himself at the mention of Mylie's granny. In fact, he was a little surprised the old woman hadn't come out already. Of course, if she had, he'd probably already be dead.

"You weren't supposed to be here until next week," Mylie continued. "I mean, that's what I heard at least."

"So, the word's out, I guess," Ben replied. He couldn't decide if he should get closer to her or back away slowly with his hands out. He remembered Sheriff Oakes. He was just as likely to shoot as Granny.

"Looks like it."

Two more women appeared behind Mylie. One of them, Ben recognized as Granny. The other, he knew, had to be Mylie's baby sister, Cassie. Wow, it really had been ten years.

Granny shoved past Mylie and stalked out to where Ben stood, a black eye mask shoved half-way up her forehead.

"Well, Benjamin Lawrence, as I live and breathe," she said. "So, it was you, and not a rabid raccoon making all that ruckus."

"I'm sorry . . . ma'am," Ben replied, remembering at the last second he needed to use the Southern manners his grandfather taught him. "I got the wrong house."

"Clearly," Granny said, folding her arms across her chest. Then, turning her attention to Mylie, continued, "Good Lord, child, go and put on some decent clothes before the sheriff gets here. I don't want him arresting you for indecent exposure!"

Mylie looked down at herself and then up at Ben, who, despite himself, still couldn't stop staring. She bit her lip, and as Ben was internally begging her to please *stop doing that*, she turned just as Sheriff Oakes pulled into the driveway.

By now, they had quite the audience. The house down the street had its lights on, and they were all standing there, watching.

"What's the problem here, Granny?" Sheriff Oakes asked. He shone his flashlight into Ben's face, despite the light of the porch. "This fella here bothering you?"

"Tell me, Sheriff," Granny said. "Do you recognize this young man?"

The sheriff took a step closer to Ben and his eyes widened. "Well, I'll be a monkey's uncle!" he exclaimed. "Benjamin Lawrence! How in the hell are you, son?" He lowered his flashlight and stepped toward Ben and engulfed him in a hug. "I barely recognized ya!"

Ben noticed that the man smelled slightly like bourbon and decided it was probably in his best interest not to respond.

"It was all a misunderstanding," Granny said, once the sheriff released Ben.

Sheriff Oakes turned his attention to Granny. "I ought to give you a ticket for making a false call. Gettin' me out of bed at all hours."

Granny cocked an eyebrow in the sheriff's direction and said sweet as cinnamon, "And whose bed did you roll out of, *Sheriff*?"

Ben choked back a laugh.

The sheriff's face reddened. He pointed his flashlight at Granny. "We'll keep this between ourselves, if that's all right with you, Granny."

"That's what I figure is best," Granny replied. She looked at

Ben. "Now, Benjamin, you must be exhausted. Nobody here will keep you."

Ben looked past Granny to the doorway where Cassie stood, wide-eyed, but there was no sign of Mylie.

"She won't be back out," Granny said. "I'll tell her you said good night."

Ben cleared his throat, embarrassed to be caught out. "Um, thanks, Granny."

"I'll escort you over," Sheriff Oakes said to Ben. "Don't need any more calls like this tonight."

"I heard you was comin' back into town," the sheriff said as they walked up the front steps of the right house. "But not until next week."

"That was the rumor, apparently," Ben said dryly.

"You should have told someone you were early," the sheriff continued. "So there wasn't no surprises."

"Who was I supposed to tell?" Ben asked, sliding his key into the lock. This time, the door swung open.

"I reckon you're right," the sheriff replied. "Seeing as how you don't have family here at present."

Ben nodded. "No, sir. I don't."

"We was all real sorry to hear about your mama," the sheriff continued. "Real sorry."

"Thank you," Ben said.

"You be careful out here at night. If Granny don't get ya, Fat Tony sure will!" Sheriff Oakes said, before waving goodbye.

Ben couldn't decide if he was glad or worried that Sheriff Oakes hadn't elaborated on exactly who Fat Tony was before collapsing into the dusty recliner in the living room. This had not been the way he'd planned . . . anything. He'd made a list. He had an agenda. He knew exactly what he was going to do each day in Clay Creek, and none of those days involved nearly getting shot by his former best friend in a see-through nightgown.

Jesus fucking Christ, that nightgown. He might never get to sleep.

It occurred to him that he really *should* have tried to reach out to her—to call her and let her know his plans. It had to have been a shock to see him standing there. The very least he could have done was reach out.

But he hadn't known how. It had just been so long. The few phone calls and emails over those first years dwindled, and then . . . well, they'd just lost touch. After a while, he figured she didn't want to hear from him anymore. This hadn't been the way he'd thought their first meeting would go.

Maybe in the morning, he'd wake up in Chicago and realize this had all been a bad dream. Somehow, though, he doubted it, and if this was his first night back in Clay Creek, what would the rest of his visit bring?

He didn't know. And for Benjamin Lawrence, PhD, not knowing was just about the worst thing he could imagine.

Mylie hadn't wanted to be his friend. In fact, the minute Granny said she had to be his friend, one morning at the breakfast table, Mylie decided that was the last thing she wanted to do.

"He's not from here," Granny said. "He's lived in Chicago his whole life, and his mama is moving him down here to live with his granddaddy."

"Old Dr. Washburn?" Mylie asked.

"Yes, and don't call him that," Granny replied, pointing a spoon at Mylie. "It's disrespectful."

"He doesn't mind it," Mylie said, and Granny kicked her under the table.

"*I mind*," Granny said.

"Is his mama from here?" Mylie continued on. She didn't know a lot of people who weren't from here. She scrunched up her nose trying to think of any.

Granny nodded. "Yes, she's from here. She's a few years older than your mama."

Granny could see the question on Mylie's eleven-year-old face before she asked it. "No, his mama isn't leaving him here. She's coming, too."

In other words, Mylie thought, his mama wasn't like her mama. She didn't just leave him places and run off. The thought made her jealous.

"But his daddy just died," Granny said. "So, I want you to be extra-special nice to him, you hear?"

Mylie shrugged. "My daddy's dead, and nobody's extra-special nice to me about it."

For a moment, Granny's face softened, and she looked sad. That made Mylie feel worse than just about anything, so she said hurriedly, "I'll be nice to him, Granny. I promise."

At school, Mylie looked for the new kid. She figured he'd come in first thing in the morning the way most new kids did, but he didn't show up until nearly lunchtime. He was tall and skinny, with scabby knees and big, ugly glasses. He looked miserable.

Ms. Jones introduced him as Benjamin Lawrence, and he'd mumbled, "Just Ben."

Just Ben hadn't sat with anyone at lunch, and Mylie knew she should have invited him to sit with her and Jodi and the rest of their friends, but they'd been too busy staring at him and wondering about him to consider actually speaking to him.

"Do you think he knows any famous people?" Jodi whispered.

"I bet he does," their friend Sarah said. "He's from Chicago."

"There's nobody famous in Chicago," Mylie scoffed. Really, she didn't know if that was true, but whenever she read her granny's *Cosmopolitan* magazine (secretly in the bathroom so Granny wouldn't catch her), all it ever talked about was Los Angeles and New York.

"There's a basketball team in Chicago," Jessica piped up. "My brother watches them on TV."

They all agreed that probably counted as famous.

At recess, Mylie watched Ben take a book from his backpack and walk alone to the swings, where he sat down and started to read. If he did know anybody famous, he sure wasn't acting like it.

Finally, she trotted over to him and plopped down in the swing next to him. When he didn't say anything, she said, "Hi. I'm Mylie. Whatcha reading?"

No answer.

"Do you know anybody famous? My friends think you do, but I don't believe them."

No answer.

Mylie sighed. This was tough. She usually didn't have a hard time getting people to like her. It was one of her gifts, her granny always said. She tried again.

"My granny says your daddy's dead. So's mine. He died when I was a baby, so I don't even remember him, but my granny says he was a real piece of work, whatever that means."

Ben looked up at her, so she continued.

"She also says I have to be nice to you, you know, because of your dead daddy. But I told her that wasn't really fair because nobody's nice to me about it. Sometimes Robbie Price tells me my daddy died because he couldn't stand to look at my stupid face. Stay away from him, by the way. He's a real asshole. I'm not supposed to say that word, but Granny says it's okay to say that about Robbie Price."

For a moment, Ben's expression didn't change. He just stared at her as if she were a bug on the sidewalk. And then, ever so slowly, he shut his book, adjusted his glasses, and smiled.

"I'm Ben," he said. "You talk a lot."

"I know," Mylie replied. "Do you want to come over after school? Granny will make us pizza rolls."

"What's a pizza roll?" Ben asked.

Mylie stared at him. "They don't have pizza rolls in Chicago?"

"I don't know." Ben shrugged.

"Do you want to come over or not?" Mylie asked.

"Okay," Ben replied. "But I have to ask my mom first." He closed the book he was reading and adjusted his glasses again on the bridge of his nose. "Don't say *asshole* in front of her, or she's going to say no."

"I won't," Mylie said. "But if you're going to be my neighbor, you're going to hear Granny say it plenty."

Chapter 8

"So, you're telling me Ben Lawrence, the nerd you've been in love with since sixth grade, is back in town, and you threatened to shoot him?"

Jodi sat cross-legged on the floor, perfecting a feather jig—a weighted fishing lure. It was Saturday, but with the fishing tournament coming up in just a few weeks, they'd been spending weekends at the warehouse working on the welcome bags for the competitors. The warehouse had been where Hook, Line, & Sinker made their products for the last five years. Before that, Mylie and less than a dozen employees rented a cramped building downtown in between the ice-cream parlor and a jewelry shop. When they'd finally begun to make a profit, Mylie decided that the business was here to stay, and she could take a risk on buying a building. The warehouse, located on the edge of town, had once been a shoe factory in the 1970s. It was, to say the least, a lot of work to make the space usable again, but it was the only thing they could afford. Now, it was her pride and joy and employed nearly fifty locals.

Mylie held up a naked hook at her friend. "Don't say it like that. It sounds bad when you say it like that. And trust me, he doesn't look like a nerd. Not anymore."

"Oh really?" Jodi placed a jig with hot pink feathers into a plastic case and looked over at Mylie.

Mylie shook her head. "Nope."

"So, he's hot now?" Jodi asked. "Is that what you're telling me?"

"What I'm telling you is that I have never been so embarrassed in my entire life," Mylie replied, avoiding Jodi's question. Honestly, she didn't know how to answer it. Yes, Ben Lawrence was hot. There was no denying that. But since she'd always been attracted to him, well, the way he looked now just felt like a bonus. He still looked like Ben, just older. She thought about the way he'd stared at her in her nightgown the night before. From the look on his face, he'd been surprised by her appearance, too.

"It wasn't your fault," Jodi said. "*He* tried to break into *your* house."

At least that part was true.

"You haven't even Googled him?" Jodi pressed.

Mylie looked down at the hook she was still holding in her hand. "I mean, sure, I Googled him once or twice over the years, but he has like, *zero* online presence. All I knew was that he was living in Chicago, and last I checked, he was working on his doctorate degree in economics."

"Sexy," Jodi said dryly.

"Says the woman who looks at spreadsheets for a living," Mylie shot back.

"The man hasn't been in town twenty-four hours, and you're already defending him." Jodi made a little clucking noise with her tongue. "I mean, I get it. I always liked Ben. He was a good friend to both of us."

"He was," Mylie agreed. "But that was a long time ago, and now I feel like we don't know each other anymore."

"Because you don't," Jodi replied. "But that doesn't mean you can't get to know him again."

"I guess," Mylie said.

"Hey," Jodi said. "Seriously, are you okay?"

"I'm fine," Mylie replied. "It's just weird, that's all."

"Well, if it makes you feel any better, Sheriff Oakes didn't say a damn thing about it this morning at the Cracked Egg," Jodi said.

"Really?" Mylie asked. "I'm pleasantly surprised."

"He couldn't get a word in edgewise," Jodi continued. "Robbie Price was there bitchin' up a storm about how you fired him."

"You were there, too," Mylie grumbled.

"He's telling everyone who will listen that you fired him because you didn't like him," Jodi said. "You know, because it had nothing to do with him stealing and drinking on the job."

Mylie groaned. "I bet everyone within a three-mile radius knows about it by now."

"Let's stop for the day," Jodi offered. She stood up and walked to where Mylie stood near the office door. "We're weeks ahead of schedule, and the lake is so nice right now. Let's take the boat out, find us a cove, and enjoy the rest of our Saturday."

"Far away from people," Mylie added.

"Yes, of course," Jodi agreed. "Far away from people *and* hot neighbors."

"And the sheriff," Mylie continued, shutting off the lights. "And everyone at the Cracked Egg!"

"You got it, sister!" Jodi called after her. "You got it!"

MYLIE HADN'T REALIZED how much she needed this. Jodi's pontoon boat bobbed in the lake as the two women lay out in the sun. It was still a little chilly outside, but by this point, people were ready to be on the water. Besides, with the sun on them, it was almost warm enough to justify a bathing suit.

Jodi handed Mylie a White Claw. "Isn't this nice?"

"Mmmhmm," Mylie murmured.

"So, I probably shouldn't ruin it by asking you about Ben, huh?"

Mylie sat up, adjusting her hot pink bikini top. She loved this bikini. It was a boat-stopper. In the summertime, she and Jodi had garnered many a free drink with this bikini.

"Do you remember that time you nearly crashed Kelly Parker's pontoon boat on the Fourth of July?" Jodi asked. "Lord, I thought we were headed straight to jail."

"It was her *daddy's* pontoon," Mylie corrected her. "And I was only driving it because Kelly was drunk as a skunk and had been since noon."

"Yeah, well, you drove like you'd been drinking since noon," Jodi replied. "I still can't believe we just anchored it right there in the water and left it."

"I didn't know what else to do," Mylie said. "Besides, Ben and I went back later and got it in the slip just fine."

"You mean *Ben* got it in the slip."

Mylie smiled at the memory. She'd gone home a wreck because she was convinced she was going to be in trouble for leaving a boat on the water. Ben, who'd refused to go out on the boat that day, probably for good reason, had been the one to calm her down. They'd taken his grandfather's speedboat out that night, and he'd managed to get the pontoon started and back in the slip before anyone found out.

"He was in love with you, Mylie," Jodi continued.

"I wish that were true," Mylie said.

Jodi raised herself up on one elbow and caught her friend with a look. "You aren't an insecure person. I never understood why you didn't just tell him how you felt. You always tell everyone how you feel."

"It was different with him," Mylie admitted. "I always knew he was going to leave after graduation. I always knew I was going to stay. I didn't want to mess up our friendship."

"You can't always know anything," Jodi replied. "But I understand not wanting to be hurt."

"It was easier to just be friends," Mylie said.

"Well, now you can change it." Jodi took another drink. "You've been given a second chance."

Mylie felt her cheeks warm. "I don't know him anymore," she said. "He could be a completely different person."

"Yeah, a hot person," Jodi replied.

"I don't care about that."

"Bullshit," Jodi said. "He's hot. You're hot. And you're not kids anymore. I don't see the issue with the two of you hooking up, at least while he's here."

While he's here. The words rang in Mylie's head. That was it. The reason she didn't want to talk about Ben, about his being here. He wasn't going to stay. She didn't even have to ask him. She knew the answer. Maybe they were ten years older, maybe they looked different, but really, nothing had changed.

Nothing ever changed around here.

Chapter 9

Ben hadn't been able to sleep the night before. He'd tossed and turned and eventually gotten up and powered on his laptop, trying to find something interesting to watch. But the whole time he just kept thinking about her standing there, in front of him, in that damn nightgown, so close he could have reached out and touched her.

He hadn't. He'd never touched her. He'd wanted to so many times before, but he never, ever acted on it. He couldn't imagine how she would have reacted—his outgoing, popular neighbor in high school, and him, the scrawny, insecure boy with whom she'd been forced into friendship by her grandmother. Ten minutes in Clay Creek, and that was all it took for all those memories to come flooding back.

He hadn't really gained any confidence at all in himself until the summer before his sophomore year in college. And although he knew it didn't happen overnight, it felt like he just woke up one day good-looking. Where he'd been tall and lanky before, he was broad and toned now. His jawline was defined. When he looked in the mirror, he barely recognized himself. Women stared at him in his classes and at the coffee shop where he worked on the weekends. He got phone numbers when he went to bars, and he even rushed a frat.

His first few years in college had been nothing short of amazing.

He'd learned about more than just economics. Now, most of the time, he felt confident in who he was, and it wasn't just because he'd finally grown into himself. It was because somewhere along the way, Ben figured out who he was. And who he was now was just about as far away from who he'd been in Clay Creek as a person could get. Maybe that's why he and Mylie lost touch. Maybe it was his fault. He'd become someone else.

Ben looked around his grandfather's house and tried not to groan. He was on his own in deciding what sold with the house and what didn't. He didn't think his mother understood how hard it would be for him to be back in this house, alone, after all these years. He missed her. He missed his grandfather. Since his mother's death, he'd put his studies into overdrive, so he didn't have to think about or feel anything. Now he was here with virtually nothing to do but pick at the remains of his former life and wait for the house to sell.

There wasn't much, if any, work that needed to be done. The house was kept in shape by a management company. When repairs were necessary, they sent a bill, and his grandfather had provided for years' worth of upkeep in his will. They'd even updated the interior a few times before the summer rush of tourists, to rent the place out. Overall, it was a lovely house, and anyone would be lucky to live there. When he'd spoken to the Realtor earlier that morning, he'd been informed that he should be as ready as he could be for potential buyers. The only upside to that news was if the house sold quickly, he'd be on his way home to Chicago in no time at all.

Ben was just about to make a trip to the grocery store to fill the old refrigerator when the doorbell rang. Through the living room window, he could see a woman he vaguely remembered standing on the front porch, a Pyrex dish in her hands.

He opened the door and smiled at the woman, trying to place her. "Hello," he said. "Can I help you?"

"Oh, Benjamin, you silly thing!" the woman said. She handed him the dish. "It's me! Mrs. Ship! Your Sunday school teacher!"

Ben squinted. His mother had taken him to the Presbyterian church a few times the year they'd moved to Clay Creek. It was the only time in his life he'd ever been to church, and that was only at his grandfather's insistence, much like the failed Boy Scout attempt the following summer.

"Yes," Ben said finally. "I do remember you. How are you, Mrs. Ship?"

He didn't actually remember her, but he had a hazy memory of someone who looked at least a little like the woman standing in front of him.

"Oh, I'm just fine," she said, grinning at him. "When I heard you were back in town, well, I had to come and see for myself. And I figured a young man like you wouldn't have a stitch of food in the house, so I baked my famous green bean casserole. Just heat it up for about twenty minutes in the oven at three seventy-five, and ta-da!"

Mrs. Ship stared at Ben expectantly.

"Thank you!" Ben replied, with as much enthusiasm as he could muster. "I, uh, love green bean casserole."

"I was so sorry to hear of your mama's passing," Mrs. Ship said. "We . . . all of us over at Bethel Presbyterian were."

"Thank you," Ben replied. "I appreciate that."

"Now, tell me," Mrs. Ship continued. "Are you married? Do you have yourself a family back in Chicago?"

Ben looked down at the dish in his hands and then up at Mrs. Ship. "No," he said slowly, confused.

"So, you're single?"

"I am."

Mrs. Ship's grin broadened. "Do you remember my daughter,

Lucy? She was just a few years younger than you in school—real sweet girl. Played the trombone in the band?"

Ben didn't remember. He hadn't been in the band. "I'm sorry," Ben replied. "I don't think I do."

Mrs. Ship's face fell.

"But I'm not very good with names," Ben said hastily. "So, that's probably why."

"Lucky for you I have her picture right here!" Mrs. Ship said, pulling her phone out of her pocket and scrolling for so long that Ben thought maybe she'd forgotten he was standing there.

"Here we are," she said finally. "Look at her. Isn't she just gorgeous? Surely you remember her."

Ben looked at the picture. He didn't remember her, and he was becoming increasingly confused about why this woman he barely knew was standing on his porch at one o'clock in the afternoon asking if he remembered her daughter. Maybe the fastest way to get her to leave was to just pretend like he knew her.

"Oh, yes, *Lucy*," Ben said. "Of course I remember her."

Mrs. Ship beamed. "I knew it!"

Ben continued to smile, but his hands were getting tired of holding the dish. "Well," he said. "Thank you again for this. I appreciate you thinking of me."

Sensing her time was running short, Mrs. Ship grabbed Ben's forearm admiringly. "Honey, a good-looking man like you shouldn't be without a woman to cook for him. My Lucy is single, too, and she's just the best cook in town, aside from me, of course. Would you like her number?"

"I, uh . . ."

"Listen," Mrs. Ship said, touching his arm. "I could just send her over with lunch one afternoon. Are you going to be at the town clinic?"

"Clinic?"

"Well, I heard the clinic downtown was looking for another doctor," Mrs. Ship said. "Of course, we could always use another practice in town."

Now it made sense. Mrs. Ship thought he was a medical doctor. The rumor mill in town had missed one crucial piece of information. Everyone heard *doctor* and just assumed he was coming back to town to take up where his grandfather left off all those years ago. Mrs. Ship was hoping to marry her daughter off to a successful doctor, when the reality was that he would be lucky to make his student loan payment when and if he ever secured a job teaching.

"I think there's been a misunderstanding," Ben began. Before he could finish, two cars pulled up, one right after the other. Two more vaguely familiar women stepped out, one of them carrying a picnic basket and the other a Pyrex dish just like Mrs. Ship's.

Mrs. Ship turned around to glare at them, but her tone was dripping with honey. "Hello, ladies," she said. "Benjamin and I were just discussing my Lucy."

"Oh, Lucy's just the sweetest," one of the women replied. "And that little boy of hers, just a lamb, don't you think so, Candy?"

The second woman, who was apparently Candy, nodded. "Yes, just a lamb. You know, I've been begging Lilly to give me grandbabies for years, but she's just not ready." She leaned in closer to Ben and whispered loud enough for all four of them to hear, "She wants to wait for marriage, you know. She's a *traditional* girl."

Beside him, Mrs. Ship made a wheezing sound through her nostrils. "It's too bad that boy from Rockbridge left her at the altar. They would have made you lovely grandchildren."

The three women stared at each other in what could only be described as the politest standoff in Arkansas history. Ben wished he could back away and into the house. He knew better. Pyrex dishes were used for only two things—funerals and bribery.

And standing there watching the three of them argue silently, he wasn't sure if he was about to witness a crime or get set up on a date.

Possibly both.

And if the women standing in front of him were any indication, he was in for a very, very long afternoon.

Chapter 10

Mylie and Jodi watched the scene across the street with growing interest. They'd barely managed to maneuver the truck into Mylie's driveway without hitting a pedestrian.

"What the hell is going on over there?" Jodi asked. "Is Ben having a party?"

"With every Sunday school teacher we've ever had?" Mylie asked. "Seems unlikely."

"They've all got food," Jodi said. "Did somebody die?"

"Hey," Mylie said, pointing to the crowd of about six women. "Isn't that your mom?"

"Oh shit." Jodi reached into the back seat for a shirt to throw on over her bikini top. "It's worse than death!"

She flung open the passenger's side door of Mylie's truck and hopped out. Mylie barely had time to find her own clothes before Jodi was halfway across the street, making a beeline for her mother, who stood next to Ben. She was alternating between staring up at him adoringly and pointing down to her phone.

"I'm telling you, Benjamin," her mother was saying.

"MOM!" Jodi yelled, her bare feet making slapping noises on the concrete sidewalk.

Jodi's mother looked over at her, guilt and surprise written all over her face. "Oh, hi, sweetheart," her mother said. "We were just . . ."

"We were just going home," Jodi replied, her tone just above boiling. "I cannot believe you! I have a boyfriend, you know!"

"It's been five years, Jodi! If he wanted to marry you, he would have done it by now!"

Mylie snuck a glance over at Ben. He was staring at the scene like a victim of a car crash, glassy-eyed and confused. Behind him, there was a mountain of food. If Mylie hadn't been so horrified on his behalf, she would have laughed.

Jodi's mother was undeterred. "Ben, you remember my daughter, Jodi, don't you?"

Beside her mother, Jodi rolled her eyes. "Of course he remembers me, Mom. We were in the same class."

"Hey, Jodi," Ben said. "Nice to see you."

Jodi's face reddened. "Hi, Ben. I'm so sorry for my mother."

Mylie couldn't help it, she let out a snort. It was just too much.

Ben looked over at Mylie and grinned. "Enjoying this, huh?"

Mylie covered her mouth. "I'm sorry," she said. "I just didn't realize what a hot commodity you were in town."

"Really?" Ben asked, his bare arm brushing up against hers as he spoke. "You hadn't noticed?"

Now it was Mylie's turn to blush.

"I guess it was kind of hard to get a good look while you had a shotgun pointed in my face," Ben continued.

"You were breaking into my house," Mylie replied.

"I thought it was my house," Ben said.

"But it *wasn't*."

His arm was still pressed up against hers, and she turned to look at him. He was staring down at her through his black-rimmed glasses. They weren't too big for his face anymore. In fact, they did something for his jawline that made Mylie's lower body tingle. She wanted to reach up and take them off so he could bury his face in the right spot to make it stop.

"Mylie?"

"Huh?" Mylie blinked. Oh God. She'd been fantasizing about him while he was *standing right there.*

Ben pointed to the edge of the yard, where Granny was dashing over, Stanley at her heels, a cigarette in her mouth and a broomstick in her hand.

"What are you people doing?" Granny demanded, pointing the broom at the crowd of women. "Don't you have the sense God gave you to behave proper?"

"We were just welcoming Benjamin back to town," Jodi's mother said. She looked down at the dish in her hands. "I brought a pie."

Stanley sniffed at the woman and sneezed.

"Oh, bullshit," Granny replied, waving her off. "You ladies, and I use that term loosely, should be ashamed of yourselves. Now go on, get out of here. Get!"

With that, and the threat of a sound beating from Granny's broom, the women dispersed, muttering to themselves. Jodi followed her mother, refusing to even look back at them. Mylie couldn't wait to give her hell about it later.

Stanley let out a bark for good measure, herding a few of them as they went.

"Jesus Christ on a cracker," Granny fumed. "They've lost their minds."

Ben gave Granny a grateful smile. "Thank you," he said. "I've spent the last two hours standing on the porch."

"That damn sheriff," Granny replied. "He must've told the whole town."

Mylie shook her head. "Jodi said he didn't even mention it at the Cracked Egg this morning."

"Hmm . . ." Granny rested her chin on the handle of the broomstick. "Maybe his wife."

"She's in Missouri with her sister for the next few weeks," Mylie replied.

"Did you stop anywhere on the way in?" Granny asked. "Who's seen you?"

Ben shrugged. "I don't know. I guess I stopped for gas just outside of town."

"Was it the gas station with the red pumps or the one across from it that sells bootleg moonshine?" Granny demanded.

Ben laughed, but when he realized Granny was being serious, he replied, "It wasn't the one with the red gas pumps."

"Damn Margie," Granny said. "She's the biggest blabbermouth in town."

"So, all of this is because I stopped at the wrong gas station?" Ben asked.

"You've been gone too long, son," Granny replied. "Did you forget the way Clay Creek works?"

Ben scratched the back of his head and then gestured to the porch behind him, covered a mile high in dishes. "What am I going to do with all of this?"

Granny peered around Ben and said, "When was the last time you had a home-cooked meal?"

For a moment, it looked like Ben might not answer, and Mylie realized that the last time had probably been when his mother was still alive. Before he could say anything, she chimed in. "Granny is cooking tonight. Why don't you come over?"

Granny gave Mylie a wink. "You read my mind." She turned her attention to Ben. "Bring over some of that food, and we'll help you eat it."

"Are you sure?" Ben asked, looking first to Granny and then to Mylie. "I don't want to put anybody out."

"Hush up," Granny replied. "I won't have any of that Yankee talk around here. We'll see you in an hour."

"Yes, ma'am," Ben said.

"Anything but Doris Ship's green bean casserole," Granny called over her shoulder. "Throw that straight into the trash."

Ben's mother, Emily Lawrence, peered across the lawn to the twin house on the other side of the street, where it appeared a woman with a cigarette hanging out of her mouth was taking a hose to a muddy dog and child.

"That's your new friend over there?" Ben's mother asked.

Ben looked down at his feet to keep from grinning. "Yes."

"The girl or the dog?"

"The girl, Mom. Come on."

"Interesting" was his mother's only reply.

If the adjustment to Clay Creek had been hard on Ben, it was equally hard on his mother. She'd grown up in Michigan, in Detroit, and then spent the majority of her adult life in Chicago. Clay Creek was . . . not either of those places. It wasn't really *anywhere* as far as Ben could tell.

They'd moved earlier than Emily would have liked, but she couldn't turn down the offer to teach English at the high school, not when her position at the elite Chicago private school where she'd taught was eliminated.

She'd asked her father, Ben's grandfather, more than once how a sophisticated city doctor like Benjamin Sr. could possibly retire here. Benji had just shrugged and said he loved the quiet, loved the fishing. He loved the part-time clinic he'd opened. He didn't even mind being called a Yankee by the locals.

Emily did, though. She chaffed against the relaxed attitudes, the way everyone waved at everyone else, the way people were so . . . *familiar* with each other. She'd come home after that first day at school, sat down at the kitchen table, and ranted about how she'd been expected to give her personal, private phone number to two faculty members just because she knew they'd be offended if she hadn't offered it.

"It's their way," Benji replied smoothly. "They just want to be able to reach you."

"I don't want to be reached," Emily replied.

"You never have," Benji joked, patting his daughter's hand.

Emily stiffened and then turned to Ben and asked about his day. Ben merely shrugged and then said shyly, carefully, that he'd made friends with the neighbor girl, Mylie.

"What kind of a name is that?" Emily asked.

"She's Violet Mason's granddaughter," Benji replied, as if that explained everything.

And now his new friend was squealing as she ran through a water hose, her ruined clothing utterly soaked, mud sliding down her tanned legs.

As they stood there, he and his mother, watching the scene unfold, Mylie looked over and grinned at them, at *him*, Ben realized. She beckoned for him.

"Come on!" she hollered.

"Don't even think about it," his mother threatened.

Ben looked to his mother and then at Mylie. Her head was thrown back laughing as she slipped and went down into the soggy grass, the dog jumping on top of her and licking her face.

"Come on, Ben!" she said again.

Ben didn't give it a second thought, running toward her, his mother yelling about his nice school clothes as he slid into the mess, Mylie's hand outstretched to meet his own.

Chapter 12

Mylie was waiting for Ben on the front porch when he got there. She was sitting on the swing, reading a book. She smiled when she looked up and saw him.

"Hi," she said.

"Can I sit?" Ben asked. He set the three dishes he'd chosen to bring over on the little table beside the swing.

Mylie nodded and scooted over to accommodate him. "So," she said. "How are you?"

Ben sat down, careful not to get too close. He didn't need a repeat of earlier when they'd barely brushed arms and he thought he might need a cold shower. "I'm good. How are you?"

"I'm good."

Silence.

Ben waited for her to say something, and when she didn't, he said, "Do you remember that game we used to play where we asked each other a question, and if the other refused to answer, we got to slap their hands?"

Mylie looked over at him. "Yeah, why?"

Ben held out his hands. "Let's play."

"I'm not twelve," Mylie replied. Then, realizing Ben wasn't kidding, she sighed and said, "Okay, fine. But I get to go first."

She placed her hands under his and said, "What are you doing here?"

Ben cocked his head to the side. "At your house or Clay Creek?"

"Clay Creek," Mylie replied. "I know why you're at my house. You're scared of Granny."

"That's true," Ben acknowledged. "I'm here because I promised my mom I'd come back at least once before I sold the house."

"Why are you selling the house?"

"It's my turn," Ben said, placing his hands on top of hers. "Are you mad at me for selling?"

Mylie stared at him, but she didn't answer.

"Don't make me slap your hands," Ben warned her. "I'll do it."

"I'm not mad," Mylie said, finally.

"Why do you sound mad?"

"It's my turn," Mylie replied. "Why are you selling the house?"

"I got a job offer on the East Coast," Ben said. "At a university. I need the money to move." Ben moved his hand. "Aren't we a little old for this game?"

"Maybe you are."

Mylie moved her hands to the top. "How long are you going to be here?" she asked.

"I don't know," Ben said. "I haven't decided."

Mylie narrowed her eyes.

"One of the women who came over today said you had your own business," Ben said. "Is it the one you always talked about?"

"Yes," Mylie replied.

"That's amazing," Ben said, truly impressed. "I always knew you'd do it."

"My turn," Mylie said. She waited until their hands were touching once again before she asked, "Did you miss me?"

Ben looked at her. Her face was a mixture of defiance and uncertainty. It was the look she got when she was ready to fight someone or burst into tears. He'd seen it a million times, but rarely had she turned that look on him. It was unnerving. He grabbed her wrists so that she couldn't squirm away from him and said, "Every single day for the last ten years."

"Then why . . ."

Before Mylie could finish her sentence, the front door swung open and Cassie and another teenager stepped out. Ben let go of Mylie's wrists and scooted away from her.

Cassie looked at the girl, rolled her eyes, and then said, "Granny says to bring that food in before the flies get it."

Ben hopped up. "Okay," he said. "You probably don't remember me, Cassie, but I'm Ben."

"I know who you are," Cassie replied. "Granny told me you used to throw me in the lake."

Ben laughed. "You asked me to, and you always wore a life jacket."

"This is Allie," Cassie said, pointing to her friend.

"Hi," Ben said. "Nice to meet you."

"Yeah," Allie replied. "You, too, I guess."

Ben followed them into the house. It looked the same as he remembered, but some of the furniture had changed. It was the same layout of his house, but it was cozier. That was probably because nobody but renters had lived in the house for a decade, but he remembered feeling the same way all those years ago. There was just something about the Masons. They welcomed everyone.

"There you are," Granny said when she saw Ben. "What did you bring me?"

Ben extended the dishes to her. "Uh, I think pasta salad, sweet potato pie, and brownies."

"I'll throw that sweet potato pie in the oven," Granny said. "It'll go perfect with this roast."

"Thanks for having me," Ben replied.

"None of that," Granny said, waving him off. "Go on and find Morris. I think he's sitting in the living room in front of the TV like always."

Ben did as he was told and sat down next to an older man who was drinking a beer and watching a hunting show on the Discovery Channel. The older man didn't even notice.

Mylie came and sat down on the chair beside the couch and said, "Morris, you remember Ben Lawrence?"

Morris didn't turn away from the TV but replied, "Of course. How are you, son?"

"I'm good," Ben replied. "Thank you."

They sat there in silence while Ben moved between trying to figure out how he knew Morris and wishing he could be alone with Mylie again. They still needed to talk. He needed to know if she'd forgiven him. He needed to know if he could touch her the way her eyes had begged him to do before they'd been interrupted. But those weren't questions he could ask her in a house full of people.

When Morris got up to replace his beer, Ben's curiosity about the man won out, and he asked Mylie, "Why does he look so familiar?"

"He was our history teacher in high school," Mylie replied. Then she scrunched up her face and said, "The Continental Congress declared freedom from Britain on July *second*, not July *fourth*!"

"Holy shit," Ben replied. "I can't believe that's him. I've never forgotten that lesson in our American History class."

"Imagine your grandmother being his *special friend*," Mylie said, shuddering.

Ben laughed. "I'm so sorry."

"I guess it's not that bad," Mylie replied. "He keeps Granny busy, and he's nice to me and Cassie. Last year, he got me a book about the Revolutionary War for Christmas, because he said he remembered I got a C in his class when I was in eleventh grade."

"His classes were hard," Ben admitted. "I had to study more in his class than in all of my college history classes combined."

"So, you're a doctor now, huh?" Mylie continued.

"Yeah," Ben said. "How did you know?"

"Well, I got a C in history, but I do know how to Google," Mylie said.

"Creepy," Ben replied. He was grinning at her, a wave of relief washing over him. She didn't seem mad at him. She was talking to him now just like she always had. He wasn't lying before. He'd missed her. He'd missed this.

"Come on!" Granny hollered from the kitchen. "It's time to eat!"

Chapter 13

Mylie noticed Ben hadn't left a single scrap of food on his plate. He'd watched them as they talked about their day, the happenings around town, never offering to join in on the conversation. He sat there and ate and watched. Occasionally, Mylie would catch him looking over at her with an expression she couldn't quite figure out. She could still feel the heat on her wrists from where he grabbed her, and it made her sweat to think about what might have happened if Cassie and Allie hadn't interrupted them.

"Mylie tells me you've got yourself a fancy PhD," Morris said to Ben when they were finished eating.

"Yes, sir," Ben replied.

"Not in history, I reckon," Morris said with a sniff.

"No, sir," Ben said. "Economics."

"Is that supply and demand stuff?" Cassie asked. "We read about that in my World Civics class last quarter."

"That's part of it," Ben replied.

Morris cleared his throat, clearly priming for another round of questions, and Mylie felt a pang of sympathy for Ben.

"What do you do with a doctorate in economics?" Morris asked. "Work for the government?"

"Or teach," Ben replied. "Which is exactly what I plan to do once . . ." He paused. "Once I wrap things up here."

"You're not staying?" Morris pulled his pipe out and began to stuff tobacco down into it.

"Just until the house sells," Ben said.

"That's too bad," Morris continued. "The community college just up the way needs a few good men. I taught a few classes there myself just after I retired. Good place. Mylie went there."

Mylie inwardly cringed. It wasn't that she wasn't proud to have gone to community college. When she was twenty-two, she went back to get a business degree. She'd done well, much better than she had in high school. But putting it up next to Ben's Ivy League education made her feel small somehow.

"Oh really?" Ben asked, interested. "What was your major?"

"Business," Mylie answered, offering nothing else. She looked to her sister for a change of topic. "Cassie, did you and Allie have a good day?"

Cassie nodded. "Yeah."

"No snaps from Ryan?"

Cassie glared at Mylie. "I told Ryan that I didn't want to talk to him until he got home from his trip."

"Good," Granny said. "I think you spend too much time with that boy."

"He sent me a text today, though," Cassie continued. "He said his dad heard you fired Robbie. You know they're related."

"Then why doesn't Ryan's daddy hire him at his boat repair shop?" Mylie asked Cassie. "Since they're *family*."

"Because he's a drunk," Cassie replied, shrugging.

Mylie threw her hands up in the air. "Well, I can't argue there."

"Robbie Price?" Ben asked.

Mylie knew why Ben was asking. Robbie was two years older than Ben and had made Ben's life hell as often as he could in high school. Ben hadn't been unpopular in high school, not by a long shot, but he was quiet and kind, two things Robbie hated in a person. Once, he'd stolen Ben's backpack and threw it in a huge vat of cooking oil in the cafeteria. How the cooks hadn't noticed before they turned on those fryers, Mylie would never know. That, of course, had been retaliation for some perceived slight that had been Mylie's fault to begin with.

"I didn't want to hire him," Mylie said, finally. "Granny made me do it."

"I've never been able to make you do anything, Mylie Marie," Granny said, pointing her finger at her granddaughter. "I simply put in a good word on behalf of his mother."

"The boys at the VFW and I took bets over how long it would last," Morris said, a laugh escaping past his lips. "We all lost. Nobody thought he'd make it past the first week."

Mylie snuck a look over at Ben, and to her surprise, he was laughing along with Morris. "I have to admit," he said, "I figured Robbie would be in prison by now."

"Hook, Line, and Sinker is kind of like a prison," Cassie replied.

"It's absolutely nothing like a prison," Mylie said. "You just hate to work."

"I'm a *child*," Cassie said.

Mylie rolled her eyes.

"Well," Ben said, standing up. "I should get back over to the house. It's getting late, and I still have a lot to do."

"What do you have to do?" Granny asked. "That place is immaculate. I was just in there last summer when there were renters for the season."

Ben shoved his hands down into his pockets and said, "There are a few sentimental things I want to take with me, but mostly I have to work on a paper I'm writing for publication."

"About supply and demand?" Cassie asked.

"Something like that," Ben said and gave her a grin.

"I'll walk you to the door," Mylie said, standing up.

"Benjamin," Granny called after him. "We play bingo at the VFW every Tuesday. You should come."

"I haven't been to bingo in a long time," Ben admitted. "I used to go with Grandpa."

"I know," Granny continued. "Before he moved off with your mother, he donated the money for a remodel, and they have a nice dedication to him."

"Thanks, Granny," Ben said. "I'd love to."

Granny nodded and waved the two of them off. "I'm gonna hold you to it!"

Mylie stood at the front door, watching him. He seemed to be deciding whether to hug her or shake her hand. She watched his internal struggle for a few seconds before finally deciding to put him out of his misery and leaned in for a hug.

When they separated, Ben didn't leave. Instead, he said, "What are your plans for the rest of the night?"

Mylie shrugged. "You're looking at it."

"So, you don't have any plans with Jodi that involve leaving a boat in the water or stealing a stop sign or something else illegal?"

Mylie laughed. "Those days are behind me, I'm afraid."

Ben studied her for a moment. "You look almost exactly the same as you did when I left, you know? The same . . . but different."

"So do you," Mylie replied. "I mean, you actually look a lot different, but you're the same in a lot of ways."

"What ways?" Ben asked.

"Your glasses, for one," Mylie said. "But they're not too big for your face anymore."

"I tried contacts for a while," Ben said.

"I like the glasses," Mylie replied. "I always have."

The corner of Ben's mouth quirked up. "Do you want to come over?" he asked. "It's just . . . I'm not ready to stop talking to you, and I'm pretty sure there are about four desserts that I'll never be able to eat by myself sitting in my refrigerator."

"Don't you have a paper to write?" Mylie asked, narrowing her eyes.

"It can wait" was all Ben said.

"Okay," Mylie replied. She stepped out into the thick May air with him. "Lead the way."

Chapter 14

Mylie hadn't been inside the house in years, not since before Ben left. It was true, Granny had gone over a time or two to help visitors, but she'd always avoided it. Looking at the outside had been hard enough.

"It looks the same," Mylie said.

"Pretty much," Ben replied. He rummaged in the fridge and handed her a beer. "I still need to go to the grocery store. I just ran up to the gas station and bought beer and some beef jerky, but I still don't have any coffee."

"You and your coffee," Mylie muttered. She twisted the cap off the bottle. "I still remember thinking it was weird that a sixth-grader drank coffee."

"It wasn't as weird in Chicago," Ben said.

"I don't believe that," Mylie replied. "You can't just say that things are normal in Chicago to make yourself look normal."

"So now I'm not normal?"

Mylie huffed a laugh. "You've never been normal."

Ben took a swig from his own beer and then said, "I really did miss you. I was telling the truth about that."

"You stopped calling," Mylie said. "You never emailed. You never reached out on social media. I thought . . . I thought you'd forgotten about me."

"*We* stopped calling each other," Ben replied. "*You* never emailed. And I don't have social media."

"Everybody has social media," Mylie countered.

"Did you ever look for me?" Ben asked.

Mylie looked away from him. "Maybe."

"Then you know that I didn't have any profiles," he said. "I tried once, back in college. But I got overwhelmed with the constant alerts. It was too much."

"You still could have called," Mylie said. "My number hasn't changed."

"Neither has mine," Ben replied.

They stared at each other for a long moment. Mylie knew they were both right. Neither of them had made an effort to stay in touch, but she wanted so badly to blame him for all of it, for everything, the way she'd been doing for the last ten years. After all, he'd been the one to leave, not her.

"I know you're trying to think of a way to blame me for it all," Ben said when Mylie didn't reply. "And if it helps, I blame myself, too."

"That helps a little," Mylie admitted. She eased the death grip she had on the bottle.

"I'm sorry," he said, taking a step closer to her. "I was eighteen. I was stupid. And after a while, I thought you probably didn't want to hear from me anymore."

"Maybe I didn't," Mylie said, more to herself than to Ben.

Ben reached up to brush a piece of hair that had come loose from her ponytail away from her face. "I'm sorry," he said again.

Mylie looked up at the man in front of her. The man who'd once been a boy and who had changed in so many ways . . . and in others, not at all. His eyes were the same behind those glasses. He was still her Ben.

"I'm sorry, too," she said finally.

Ben didn't remove his hand from her face, and she could feel her heart pounding in her chest. After all this time, all these years, here he was, finally, right in front of her. She'd imagined this scenario over and over again.

Finally, Ben stepped away from her, clearing his throat. "Well," he said. "I guess now that we're not mad at each other anymore, I can cross that off my list."

"You have a list?" Mylie asked, the pressure in her chest finally releasing. She could breathe.

"Of course," Ben replied. "Have you ever known me not to keep a list?"

Mylie laughed. "I should go," she said. "Granny will be wondering where the hell I went, and I promised the girls we'd watch a movie."

"Okay." Ben tried and failed to hide the tiniest hint of disappointment in his eyes. "Enjoy your night."

"What about you? What are you going to do?" Mylie asked. "Oh, wait. Let me guess. You're going to go upstairs, read a book, and it's lights out at promptly eleven p.m."

Ben tilted his head back and laughed. "So, you remember?"

"All those parties you refused to attend?" Mylie asked. "Yes."

"Maybe things have changed," Ben replied.

Mylie grinned. "Some things never change."

"You'd be surprised," Ben said.

"Oh, really?"

Ben placed one hand against the doorframe and leaned down to Mylie's level, so close that she could feel the way his breath hitched in his chest, the way his jaw tightened as he replied, "There's a lot you don't know about me, Mylie."

Mylie watched his jaw tick just a bit, watched his hands clench and unclench, like he was on the brink of saying more . . . or do-ing more. He was still Ben, after all, controlled and collected, but something told her that if she'd gotten just an inch closer to him, parted her lips just a little, offered herself in any way to him, he might shatter.

He pulled himself away from her and stuck his hands inside his pockets, his easy smile returning to his face so quickly, that Mylie wondered if she'd imagined the whole thing.

"I'll see you later, Mylie," Ben said. "Good night."

LATER THAT NIGHT, Mylie looked out her bedroom window and wondered if Ben really was reading a book. It was getting close to eleven p.m. He'd be going to sleep soon if her theory held true. She figured it had to be hard, being back here all alone. She'd always had family around her, even if her parents hadn't been there for her. First it was Granny, and then Cassie came along, and Mylie couldn't imagine her life without them.

She wondered idly what Ben thought about her still living at home with her family. It wasn't something she'd ever really considered— moving out on her own. Granny and Cassie needed her, and she knew she needed them. Mylie knew most people moved out of their childhood homes and started a life on their own, but she'd always known that she wanted to live with Granny, at least until Cassie graduated from high school. She'd always wanted to take care of her little sister. At first, Granny tried to remind Mylie that Cassie wasn't her responsibility. She didn't have to stay there. She could go out and see the world if she wanted, but Mylie had ig-nored her, and eventually, Granny stopped talking about it.

Mylie was about to go to bed when she saw a light in a window at Ben's house. It wasn't his old room, which was directly across from hers, but she could still see it. It was flashing on and off, on and off.

She turned and rummaged around in her desk drawer until she found a flashlight. She hadn't used it in forever, but it still worked. This had been their way of saying good night to each other for years, and Mylie couldn't believe Ben remembered.

She turned the flashlight on and pointed it out her window. On and off. On and off.

There were a few more flashes from Ben's side, and then it went dark. Mylie stood there for a while longer, smiling, remembering, and thankful that for now at least, her Ben was back.

"Look at that mama's boy." Robbie Price jabbed his thumb in Ben's direction. "He gonna let her nurse him at the lunch table?"

Everyone sitting near Robbie in the school cafeteria laughed. Mylie looked over to where Ben sat, at the teachers' table, with his mother. Most of the time, he and Mylie sat with her friends, or they ditched the cafeteria all together and sat on the picnic tables outside, Ben drinking his water and Mylie enjoying a Dr Pepper.

Mylie knew why Ben was sitting with his mother that day. She'd recently been diagnosed with cancer, and nobody knew. In fact, Ben had sworn Mylie to secrecy when he'd told her the week before. It wasn't as serious as it could have been—a thyroid cancer that doctors thought they could remove, but it was still scary. Especially for Ben, who had only his mother.

Mylie also knew a little bit about that. Her own mother was often in and out of her life, and her father had been dead since she was a baby. She knew what it felt like to live without parents and how upsetting it must be for Ben to face it.

From where she stood in line to get the day's serving of limp pizza and cold French fries, Mylie could hear Robbie continue to mock Ben, and it made her blood boil. He'd always been a bully, picking on the kids he thought were weaker than him. Probably the only reason he didn't try it with Mylie was because he knew her granny would run him over in front of the Kroger.

Ben ignored Robbie, mostly. They all did. It was easier than standing up to him and finding yourself in a trash can or a locker. Besides, all they had to do was get to the end of the year, and with any luck, Robbie would eventually graduate and move on to the Arkansas State Penitentiary, where he belonged.

Still, it didn't make it any easier for Mylie to listen to Robbie when she knew what Ben and his mother were going through.

"He's such an asshole," Mylie's friend Jodi said, picking up the tray one of the lunch ladies had slid out to her.

"I hate him," Mylie spat, a little louder than she meant to. "I hope he drowns in the lake." So much of the time, Mylie felt bad for Robbie, but today, when Robbie's anger was aimed at Ben and his mom, all she felt was rage.

"Not even the lake wants him," Jodi replied. "Did I tell you he asked Sarah out on a date? She said no, and the next morning, she woke up to rotten eggs smashed all over her car. It had to be Robbie."

"I'd take the rotten eggs over prom with Robbie Price," Mylie replied.

"Same," Jodi said.

The line lurched forward, and Mylie took her own tray. "Hey," she said. "Why didn't I get pizza?"

"We're out," the lunch lady said. She pointed a ladle at Mylie. "You should get here earlier if you want pizza. We're down to chili now."

Mylie sighed. Could this day get any worse?

"That chili looks disgusting," Jodi said. "Do you want to throw it away and get something from the snack machine?"

Mylie was staring at Robbie. He was still laughing with his buddies, and from the teachers' table, she could see that Ben looked miserable. But when he caught her looking at him, he gave her a half smile and a little wave.

She waved back and then said to Jodi, "Yeah, I'm gonna throw this away. I'll be right back."

"Hey!" Jodi called after her. "The trash can is the other way!"

But it was too late. Mylie was already making her way toward Robbie's table. As she neared him, she tripped over an invisible crack in the linoleum, her lunch tray flying out of her hands and landing squarely on top of Robbie and his friends.

"What the fuck?" Robbie screeched, pushing up from his seat.

From her position on the floor, Mylie looked up at Robbie, who was now furious and covered in chili. It was hard not to burst into laughter, but Mylie mustered all her strength and said, as apologetically as she could, "I'm so sorry! I tripped!"

The entire lunchroom erupted in hysterics, including Ben, who once again caught Mylie's eye and mouthed *thank you*.

"You bitch!" Robbie ranted. "You did that on purpose!"

"I tripped!" Mylie repeated, but now she was laughing, too.

"Mr. Price," the principal said, stepping in between the two. "Language."

"She spilled her fucking chili all over me!"

"That's it," the principal replied. "Clean up and see me in my office. Now."

Robbie glared at Mylie, who by now had stood up and was watching him in smug satisfaction. He opened his mouth to say something, but the principal pointed to the door, and Robbie skulked out, cursing under his breath.

"He's gonna get you for that," Jodi whispered to Mylie. "He's pissed."

"He can try," Mylie replied, crossing her arms over her chest. "But it'll be Christmas before he gets all that chili scraped off."

Mylie felt a tap on her shoulder and turned around to see the lunch lady standing there with a paper bag in her hand. She held it out to Mylie.

"What's this?" Mylie looked inside and saw two pieces of pizza. "I thought you were out."

"We always keep some back just in case," the lunch lady replied. She winked at Mylie.

Mylie grinned. "Thanks."

"Don't tell nobody," the lunch lady said with a wink. "Can't have Robbie Price full of chili every day."

"What about soup?" Jodi asked.

The lunch lady gave them a toothy grin. "Next week is clam chowder."

Chapter 16

When Ben woke up the next morning and remembered there was no coffee in the house, he knew he needed to make a trip to the grocery store. He'd laid awake for hours the night before, thinking about how nothing on this trip so far was going according to plan. He hadn't accomplished a single thing except chaos. He needed to go through the house, meet with the Realtor, and more than anything, he needed to sell. But all he could really think about was Mylie. God, she made him feral.

He couldn't act on it. He couldn't, wouldn't, act on it, he told himself, for the same reason he couldn't act on it ten years ago—he was leaving. That was a cop out, and he knew it. For one thing, he'd been too shy and immature to even *consider* some of the things he was fantasizing about right now, at this absurd hour in the morning. But he'd always known there was something between them. He'd known, and for the sake of both of them, he'd let it go.

It was proving more difficult this time around. For one, they were both adults. There wouldn't be any fumbling around the bedroom . . . *if* they even made it as far as the bedroom. He'd wanted so badly to pull her up there last night. Would have if she hadn't left when she did.

Back to coffee. If he wanted his brain to work, he had to find coffee.

Coffee was how he'd gotten through college. It was how he'd

managed to write his thesis. It had been there for him during late-night study sessions and early-morning exams. It was his constant in life, and yes, Mylie had been right—he'd had coffee nearly every day since sixth grade. It was a habit he and his mother had gotten into after his father died. He'd never grown out of it.

Ben stumbled to the shower, dressed, and headed out the door, trying to remember where exactly the grocery store was. He wasn't amused when he parked and got up to the door to find that little Town & Country market was closed.

He looked down at his watch. It was nearly nine a.m.

"We don't open until eleven," a voice behind him said.

Ben turned to look at an elderly woman wearing a red vest and matching lipstick. She was smiling at him and pointing to the locked sliding glass doors.

"Oh," Ben said. "Okay, thank you."

"Church and all," the woman continued as if she hadn't heard him. "I take myself to the early service, but not everybody is an early bird like me."

"Do you know where I could get some coffee?" Ben asked, trying to keep the desperation out of his voice.

She squinted her eyes and tilted her head to the side before she said, "Hmm, I think you can get some at the Cracked Egg. It's just down the street to your left. You can't miss it."

He sighed with relief. "Wonderful."

"Buncha nondenominationals over there," the woman replied. "They go to church whenever they feel like it. I'm a proper Baptist, you know."

Ben decided this probably wouldn't be the best time to tell her that half of the Baptist women's coalition had been in his front yard yesterday auctioning off their eligible daughters. Instead, he said, "I appreciate the help, ma'am."

"Ma'am," the woman said. "Oh, aren't you sweet. The kids these days don't know how to be polite. I'm glad someone raised you right."

After he said goodbye to the older woman, Ben made his way over to the Cracked Egg. It wasn't a restaurant he remembered from his years in Clay Creek. Most of the restaurants in town closed for the season and didn't open until the tourist season, in June, but there were always a few small mom-and-pop-type places that stayed open year-round for the locals.

The Cracked Egg was on the outskirts of town close to the marina. When he pulled into the parking lot, Ben realized that this place had once been a boating repair shop. He wondered how they'd managed to turn it into a restaurant, but if they had fresh coffee, he guessed it didn't really matter.

It was crowded for a Sunday morning, but he found an empty stool at the counter and sat down. A harried-looking waitress appeared in front of him a few minutes later.

"What can I get ya, hon?"

"Coffee, please," Ben said.

She looked at him, pen poised on a small pad. "That it?"

"For now, I think," Ben replied. "Thanks."

"Hey," the waitress said. "Don't I know you?"

Ben looked at her. They were around the same age. She had red hair and a face full of freckles. He realized who she was at the same time she recognized him.

"Ben Lawrence!"

"Melissa Miller!"

"Well, it's Melissa Sutherland now," Melissa said, grinning. "I'll be damned. It is you. I heard you were back in town."

While Ben often thought that Mylie was his only real friend in Clay Creek, that hadn't technically been true. He'd had a few friends, especially by the time he got to high school. Melissa had been one of them. They'd been in math club together, and even though Melissa was a year younger, they'd nearly always found themselves in the same advanced placement classes. That was why he was surprised to see her behind the counter of a diner taking orders.

Melissa narrowed her gaze at him and said, "You're judging me."

"What?" Ben shifted on the stool. It was suddenly uncomfortable. "No, I'm not."

"Yes, you are," Melissa replied. "You're wondering how the smartest girl in school ended up waiting tables at a greasy spoon."

Goddamnit.

"I have a master's degree in English," Melissa said, pointing her pen at him. "I teach at the college in Rockbridge. My aunt owns this place, and I help her out on the weekends."

"I'm sorry," Ben replied. "You're right. I was judging you."

"I know," Melissa said. "I'm just as smart as you are, Mr. Fancy Pants."

"You're smarter than I am," Ben admitted. "You always kicked my ass in mathletes."

Melissa laughed. "That's true."

At the back of the diner, there was a loud crash and a round of cursing. Ben craned his neck to see a booth full of men scrambling to pick up the pieces of a shattered plate of biscuits and gravy.

"Cleanup on aisle eight!" one of them quipped.

Melissa shot them a look, and the man immediately paled. "Sorry, Missy! We'll get it taken care of!"

"You better!" Melissa yelled. "I ain't bringing you another plate until that floor is spotless!"

"Yes, ma'am!"

"They're all drunks." Melissa poured Ben a cup of coffee and then leaned on the countertop with her elbows. "They come in here every Sunday, hungover and stupid."

"Sounds awful," Ben replied.

"They're harmless, mostly," Melissa said. "Except when he's with them."

A man was walking toward the counter with the remnants of the plate, bits of gravy sliding off the jagged ends onto the floor.

"You're making a mess!" Melissa said when the man dropped the plate unceremoniously on the counter.

The man wiped his hands on his jeans and said, "I reckon you better get a mop."

If looks could have killed, the man would have been dead. Melissa put her hands on her hips. "Maybe you should get the mop."

"I don't work here," he replied, turning around to walk back toward the booth.

"Well," Melissa called after him. "From what I hear, you don't work anywhere."

Ben watched the man stop in his tracks and turn around. He sauntered back over to them, a sneer on his ruddy face that Ben recognized immediately. The man was Robbie Price.

The diner was silent.

Robbie leaned over the counter and said, "I think it's best if you mind your own business, Missy."

Melissa still had her hands on her hips, but she looked less sure of herself. "Oh yeah? Or what?"

"Or that bitch Mylie Mason won't be the only one in town with problems she can't solve," Robbie replied. His tone was low and cool, but his fists were clenched tight at his sides.

"You really wanna get yourself sideways with the Masons?" Melissa asked. "Come on, now, Robbie."

Robbie sniffed.

Ben set his coffee cup down onto its saucer, careful not to spill any of the precious liquid and stood up, forcing Robbie to take notice of him for the first time. He towered over Robbie by at least three inches, and Ben looked down at him, a polite smile plastered on his face.

"Do we have a problem here?" he asked Robbie.

"Well, I'll be damned," Robbie replied. "Little Ben Lawrence. Never thought I'd see the day."

Ben was surprised at how old Robbie looked. It was clear his football-playing days were long past him. His face was sallow and his eyes red-rimmed. Most of what he had left by way of bulk pooled in his midsection like a flat tire. He didn't look like he could be knocked over by a feather, but he was no match for Ben.

And they both knew it.

"Hey, Robbie," Ben said. "It's been a long time."

Robbie looked over at Melissa and then back at Ben. He took a step back from the counter and released his fists. "I ain't cleanin' this mess," he said, finally. "Georgie can do it."

"You tell him the mop is in the back," Melissa replied.

They watched him skulk off to the booth, and Melissa let out a long-held breath. "See what I mean? He's still causing trouble wherever he goes."

Ben took a sip of his coffee. "Is he making trouble for Mylie?" he asked Melissa.

"He's gonna do his dead-level best," Melissa replied. "But don't worry. Everybody in town loves Mylie. Besides, Robbie's a blow-hard. Always has been."

That didn't make Ben feel better. He wished Mylie had never hired him, favor or not. He might not look like the old Robbie, but he sure as hell acted like him. Years ago, Robbie had been a bully, there was no doubt about it, but it had been in high school, when he'd started drinking, that his behavior got worse. It was clear now that the drinking had never stopped.

"Don't go judging Clay Creek by Robbie Price," Melissa said, refilling Ben's cup. "And don't go thinking you're better than the rest of us, either."

"I don't think I'm better than the rest of you," Ben replied. "I lived here, remember?"

"Mmmhmm," Melissa said.

"I'm not here to stay," Ben said. "I'm just here until the house sells."

"House or not, you've got ties here you can't break," Melissa replied. "And sooner or later, you'll figure that out."

"If you say so." Ben looked back over to the booth where Robbie sat, his arms crossed over his chest, clearly still fuming.

"I'm smarter than you, right?" Melissa asked him.

Ben sighed. "Since you're so intuitive, what am I going to order for breakfast?"

Melissa touched her index finger to her nose and said, "One order of country fried steak and eggs, coming right up!"

Chapter 17

"How has practice been going?" Mylie asked the following Monday when the four women on the Hook, Line, & Sinker angler team crowded into her office. "I think we stand a pretty good chance at winning this year."

Jessica, the team's lead, grinned. "It's going good! Don't you think so, Louise?"

Louise, who was at least as old as Granny, nodded. "Yeah, honey, I think we're gonna whoop some ass."

Angel and Nevaeh, identical twins and Louise's daughters, agreed.

People had been fishing in Clay Creek since, well, forever. The lake brought all kinds of sportsmen to town, and fishing was no exception. There was something about being out on a boat with a rod and reel that was like a balm for the soul. Mylie loved baiting a hook and casting a line into the clear, cool water. The competition was just another way to bring revenue into the town, and Mylie was proud to sponsor a team.

"How many teams are signed up?" Mylie asked Jodi. "I looked last week, and twenty teams had paid the entry fee."

"Let me look." Jodi squinted into Mylie's computer.

"Okay, while she's doing that," Mylie began, opening a cardboard box in the corner of the office. "Look! The new team shirts came in!"

They were baby blue with each woman's name written in black across the back with the Hook, Line, & Sinker logo across the front.

"They're perfect!" Angel squealed.

Louise rolled her eyes. "They could be a little less girly," she said, holding up her shirt and wrinkling her nose. "I asked for gray."

"We had gray last year," Nevaeh pointed out. "It was our turn to choose this year."

"Uh, Mylie?" Jodi said, turning away from the computer to face the women. "We might have a problem."

"What is it?" Mylie asked. "Did a team drop out? We need at least twenty to thirty to be a decent competition."

"No," Jodi replied. "There's a new team signed up."

"We'll beat them, too," Jessica said, dismissing Jodi with a flick of her wrist. "No problem."

"It's Robbie Price." Jodi's mouth set in a grim line. "He just signed up his own team."

The women looked between each other.

"Who's on his team?" Louise asked.

"His two brothers and a cousin," Jodi replied.

"Aren't those three usually on a team with someone else?" Mylie asked.

"Yeah," Jodi said. She scrolled through the list of names. "It looks like they've quit that team and joined with Robbie."

"They won't give us any trouble," Louise said. "They never have before."

"Robbie's never been on their team before," Mylie pointed out.

"Well, it's against the rules to sabotage another team," Jodi said. "Robbie knows that. He's just doing this to get into our heads."

"*My* head," Mylie replied.

There was a knock at the office door, and Janet, the front office secretary stuck her head inside. "Mylie, your sister is here with her friend."

Mylie looked down at her phone. 3:30 p.m. Shit. She'd forgotten her promise to take Cassie and Allie shopping for the community-wide Sadie Hawkins dance that weekend. It was a Clay Creek tradition. Every May, the town held a Sadie Hawkins dance. The real Sadie Hawkins Day was in November, but nobody in the community wanted to have a dance in November when it was freezing cold. So, they did it every May instead.

"Janet, you don't have to announce us," Cassie said, shoving her way into the already overcrowded room. "She knows we're coming."

"She forgot about us," Allie said from behind Janet.

"I didn't!" Mylie protested. "I just got distracted. But it's fine! We're done in here, aren't we ladies?"

Louise tucked her shirt under her arm and grumbled, "Watch who you're calling a lady."

"All right," Mylie said, clapping her hands together. "Who's ready to go dress shopping?"

ROCKBRIDGE WAS THE town that had everything. It was the "big" town in the center of several smaller towns, which meant it was a hub for restaurants and shopping. As a kid, Mylie loved going there with Granny. Now, she enjoyed taking Cassie.

"I feel like I cheated the dance rules," Cassie said as they parked the car to go into the first department store. "I didn't have to ask Ryan since he's my boyfriend."

"You can't go unless you officially ask him," Allie joked.

"You haven't asked anyone," Cassie pointed out.

"I'm going alone," Allie reminded her. "Like a loser."

"Going to a dance alone doesn't make you a loser," Mylie said. "I went to almost every dance alone."

"I think that's her point," Cassie said.

"I'm not a loser!"

"You're not married, either," Allie replied.

"Yeah, and that's on purpose," Mylie said, getting out of the car. Damn. This teenager stuff wasn't for the faint of heart. How had Granny done it?

"I want one of those dresses with a slit up the side," Allie said, ignoring Mylie. "Like all the way up to here." She pointed to the middle of her thigh.

"Remember, I have to send pictures of every dress you try on to your mother," Mylie reminded Allie.

Allie rolled her eyes. "Fine. Maybe a shorter slit."

"I think that's a good idea."

Mylie walked slightly behind the two girls as they hurried toward the formal-dress section of the store, allowing them their excitement. It was their first dance as high schoolers, after all. Freshmen weren't allowed to go to homecoming or prom in Clay Creek. Only upperclassmen, and Mylie remembered exactly how she and Jodi had felt the first time they'd been allowed to buy fancy dresses for a dance.

They'd been ridiculous about it. Poor Granny had stood there for hours as they tried on every style under the sun, imagining that their final choice would be *the* dress to make them the absolute belles of the ball. It made Mylie laugh to think about it. They'd mostly looked silly.

It was a rite of passage, and it made Mylie's heart swell that she got to be a part of it for Cassie. Allie's mother had already been through it three times with Allie's older sisters, and Granny hated going into Rockbridge. Mylie wondered if Cassie wished their mother was there, the way she had the first time.

Mylie doubted it. Cassie didn't even remember their mother. She'd taken off for the last time when Cassie was just an infant. She'd never made any promises to Cassie the way she had to Mylie. Cassie had never stood outside waiting for their mother to show up, never looked out into the bleachers at a basketball game looking for her. She'd never waited for a phone call that didn't come.

Small mercies, Mylie thought.

"Mylie!" Cassie called from the dressing room. "Come here!"

"What is it?" Mylie asked, slightly panicked. "Are you okay?"

Cassie stood in the dressing room hallway, wearing a purple, off-the-shoulder dress that came just above her knee.

"Oh, I love that," Mylie said, admiringly. "You look so pretty."

"It's okay," Cassie said, twisting around to look at herself. "I don't know if I like it in the back."

"What about this one?" Allie asked, stepping out of a room.

"Absolutely not," Mylie replied, stepping in front of Allie just in case anyone was to walk in. "I can practically see your nipples!"

"Gross, Mylie," Cassie said.

"I agree," Mylie replied. "It is gross. Please try to pick something that won't get you kicked out of the high school gym."

"Dress codes are unfairly restrictive toward girls and women," Cassie said, throwing a pointed glance at Mylie.

"Yes, they are," Mylie said. "But I'm pretty sure you can't show your nipples anywhere, not just at school."

"Free the nipple!" Allie shouted.

Despite herself, Mylie dissolved into giggles. "Okay," she said, finally. "I'm not taking a picture of that to show your mother. She'll never let me take you anywhere ever again."

"You try it on," Allie said to Mylie, going into the dressing room and shutting the door. "You've got enough . . . uh, up on top to keep it on."

"No way," Mylie said. "I'm not going to the dance."

"Yes, you are," Cassie said.

"No, I'm not," Mylie replied. "I haven't gone to that dance in years."

"Please just try it on," Cassie begged. "Please. It'll be funny!"

Mylie took the dress out of Allie's hands and said, "If I do this, will you promise to pick more appropriate dresses from now on?"

"Pinky promise," Allie said, grinning.

"I don't believe you," Mylie said. "And pinky promises are sacred, so you better not be lying."

"Just try it on."

Mylie sighed and went into an empty dressing room. The dress was at least two sizes too small. "I need you to zip this up," she said once she'd gotten it, on a breath and a prayer, over her hips. "I can't reach it."

"I don't think Jesus himself could zip this up," Cassie said, yanking on the zipper.

"Thanks a lot," Mylie replied.

"It looks good in the front," Allie offered.

This time, Allie was wearing a long black dress with thick straps. She looked beautiful. "I love this one," Mylie said, touching one of the straps. "This is the one you should get."

"I'm going to need taller shoes," Allie said. "But I think you're right."

"We said we were wearing tennis shoes!" Cassie protested, still in the purple dress. "I was going to get Converse to match!"

"Maybe we can find tennis shoes with a heel," Allie replied, thoughtful.

"Like the Spice Girls," Mylie said.

"Who?" both girls asked.

Mylie was about to break into a rendition of "Wannabe" when Cassie said, "Uh-oh."

"What?" Mylie asked. "What does *uh-oh* mean?"

"The zipper is stuck," Cassie replied. "I can't move it."

Allie walked around behind Mylie and yanked on the zipper. "Me either. It's really stuck."

"I have to get this thing off!" Mylie said. "Without ripping it!"

"You're gonna have to wear that thing home," Allie said. "Maybe even sleep in it."

Mylie was about to respond when Cassie pointed to a figure walking toward them and said, "Hey, is that Ben?"

Sure enough, Ben was walking toward them carrying two shopping bags and an amused expression plastered across his face.

"Oh my God," Mylie gasped, ducking back into the dressing room.

"Hi Ben!" Cassie called out.

"I'm going to murder you in your sleep!" Mylie hissed from behind the locked door.

Ben stopped. "Hi Cassie, and . . . Allie, right?"

"Hi," Allie said.

"Where's Mylie?" Ben asked. "I thought I heard her voice."

"She's hiding in the dressing room," Cassie replied. "She's stuck in a dress."

"I'm not stuck!" Mylie yelled through the door.

"Then take it off!" Cassie called back.

Mylie reached around to her back to try to pull part of the zipper down. It was jammed midway. She couldn't move it. She tried pulling it up over the top of her head, but it was stuck on her hips.

There was a knock on the door. "Do you need some help?"

"You're not supposed to be in the women's dressing room!" Mylie hissed to Ben.

"There's nobody back here but you three," he said. "Do you want help or not?"

Reluctantly, Mylie opened the door. "Don't laugh."

"I wouldn't dream of it," Ben replied, his lips twitching upward.

"Stop!" Mylie said, her own laugh threatening to escape.

"Turn around," Ben instructed.

Mylie did as she was told. "It's stuck there in the middle," she said.

"I can see that," Ben replied. He set his bags down.

"What are you doing in Rockbridge?" Mylie asked as he tugged at the zipper. She tried not to think about how close he was standing to her or the way she could see him behind her in the mirror.

"I needed sheets," Ben said. "I've washed the sheets in the house five or six times, and they still smell like mothballs."

"Did you miss having to drive an hour for something as regular as sheets?" Mylie asked. "You probably could have gotten some at the Piggly Wiggly."

Ben laughed. "Damn, this thing is really stuck."

"I never should have put this dress on," Mylie lamented.

"Why *did* you put it on?"

Mylie shrugged. "The girls asked me to. We were just being silly."

"Well," Ben said, looking up at her from the mirror. "It looks good."

"I'm stuffed in here like a sausage," Mylie protested. Her breath hitched in her throat when she felt his fingers on her bare skin. "But you know, it's the Sadie Hawkins dance this weekend. That's why we're here."

"I forgot about that," Ben replied, thoughtful. "I always hated that dance."

Mylie had to reach up and catch the fabric around her breasts before it fell down. "Thanks," she said.

"Anytime," Ben replied, taking a step back from her. "I guess I better leave you to it." He backed out of the dressing room.

"Ben?" she asked.

"Yeah?"

"Do you want to go to the Sadie Hawkins dance?"

"With you?" Ben replied. "Are you asking me to go with you?"

"Only if you're going to say yes," Mylie said, feeling her cheeks flush and hating herself for it.

"Sure," Ben said. "I'd love to go."

"Really?"

Ben gave her another look that made her skin prickle and replied, "Only if you wear that dress."

By the time Mylie got out of the dressing room, Ben was gone. The girls had their dresses hanging over their arms and were arguing about Converse or heels. They didn't even notice as she slipped around them and asked the saleswoman to help her find the dress in her size. She'd try it on at home to make sure it fit.

"Let's go pay for these dresses," Mylie said to Cassie and Allie when she returned, trying to shake the anxiety that had begun to gnaw at her stomach.

"Shoes next," Cassie said, tugging on Mylie's arm. "You can tell us about the Spice Girls on the way."

Chapter 18

What had he just agreed to? All he'd wanted to do today was find some sheets that didn't smell like 2013. But he couldn't stop thinking about Mylie in that dress. He hadn't been able to take his eyes off of her. He could barely breathe the whole time he'd been in that dressing room.

Ben started his car and turned out of the shopping center's parking lot. It had been Mylie in that dress, that's all this was. But it had also been the way she looked at him in the mirror. It had been the way her skin felt against his knuckles.

Ben was forced out of his thoughts when his phone rang. He'd forgotten it was connected through Bluetooth to his car, and when the ring blasted through his speakers, he nearly drove off the road.

"Hello?"

"Ben, hello. This is Courtney."

"Oh, yeah, hi," Ben said.

"Your Realtor."

"I know," Ben replied. "We've spoken before."

"Right. Well, exciting news. I have a couple interested in looking at the house," Courtney said, her words coming out in a rush, like she was the White Rabbit late for a meeting.

"That's great," Ben replied. "When are they coming by?"

"Would tomorrow morning work for you?"

Ben nodded, even though Courtney couldn't see him. "That should be fine."

"Anything you can do to make the house look presentable would help," Courtney continued.

"Got it," Ben said.

He wondered who the couple was and if he knew them. Ben was beginning to realize that there was no length of time a person could be gone from Clay Creek that would make people forget. It seemed like no matter where he went, he knew someone. He'd already fulfilled his promise to his mother. There hadn't been a requirement as to *how long* he stayed. If the house sold tomorrow, that would be fine.

Wouldn't it?

This place wasn't his home. It was just a stop in the road. He'd spent the majority of his life in Chicago. THAT was home. Still, it shocked him just how easily he found himself falling back into life in Clay Creek, despite having no intentions of living there permanently.

Yes. He needed to sell this house before he was in too deep. New sheets and one dance with Mylie. That was all he was going to give to this Arkansas spring. That was all he had time to give.

Chapter 19

Tenth grade

"You can't seriously be thinking of asking him to the dance," Jodi said to Mylie one morning before first period English. "You could go with anybody. Why would you ask *him*?"

Mylie looked over at Ben, who was sitting on the concrete floor beneath his locker, reading a book. She smiled when he absently shoved his glasses farther up onto the bridge of his nose. Ben was her friend. He'd been her friend for a long time, and Jodi knew that.

"Oh my GOD," Jodi squealed.

"What?" Mylie asked.

"You like him!" Jodi said. "You *like like* him!"

"I do not," Mylie replied. "He's my friend."

"Whatever," Jodi said, grinning. "I can't believe it took me so long to figure it out."

"I don't like him," Mylie protested, inwardly cringing at how terribly she was lying. Of course she liked him, but she would have died before telling anyone.

"Want me to see if he likes you back?" Jodi asked,

"Please don't!" Mylie said, a little louder than she'd meant to. A few people turned to look at them. Ben hadn't noticed. He never noticed anything when he was reading.

"Okay, okay," Jodi said. "Sorry, I didn't realize it was that serious."

"It's not *serious*," Mylie replied, her voice now at a near whisper. "Just please, please don't say anything to him."

"Hey," Jodi said, touching her friend's arm. "You know I'd never do that, right? I mean, not unless you wanted me to?"

"I know," Mylie said, breathing a sigh of relief. Honestly, she hadn't known. Sometimes Jodi did things without thinking, and that got them both into trouble . . . a lot.

"So, are you going to ask him?" Jodi wanted to know. "To the dance?"

Mylie shook her head. "I can't," she said. "He'd say no."

"He would not."

"He would," Mylie said. "He told me last week he wasn't going."

"Maybe that's because you haven't asked him yet," Jodi offered. "Jason said he wasn't going to go, and then I asked him. Now we're going together."

"He's your boyfriend," Mylie replied, rolling her eyes. "That's different."

"Ben could be your boyfriend, too," Jodi said.

"No," Mylie replied. "I don't think he'll ever be my boyfriend."

"Well, he won't be if you never tell him," Jodi replied. "That's for sure."

Mylie knew Jodi was right. She also knew, deep down, that she'd never tell him. She couldn't. She knew who she was. Even at fifteen, she knew. She was her mother's daughter, after all. She'd watched her mother search for a man to stay her entire life. All they ever did was give her children and run away. That's how Mylie had been born. That's how her new baby sister, Cassie, had been born—straight into the chaos and fire of the Mason women.

Eventually, everyone left.

Mylie didn't think she could bear it if Ben left, too. Ben looked up when the bell rang and caught Mylie looking over at him. He gave her a half grin and waved.

Mylie waved back. It was better not to tell him. It was easier this way, wasn't it?

Chapter 20

The couple standing outside Ben's house looked excited, and Courtney, the only Realtor in town, looked absolutely predatory. If the skin stretched across her bones and Botoxed to perfection could have contorted into an evil smile, Mylie was sure that's what she would have been doing.

"As you can see," Courtney was saying, her arms outstretched and waving around the yard. "This property has been immaculately kept."

Mylie tried not to snort. She'd come home from work that morning to grab the lunch she'd left in the refrigerator. Normally, she wouldn't bother, but leftovers of Granny's meatloaf made for a mean meatloaf sandwich. It was only 10:30 a.m., and Mylie was starving.

Courtney threw a glance over at Mylie. The two had never been fans of each other. Mylie was certain that Courtney believed the fact that she lived across the street devalued the property.

"Oh, look, honey!" the woman in the couple said, turning around. "The house across the street matches! How cute!"

Mylie waved and made to go inside but stopped short when she heard Courtney calling her name.

"Mylie! Mylie, honey!"

Mylie closed her eyes and tried not to think about the meatloaf sandwich.

"Hi!" Mylie said, plastering on a smile. It gave her some satisfaction to know Courtney couldn't smile if her life depended on it. "How's it going?"

Courtney tottered across the little road separating the houses, her heels digging into the gravel. "Have you seen Ben this morning?"

"I haven't," Mylie said.

"I just tried calling him—I realized I don't have a key for the basement in case the potential buyers want to see it."

"I've been at work since seven thirty," Mylie said. "I just ran home to grab my lunch."

"I don't know where he could be," Courtney said, touching her tongue to the roof of her mouth.

"What time was the appointment?" Mylie asked.

"Eleven," Courtney replied.

"Well, you are half an hour early," Mylie said. "Did you knock?"

"Of course," Courtney said. "Anyway, I just thought you might know."

"I don't," Mylie replied. "I'm sorry." She turned to walk inside the house when a new voice from behind stopped her.

"Hi!" the woman in the couple said, walking up to where Mylie and Courtney stood. "Are you the neighbor?"

"I am," Mylie said. "I'm Mylie Mason."

The man in the couple wrinkled his brows. "I feel like I've heard your name before."

"Oh, surely you have," Courtney cooed. The sound made Mylie want to claw at her ears. "Mylie owns Hook, Line, and Sinker. You know, it's that big building when you first come into town?"

"That's right," the man replied. "Sorry, we're from out of state, so we don't know much about Clay Creek."

"But you have that adorable festival every year," the woman cut in. "Of course, we won't be moved here in time to go, surely, but it's one of the reasons we love it here."

Mylie wasn't sure the bass tournament was adorable, but she didn't say otherwise, especially not after Courtney gave her a look that told her to keep her big, fat mouth shut.

"It was nice to meet you," Mylie said to them, resisting the urge to flip Courtney the bird.

Courtney turned her back to her and continued espousing the perks of Clay Creek as Mylie hurried up the front steps and headed inside.

"Jesus Christ on a cracker," Mylie said once she'd shut the front door.

"Mylie?" Granny called from the kitchen. "Is that you?"

"It's me," Mylie said. "I forgot my lunch!"

"Come in and sit down!" Granny called.

"I can't," Mylie said. "I've got to get back to work. Hey, did you know Courtney is out there with a couple . . ." She trailed off when she saw Ben sitting at the kitchen table with Granny.

He lifted a coffee cup up in greeting to her. "Hey, Mylie."

Mylie narrowed her eyes at him. "Are you hiding from Courtney?"

"*Hiding* is a strong word," Ben replied.

"Well, she asked me if I'd seen you, and I'm going to look like a liar when you come out of my front door," Mylie said.

"Technically, it's my front door," Granny said. "Besides, who cares what that woman thinks."

"You should be nice to her," Mylie replied, grinning. "Courtney is in charge of the liquor license for the fishing tournament, and if you piss her off, she'll hold it up just for spite."

"She would do that, wouldn't she?" Granny asked.

"When is this fishing tournament?" Ben asked.

"Three weeks," Mylie replied. "We've got teams coming from all over the state to compete, and we always have a big celebration after the tournament ends. It's kind of our kickoff to summer."

"I don't remember anything like that happening when I lived here," Ben said.

"We started it the year after you left," Mylie replied, lingering a little longer than she meant to on the word *left*.

"Oh."

"You plan on being here that long?" Granny asked Ben.

"I'm here until the house sells," Ben replied. "I gave up my apartment in Chicago, and I can't sign a lease on a new place on the coast until I sell."

"Well, those two over there seem pretty interested in the house," Mylie said, going over to the refrigerator to grab her sandwich. She was trying not to sound irritated. It wasn't that she wanted the house to sell and for Ben to move. That wasn't it at all. In fact, that was the opposite of what she wanted. But the whole thing felt like a waiting game. Nothing was set in stone, and it was the waiting that she hated. How long did she have with Ben before he was gone again?

"Then they'll wait," Granny replied, giving Mylie a look that told her to snap out of it.

Ben was up and peering out the front window, absently stroking Stanley's ear. "She's opening the house up," Ben said. "I guess I should get over there."

"Okay, bye," Mylie said into the refrigerator.

Granny grabbed the Tupperware container with the meatloaf sandwich out of Mylie's hands and handed it to Ben. "Take this for lunch," she said.

"Thanks, Granny," Ben said.

"Hey!" Mylie said. "That's mine!"

"Not anymore," Granny said. "Bye, Ben! We'll see you for bingo tonight at the VFW! Don't forget. Six o'clock sharp!"

"Give that back!" Mylie demanded. "That's the whole reason I came home."

"Sorry," Ben said, grinning at her. "See ya tonight!"

"Thanks, Granny," Mylie said once Ben was out the door. "I'm starving."

"Oh, you hush," Granny replied. "Sit down, and I'll make you something."

"I need to get back to work," Mylie continued, fully aware that she was being ridiculous.

"You're the boss," Granny said. "Now, why don't you tell me why you were acting so strange to poor Ben? When I invited him over for coffee this morning, he seemed excited about that dance."

"I don't even know why I asked him," Mylie replied. "I feel stupid about it now. It feels like we're falling right back into step with how it was when we were teenagers."

"Is that a bad thing?" Granny asked.

"I don't know," Mylie said honestly. "At least he agreed to go to the dance. That's not something he ever did before."

"Well, there you have it," Granny said.

"Did you really invite him for bingo at the VFW tonight?" Mylie asked her.

"Sure did," Granny replied. "I reckon that means you'll be going as well?"

Mylie only shrugged.

Granny set a fresh sandwich in front of Mylie. "Listen," she said, sitting down next to her. "I know it must be hard watching Ben Lawrence come back after all these years. I know things between you didn't . . . end well."

"There was nothing to end," Mylie replied. "He left. I stayed here. That's all."

"Nevertheless," Granny continued. "I know it's been hard. But I think it's important for you to remember that Ben is your friend. Don't shut him out because of something that happened a decade ago. You'll regret it if you do."

"I know," Mylie said. "I'm trying."

"I know you are, sweetie," Granny replied.

Mylie bit into the sandwich and tried not to look out the window, where she knew there was a house across the street with strangers inside.

Chapter 21

The VFW in Clay Creek smelled a little bit like stale beer and arthritis cream, but Ben didn't mind spending time in the little tin can building at the edge of town. His grandfather had taken him there a few times when he'd been younger after he'd promised that under no circumstances would he tell his mother. It was where he'd learned to curse and also where he'd had a sip of his first beer while his grandfather was playing pool and his drink was left unsupervised. He'd thrown up in the hedges when he got home, and his grandfather said that was punishment enough.

There was indeed a wall of thanks dedicated to Ben's grandfather, and he stood staring at it for a few minutes after he arrived, while Granny, Morris, Cassie, and Mylie secured a table. It was surprisingly packed for a Tuesday night.

Ben admired the picture of his grandfather in his service uniform. He'd served in the Korean War as military intelligence and used the G.I. Bill to go to college and become a doctor. Ben hadn't seen many pictures of his grandfather as a young man and even fewer of him in uniform. He felt a sense of pride at realizing he looked quite a lot like his grandfather, even though the only uniform Ben had ever worn was a cap and gown at various graduations. He knew all the work his grandfather put into becoming a doctor and raising his mother, primarily on his own, had paved the way for Ben's own education.

"Your grandfather was a good man," Granny said from behind Ben. "I miss him."

"Me, too," Ben said.

"I didn't think he'd last a month when he moved here," Granny continued. "Such a city slicker, that one. But you know, he surprised us all. Opened that clinic and cared for the people of this town like we were his own. I suppose after a while, we were."

"He loved it here," Ben replied, still staring at his grandfather's picture. "My mom thought he was crazy, but he just said, 'Now, Emily, you ought to give it a try. Clay Creek will surprise you.'"

Granny croaked out a laugh. "I don't suppose your mother ever got used to it, did she?"

Ben turned to face Granny. "She didn't," he admitted. "But I think she tried. It's because of her I'm here, you know."

"Oh?"

Ben nodded. "When she got very sick, I went to live with her for a while. I took a few months off from school and stayed with her at her apartment."

Granny squeezed his arm.

"She said she knew that when I inherited the house, I'd sell it." Ben didn't know why, but he felt shame saying those words out loud. "She made me promise that before I did, I'd come down here and visit, made me promise to spend time here before I made any final decisions."

"And here you are," Granny replied, still gripping him. "You've upheld her wishes, and that's all she ever could have asked for."

"I'm trying," Ben said. "But I still don't know why she wanted me to come back. No offense, but she was glad to go back to Chicago."

"None taken," Granny said. "Perhaps your mother knew something you didn't about Clay Creek."

"Maybe," Ben said, unconvinced.

"They're starting!" Mylie called from the table across the room. "Hurry up!"

Ben followed Granny over to the long white table and took a seat in a rickety folding chair.

"Here," Mylie said, handing out three large bingo cards to each of them. "This is the marker." She held out a marker with a broad foam tip. "Press it down when you hear a letter and number that corresponds to your card."

"Thanks," Ben said. "But I have played bingo before."

"You've never played bingo at the Clay Creek VFW," Granny pointed out. "We play for blood. See those women over there?" She pointed to a table where a group of women sat, concentration written on their wrinkled faces. "Those are the bingo queens. They nearly always win. Agnes paid her house off last year with her bingo winnings."

Ben whistled under his breath. "I didn't realize bingo could be so lucrative."

"Quiet over there!" one of the women shouted, glaring at Granny.

"Calm your tits, Bernice!" Granny shot back. "Turn up your hearing aid!"

Bernice flipped Granny the bird.

"Tough crowd," Ben said, leaning over to Mylie. "I thought this would be a bunch of sweet senior citizens."

Mylie snorted. "You thought wrong, Dr. Lawrence."

"Is that Dr. Benji's grandson?" Bernice asked, standing up and pushing a walker over to where Mylie and Ben sat. "Did I hear that right?"

Granny narrowed her eyes at Bernice and mumbled, "She turned the damn thing up too high."

Bernice ignored Granny, focusing her attention on Ben. "I should have recognized you!"

Ben gave Bernice a tentative smile, still unsure if Bernice was going to hug him or bite his head off. "You're a doctor, too?"

"Well," Ben began.

"You know; I have this goiter . . ."

"Shove off, Bernice!" Granny growled. "He ain't that kind of doctor."

Bernice opened her mouth to respond, but the announcer walked to the front of the stage next to the large spinning machine where they pulled the numbers. "Welcome to this week's VFW bingo! Is everybody ready?"

Shouts came from the crowd, and Bernice hobbled her way back over to her table.

"Get ready," Mylie said. "Things are about to get interesting."

THERE WERE SEVERAL bingos over the next hour, mostly from the table of crones where Bernice sat. Every time someone at that table won, they'd look over at Granny and smile. Granny, to her credit, only cursed under her breath.

"Stop looking at my card," Mylie said, elbowing Ben in the side.

"It's not like I can cheat at bingo," Ben hissed, rubbing his sore ribs.

Mylie narrowed her eyes at him. "I'm going to make you go sit with Bernice if you're not careful."

Ben shuddered. "Okay, I won't look anymore."

Ben enjoyed the easy way everyone at the table existed with each other. Sometimes Morris would reach over and hold one of Granny's hands when no one was looking, and the old woman would smile. Cassie stayed close to Mylie, drinking a Coke out of a glass bottle and paying little attention to the card in front of her. He'd thought maybe he would feel uncomfortable going out with them, since he wasn't really part of the family, but it wasn't that way at all. Everyone took measures to include him, and it began to feel like this was something he'd always done—played bingo at the foul-smelling VFW with this band of misfits.

"I think I have a bingo," Ben whispered to Mylie after a couple of hours.

"What?" Mylie said, looking over at his card. "Holy shit, you do. Yell bingo!"

"Bingo!" Ben said, raising his hand. "Bingo!"

"Louder!" Mylie said at the same time Bernice yelled *"Bingo!"*

"He said it first!" Mylie shouted, jumping up from her seat. "Ben said it first!"

Bernice and her table glared at Mylie. "No, I'm first!" Bernice said.

"Bullshit!" Granny said, standing up. "We all heard him say it."

The two elderly men at the front of the room glanced at each other uncomfortably. People didn't usually protest when Bernice claimed a win.

Bernice held up her card. "I said it loudest!"

"That doesn't matter," Mylie cut in. "Ben had a bingo first!"

"It doesn't matter," Ben said, genuinely afraid this might come to blows. "Let her have it."

Bernice made to walk toward the stage, but Granny stepped in front of her, hands on her ample hips. "Not another step, Bernice," she said.

"Or what, *Violet*?" Bernice countered, shoving her walker into Granny. "You aren't *my* granny, so I ain't callin' you anything other than your Christian name."

"Your granny had a full beard," Granny replied, steady despite the threat of the walker. "So, I guess I should take that as a compliment."

That was all it took for chaos to break loose at the Clay Creek

VFW. Granny ducked just in time to miss Bernice's right hook, but not fast enough to dodge Agatha's shoulder. Granny knocked into the table behind her, sending bingo cards flying.

Ben watched in horror as women, literal grandmothers, began to brawl. Bracelets and clip-on earrings came off, fists went flying. One woman, a rounder, plumper version of Bernice, swung her beaded necklace around like a pair of nunchucks.

"Now you've done it," Mylie said to Ben, motioning for Cassie to duck as an empty soda bottle went flying. "You just had to have a bingo, didn't you?"

"*ME?*" Ben gasped. "I didn't even want to say it!"

In front of them, Morris grabbed Granny around the waist, hauling her kicking and screaming back toward the table.

"THAT'S ENOUGH!" A voice bellowed into the microphone from the front of the room.

Nobody paid any attention.

"BINGO NIGHT IS CANCELED INDEFINITELY!"

Everyone paused, as if involved in a sadistic game of freeze tag.

"Sit down!"

Ben was surprised to see Melissa at the stage, mic in hand, staring out into the abyss of pandemonium, eyes narrowed.

"Bernice," Melissa continued. "You know good and well someone else called bingo before you. And *Granny!* You know better than to insult Bernice's family. Everybody sit down right now and act like the adults you are."

Everyone sat.

Granny harrumphed into her chair, a cut across her cheek and two fingernails chipped and jagged. Bernice, who'd been wielding her walker like a battering ram, did the same.

"Now, who called bingo?"

Ben's mouth went dry.

Mylie nudged him. "Say it," she said.

"Am I going to get stabbed in the parking lot after this?" Ben whispered.

"Maybe," Mylie said with a shrug. "It's been known to happen."

"She's kidding," Morris said with a nervous laugh. "It only happened the one time."

"Hello?" Melissa said. "Who said bingo?"

Slowly, Ben stood up. "It was me," he said.

"Come on up, Ben!" Melissa said into the mic, eyes shining with delight. "You're tonight's grand prize winner! Last bingo of the night!"

Ben made his way to the stage, aware that everyone was staring at him. He had no idea how the night had taken such a turn, but he knew one thing for sure—he never wanted to piss off another senior citizen for as long as he lived.

"Congratulations," Melissa said as he neared her. "You've won our five-hundred-dollar weekly pot."

Ben gawked at her. "Five hundred dollars?"

Melissa nodded and then leaned in to whisper, "Bernice has won every week for a month. We think she's cheating, but for the life of us, we can't figure out how."

Ben handed over his card while the men behind the table on the stage checked it over. When they were satisfied, they nodded to Melissa who handed Ben five crisp hundred-dollar bills.

"Thanks," Ben said, not knowing what else to say while the rest of the room watched the transaction.

"I'd leave now if I were you," Melissa said with a wink. "You saw how Bernice can be with that walker."

"This is the most terrifying group of people I've ever been around," Ben muttered, walking back toward Mylie and the group, who were already readying themselves to leave.

"See you next week!" Melissa called after him.

"Not if I can help it," Ben said, shoving the money down into his pocket.

Bernice eyed him as he walked by, and he was nearly to the door when he changed his mind. He turned and walked back toward where she sat and laid down one of the hundred-dollar bills Melissa had just handed him.

"What's this?" Bernice asked him, her eyes narrowing.

"That's for you," Ben said.

"Why?" Bernice asked.

"Just trying to be gentlemanly."

"$300," Bernice countered.

"$200," Ben replied, placing another bill down in front of her.

"Fine," Bernice growled. "But . . ."

"No buts," Ben said, cutting her off. "And you should definitely get that goiter looked at."

For a moment, Ben thought Bernice would balk, but instead, her face broke out into a wide grin and she began to howl. "Oh, I like you, kid." She turned to where Granny stood watching, her mouth hanging open. "He's a keeper!"

Chapter 22

It was Friday, and Granny was fuming. She paced around the kitchen and stopped to face Morris, her hands on her hips. He looked away from her and down at his hands.

"Now, don't take it personally, Violet," he said.

Mylie looked over at Cassie. He was using Granny's name. This was serious.

"Don't take it personally?" This just made Granny angrier. "You just told me I'm banned from the dance!"

"I didn't say you were banned," Morris replied, his tone patient. "I said you can't bring your famous down-home punch."

Mylie nearly choked on the water she was drinking. Granny had been making that punch since before Mylie was born. It was half the reason people went to the dance in the first place. It was a community-wide event, but this year, the dance was being held at the school gym, which meant that, technically, the school was responsible for any damages . . . or drunk teenagers. Even though you were supposed to present ID to drink, kids always found a way to get a nip of Granny's punch.

"To be fair, Granny," Cassie began. "Last year, two middle schoolers got drunk off their asses and then threw up in the sheriff's hedges."

"That's not my fault," Granny said.

"You added moonshine last year," Morris replied. "I tasted that punch, and it was straight moonshine."

"Moonshine doesn't count," Granny said, waving them off. "Everyone knows moonshine doesn't count."

"It counts if it's bootleg moonshine from the Wilson family hollers," Morris said. "That stuff put three of my family members in the hospital in nineteen eighty-five."

"Your family has a weak disposition," Granny sniped.

"Nevertheless."

"I have half a mind to make it, anyway," Granny continued.

"Granny, you can't!" Cassie said, panic in her voice. "You'll cause a scene at school."

"She's not going to," Mylie replied. "Are you, Granny?"

Granny crossed her arms over her chest.

"Granny?"

"No," Granny said, finally. "I reckon I won't."

Cassie breathed a sigh of relief. "Okay, I'm going to go get dressed."

"I should probably do that, too," Mylie replied. "Cass, you've got about an hour."

"That's not enough time!" Cassie said, running up the steps toward her room.

Granny sat down at the kitchen table next to Morris. "Mylie, honey, make sure you watch her tonight."

"Granny," Mylie said. "It's a dance, not a rave. She'll be fine. There will be plenty of people there to watch out for her, myself and Ben included."

"I just don't like that Ryan," Granny continued.

"You liked him perfectly fine last week," Mylie replied. "I'm going to go upstairs and try to make myself look presentable." She looked over at Morris. "Don't let her make that punch."

"Roger that," Morris said, saluting Mylie.

Mylie headed up the stairs, feeling more like she needed to nap than get dressed for a dance. The rest of the week had been exhausting. She'd had to stay late at work every day, and she'd come home every evening to a seemingly endless parade of people going in and out of Ben's house.

She laid face down on her bed and closed her eyes. Maybe she could sleep for a few minutes and still get ready on time.

"Mylie!" Cassie said from the doorway. "What are you doing? You have to get ready! I'm supposed to meet Ryan outside the gym in forty-five minutes!"

"Ugh," Mylie rolled over. "I'm so tired."

"Get untired!" Cassie replied. "Come on."

Mylie peeled herself off the bed and stood up. She ran a hand down the dress she'd bought. It fit perfectly. Granny'd had to loosen the straps a bit, but otherwise, it really did look nice. It wasn't formal, but it was right on the edge of it. She'd agreed, begrudgingly, to wear Converse with Allie and Cassie. Truth be told, she'd been thrilled that her sister and her friend asked her to match. So much of the time, she felt more like Cassie's mother than her sister. It was nice to feel like a sister once in a while. And it was nice, she told herself, to dress up and feel pretty.

BEN MET THEM outside. It was just starting to get dark, but he could see well enough to tell that Mylie looked fantastic. She was wearing that dress. Goddamn, that dress. It was just a simple black dress, but the back dipped low, exposing her skin. She smiled at him when she saw him, and he pulled out the little box he had behind his back.

"I thought you might like this," he said.

Mylie's smile widened, and Ben felt his heart crack a bit. "You got me a corsage?"

"It's a wristlet," Ben replied. "The lady at the flower shop said that's what all the kids wear now."

"You have to put it on her," Cassie said. "That's the rule."

"Sorry," Ben said. "I didn't know that."

"You've never given a corsage to anyone before?" Cassie asked.

"Nope," Ben admitted. "I never went to any dances in high school."

Cassie looked to Mylie.

"It's true," Mylie replied. "Even when he got invited to junior prom by Melissa—you know, Cracked Egg Melissa? Even then, he refused."

"Melissa is so pretty!" Cassie blurted.

"I didn't refuse," Ben said. He wanted to tell Mylie that Melissa didn't hold a candle to her, but he bit down on the words. "Well, I didn't refuse prom. I was touring a college in Chicago that weekend."

He opened the box and slid the red rose arrangement over Mylie's hand. He could have sworn her pulse quickened when he touched the tender inside of her wrist.

"Let's go," Cassie said. "We're already late."

People were streaming into the gym by the time they got there. People of all ages, laughing and rushing to get out of the muggy spring air.

"Ryan!" Cassie said, running up to her boyfriend.

Ben was pleased to see that the woman at the flower shop had been right. Nearly everyone had a wristlet rather than a corsage. He'd agonized over it all day, wondering if he'd made the right choice.

"Are you excited?" Mylie asked, one side of her mouth twitching up into a sarcastic grin. "I know you missed the gymnasium so much."

"Yes," Ben replied. "I love going back to the scene of years of humiliation."

"Oh, come on," Mylie said. "It wasn't *that* bad."

"Did Coach Pritchett leave you dangling halfway up a rope during second period to eat his tuna fish sandwich?" Ben asked. "Jodi had to find a ladder to get me down!"

Mylie laughed. "I forgot about that."

Inside, the gym looked just as Ben remembered. Nothing had changed—not the faded 1979 state basketball championship banner, not the slightly warped wooden floor, and not the scarred metal door in the back that kids used to sneak out of to smoke. He'd only done that once, and when his mom found out, he'd been grounded for a month.

"Mylie! Ben!" Jodi waved at them from across the silver balloon arch.

"Hey!" Mylie tugged at Ben's arm, pulling him over to Jodi and a man who looked about as enthusiastic to be there as Ben felt.

"Ben, this is my boyfriend, Jared," Jodi said. "Jared, this is my old high school buddy, Ben."

"Nice to meet you," Ben said, extending his hand.

"Your girl drag you here, too?" Jared asked. "Jodi makes me come to this thing every year."

"Look," Jodi said, pointing to Mylie's wristlet. "I told you that you should have gotten me one."

"I have this instead," Jared said, pulling a silver flask from his pocket.

"That's even better," Jodi replied, taking it from him. "Once the music starts and our old gym teachers start dancing, we're going to need it."

Ben wasn't usually a fan of drinking after people he didn't know, but he figured whatever was in the flask contained enough alcohol to sanitize the lid. Besides, Jodi was right. They were probably going to need it. It had been a long time since he was in a room with so many people he went to high school with.

"So, I heard Granny's punch got banned," Jodi said, leaning in toward Mylie conspiratorially.

"Yeah," Mylie replied, taking the flask and tipping it back. "And now here we are drinking out of a flask."

"She'd be so proud," Jodi said with a laugh.

"Is Morris here?" Mylie asked. "I promised Granny I'd let her know if he was dancing with Lorelei Wilson."

"Granny didn't come?"

"She's protesting," Mylie said. "You know, because of the punch and all."

"Well, Lorelei came with Mr. Pritchett," Jodi replied. "I don't think Granny has anything to worry about."

"Our old gym teacher?" Ben asked. "I thought he was married."

"She divorced him," Mylie replied. "For cheating on her with Lorelei."

"It's like I've been gone a lifetime," Ben said.

"Ten years is a long time," Jodi agreed.

"Some things never change," Mylie muttered. She inclined her head to where Robbie Price had entered the gym, arms crossed, flanked by his brothers. They cut a menacing profile as they stalked inside. Several people gave them a wide berth.

"What is he doing here?" Jodi whispered.

"Same as everybody else, I guess," Jared said.

"Shut up," Jodi replied. "He's here to cause trouble, plain and simple."

Mylie shrank back. She didn't want him to see her, didn't want the confrontation that would inevitably bring.

"Do you want to leave?" Ben asked her.

"No," Mylie said, shaking her head. "This is my town, too. I'm not going to let him intimidate me."

Ben opened his mouth to respond when the speakers began blaring music and a collective scream rippled through the crowd. They were swamped by people, making their way onto the gymnasium floor. It looked more fun than he thought it would.

"Let's dance!" Jodi said, grabbing Mylie's hand. "Forget about Robbie! He sucks!"

Mylie laughed and let herself be dragged onto the dance floor.

Ben stood there next to Jared and watched Mylie and Jodi snake around the crowd and begin to dance.

"So, you went to high school with Mylie and Jodi?" Jared asked.

"Yep," Ben replied. "I've known them both since sixth grade."

"Jodi said you moved off for college," Jared continued. He discreetly passed the flask over to Ben. "But you haven't been back in years?"

"Also, yes," Ben said.

"It's nice to see you reconnected with Mylie," Jared replied. "Jodi says she always had a thing for you."

"We're not seeing each other." Ben shifted uncomfortably on his feet. It was an automatic answer, but he didn't enjoy saying it.

Being back in this gym reminded him that, despite the fact years had passed, they were still who they were. There wasn't any changing that. Getting involved now would be a mistake.

The song ended and "Thinking Out Loud" by Ed Sheeran began to play. Jodi motioned for Jared, and he reluctantly made his way out into the middle of the dance floor.

Mylie stood there for a few minutes avoiding looking at Ben. He sighed and walked over to her, carefully avoiding two teenagers who were kissing.

"Do you want to dance?" he asked her, holding out his hand.

"Yeah," Mylie said, surprise taking over her features. She reached up and put her hands around him, her fingers grazing the back of his neck.

Ben pulled her close into his space and grasped onto the sides of her hips. He couldn't remember the last time he'd slow-danced with someone. It had to have been at one of his fraternity brother's weddings a few years ago. He'd taken dancing lessons before that event, worried he'd make a fool of himself. They'd been worth the money. He wasn't going to be stepping on Mylie's toes.

"This is a nice surprise," Mylie said. "I didn't think you would dance."

"I'm full of surprises," Ben replied, grinning.

Mylie rested her head on Ben's chest, and his grip on her involuntarily tightened. "I'm so tired," she said.

"Long week?"

"You have no idea."

"I've had people in and out of my house every single day," Ben replied. "I was too afraid to eat or drink anything inside because I thought I might mess up the kitchen. So, I ate outside. Then I accidentally attracted the largest raccoon I've ever seen, and now he expects me to feed him.

"That's just Fat Tony," Mylie said. "Everyone in the neighborhood feeds him."

Ben laughed. "I thought he was wearing a collar, but I couldn't tell."

"He's the bane of Stanley's existence," Mylie replied. "Whoever buys your house will be in for a real treat."

"I'm not going to tell Courtney about that," Ben said.

Mylie grinned into his chest. "Oh, she knows."

They danced in silence for a while until Mylie lifted her head and looked up at him. "Has anyone made an offer on the house?"

"No," Ben said. "Not yet, but Courtney called today and said that first couple want another viewing next week, so I think that's good news."

"Sounds like it," Mylie replied.

"If I'm lucky, I'll have the place sold by summer."

Mylie let her hands fall away from Ben's neck, and Ben realized why exactly a second too late.

"I mean, it's not that I'm excited to leave or anything," he said quickly. "It's just, you know, I really need to be settled before the fall semester starts."

"Right," Mylie said. "I know."

The song ended, and Ben reluctantly released his grip on her.

They wandered back to the fringes of the dance floor, and Mylie waved to Allie and Cassie. The girls were in the middle of some choreographed dance they'd clearly been practicing. They were all watching the dance so intently, they didn't notice when Robbie sidled up to them until he was talking.

"Evening," he said. Even in the dim lighting, Mylie could see the sneer on his face.

"Jump scare," Jodi said.

Mylie tried not to laugh.

"I'm surprised you'd show your face here," Robbie continued. "Seein' as how everyone in town knows you fired me without so much as a paycheck."

"The check's in the mail," Jodi said through gritted teeth. "And the only person who should worry about showing their face in town is you."

"Just ignore him," Mylie said, turning to Jodi. "Maybe he'll go away."

Robbie slid in between Jodi and Mylie, knocking Mylie out of the way with one of his tree trunk arms. "I don't ignore so easy," he said.

Before anybody else could react, Ben grabbed Robbie by his collar and hauled him out from between the two women. Robbie stumbled back, nearly falling in the process.

"Back off," Ben said.

"You don't want any of this," Robbie said, giving Ben a grin that didn't quite reach his eyes.

"Trust me," Ben said. "I do."

Robbie considered it, looking Ben up and down. Ben squared his shoulders, and Robbie took a step back. "Nah," he said, sniffing. "You ain't worth it."

Mylie resisted the urge to flip him off as Robbie turned and sauntered back toward his brothers, who were waiting for him near the exit.

"Do you think he came here just to fuck with us?" Jodi asked.

"I don't know," Mylie said, "But I'd say that's a pretty good guess."

"Are you okay?" Ben asked her.

"I'm going to go outside for some air." Mylie turned and headed toward the metal door at the back of the gym.

Jodi made to follow her, but Ben stopped her. "I'll go," he said.

He found Mylie leaning up against the railing, her arms folded across her chest. When she saw him, she said, "I'm fine."

"I didn't say you weren't," Ben replied.

"Oh."

"But now that you've brought it up," Ben continued. "I think you're lying."

Mylie turned to him. "Just go back inside."

"No," Ben said. "I think we need to talk about it."

"I don't want to talk about it," Mylie replied.

"Well, I do."

"I didn't need you to stick up for me," Mylie said. "I can take care of myself."

"I know that," Ben said. "I just really hate Robbie."

That got a small smile out of her.

"I just want to make sure you're okay," Ben pressed.

"I'm fine," Mylie replied, angling herself away from him.

"Why do you have to be this way?" Ben asked. "You won't ever tell me how you feel about anything. I thought maybe you would have grown up in the last ten years, but apparently, I was wrong."

"Would it have mattered?" Mylie asked. "Tell me, Dr. Lawrence, if I told you how I felt then or how I feel now, would it matter?"

"Of course!" Ben threw his hands up into the air.

"So, if I told you I didn't want you to leave ten years ago, you would have stayed?" Mylie wanted to know.

"That's not fair," Ben said.

"See?" Mylie replied. "It wouldn't have mattered."

"It would have mattered!" Ben tried to keep from yelling, but he couldn't. "It matters to me how you feel, but you know that I had to leave."

"And you have to leave now?" Mylie asked. "If you're so desperate to sell this house and leave, then why are you even here now?"

"I promised my mother," Ben said. "I promised her I would come back one more time before I sold it. I keep my promises, Mylie. You know that. That's why I never lied to you about leaving. I was always going to leave."

"Why?"

"Because I have to!" This time, Ben was yelling. "I have to leave. There isn't anything here for me."

"I'm here!" Mylie said. "I'm here. I've always been here."

"You don't have to be here!"

Mylie let out an exasperated groan. "Yes, I do! I have to be here. I have to stay here for Granny. For Cassie. For work."

"What about you?" Ben asked, his tone softening.

"What about me?"

"What do you want, Mylie?" Ben took a step closer to her. "What is it that you want?"

"You," Mylie said, her voice barely above a whisper.

"What did you say?" He was so close to her now. He reached out and wrapped two of his fingers around tendrils of her hair that had fallen out of her ponytail.

"I want," Mylie said, licking her lips, "you."

That was all the invitation he needed. Ben leaned down and found her mouth, pressing himself into her so that she was flush against the railing.

At first, Ben thought the surprise that registered on Mylie's face meant that she would pull away, but she didn't. Instead, she welcomed the crush of his body onto hers, and she kissed him back, opening her mouth to give him access.

Fuck, he wanted her. He'd always wanted her, and now he wasn't sure if he'd ever be able to stop wanting her. As he kissed down her jawline into the hollow of her neck, she shivered, and he smiled into her warming skin.

Behind them, the metal door banged open, and Jodi called out to Mylie.

With a groan, Ben tore himself away from Mylie, backing up enough so that she could move away and out from under him. She didn't look back at him.

"What is it?" Mylie asked Jodi.

"Uh, I uh . . ." Jodi trailed off, smirking slightly at Mylie. "I'm sorry, I didn't mean to interrupt."

"It's okay," Mylie said.

It wasn't okay, but Ben knew that Jodi wasn't talking to him. He hung back, crossing his arms over his chest, willing the rational side of his brain to stay hidden for just a little longer so that he could enjoy the moment. He knew he was going to regret this later, when he'd had time to think about it. For now, at least, he just wanted to pull Mylie back to him, to shut out the world.

"It's Cassie," Jodi said, finally. "I guess she's been trying to call you."

"What's wrong?"

"I don't know," Jodi said, sighing. "Seems like maybe a fight over a boy or something, but she won't tell me anything."

"Where is she?" Mylie wanted to know, already pulling on the door handle.

"The bathroom," Jodi replied.

With that, the two women disappeared into the gymnasium, leaving Ben behind, alone with his thoughts.

Chapter 23

Mylie found Cassie in the last stall in the girl's bathroom.

"What's wrong?" Mylie asked through the door.

"I don't want to talk about it," Cassie sniffed.

"The fifteen missed calls on my phone say that's a lie," Mylie replied. "Please, Cass. Tell me what's going on."

"R-R-Ryan," Cassie stuttered.

"Open the door," Mylie said.

After a few halting seconds, Cassie complied, unlocking the stall and allowing Mylie inside.

Cassie was sitting on the floor of the bathroom, her dress pooled around her.

"Tell me what happened with Ryan," Mylie said, her voice as soothing as she could muster. "Did he say something stupid?"

Cassie shook her head. "No, he's cheating on me!"

This surprised Mylie. She hadn't thought Ryan was the most thoughtful person in the world. Sometimes he said and did things that upset Cassie, but he was also just a teenager. He'd really seemed to like Cassie, though, despite everything.

"With who?" Mylie asked.

"Laiken Sanders." Cassie spit out the name of the girl like a bad taste in her mouth. "For months, and do you know what's worse than that?"

"No," Mylie asked, sliding down to sit next to her sister. "What?"

"Allie knew!"

With this, Cassie dissolved into sobs, leaning against Mylie.

"Oh, Cassie," Mylie said. "I'm so sorry."

Mylie stroked Cassie's hair as she cried. She wished she knew what to do or say in this situation. She was good at a lot of things, but crying always made her uncomfortable. She wished they were back home. Granny always knew what to say. Maybe she should call her.

"Do you want to go home?" Mylie asked. "Because we can leave right now."

Cassie shook her head. "No," she said, accepting the piece of toilet paper Mylie handed her. "I can't go out there right now."

"It's okay," Mylie replied. "We can do whatever you want to do."

"I want to punch Ryan in the face," Cassie said. "Then I want to punch Laiken and Allie."

"Okay, well, we probably can't do that."

Cassie gave Mylie a small smile, even as the tears fell down her face. "I know," she said. "But it makes me feel better to think about."

Mylie tugged at the hem of her dress. Minutes ago, she'd been pressed up against Ben, kissing him. She resisted the urge to reach up and touch her swollen lips. She could still taste him.

"What's wrong with your face?" Cassie asked, looking over at Mylie. "You're all red."

"I was outside," Mylie replied. "It's hot out there."

"Why were you outside?"

"Just getting some air," Mylie said. That much was at least true. "Where is Allie? Have you talked to her?"

"She asked her mom to take her home," Cassie replied. "We were arguing. She said she didn't tell me because she didn't want me to be upset, and I told her I hated her."

"Oh, Cassie."

"I do hate her!" Cassie said, her voice echoing off the bathroom walls.

"This isn't her fault," Mylie replied. "I don't think she should have kept it from you, but she also wasn't the one cheating on you. That was Ryan."

"Well, I hate him, too!"

"So do I, at the moment," Mylie agreed. "I really think we should go home. We'll stop and get something to eat. Anything you want. Then we can sit on the couch with Granny and talk."

"I can't go out there," Cassie said. "They'll all see me."

Mylie thought about it. "I have an idea," she said. "There's an exit around the corner. I'll have Morris unlock the door, and you sneak out. I'll drive the truck around and get you."

"Really?" Cassie asked, hopeful. "I won't have to see anyone?"

"Not a single person," Mylie promised. "Wait here, and I'll text you when I'm outside."

"Okay," Cassie said. "Thanks, Mylie."

Mylie found Morris and explained the situation. He pulled out his set of keys—the keys to the high school buildings he still kept after his retirement, despite repeated requests to turn them in—and unlocked the door. She found Ben waiting for her outside, where she'd left him.

"I have to take Cassie home," Mylie explained. "She had a fight with Ryan. She's waiting for me in the bathroom. I'm going to send her out the other door."

Ben nodded. "Let's go."

Chapter 24

They made a stop at the Cracked Egg after leaving the dance. Melissa was just closing up, but when she saw Cassie's red, tear-streaked face, she herded them inside and sat them down at the counter.

"What can I make you, sweet pea?" She asked. "Anything at all."

"Waffles?" Cassie asked hopefully. "With whipped cream?"

"Comin' right up."

Mylie accepted the coffee Melissa offered her, not caring that it was after ten p.m. and she might never sleep again. This night had been . . . interesting to say the least.

Beside her, Ben seemed just as grateful for the liquid dose of caffeine. He breathed in the aroma before taking a sip. Mylie tried not to look at his lips as he drank, tried not to think about those lips on her, what they might have gotten up to if they hadn't been interrupted.

"Is Cassie all right?" Ben whispered.

"She's going to be okay," Mylie replied. She looked over at her sister, who was making conversation with Melissa. She was no longer sniffling. The waffles were helping.

Melissa looked over at them, grinning. "It's nice to see you two together again," she said. "I wondered how long it would take."

Mylie felt her face flush and cursed the fluorescent lights. They'd all see.

"Well, we are neighbors," Ben replied.

"You find a buyer for that house already?" Melissa asked. "That was quick."

"Not yet," Ben said. "But Courtney thinks an offer may come soon."

Melissa looked at Mylie.

"There was a couple who looked earlier in the week," Mylie offered. "They seemed nice."

"Well, that's good," Melissa said.

"It'll be nice having someone living next door, instead of having random guests sneaking down to our dock at all hours of the night," Mylie continued.

"I didn't know that happened," Ben said, surprised.

"Just a few times," Mylie said. "You know that dock is decrepit, I don't care what Granny says. I worried someone would fall through and drown."

"I've been telling Granny to fix that dock for years," Melissa said.

"I've offered to hire someone more than once," Mylie replied. "But you know Granny."

Cassie took the last bite of her waffles and then leaned her head on Mylie's shoulder. "Can we go home now?" she asked.

"Of course," Mylie said.

Ben began to reach into his wallet at the same time Mylie went to grab her purse, but Melissa waved them off. "It's on the house," she said.

"Thanks," Mylie said, truly grateful. "I know it's late, and you were ready to go home."

"I have about fifty essays to grade," Melissa said. "I'd stay here all night if I thought I could get away with it."

Cassie wrinkled her nose. "You mean I have to write essays in college, too?"

Melissa nodded. "Yep, and don't think I'll go easy on you because you're my favorite, either."

"I'm your favorite?" Cassie gave Melissa a genuine smile.

"Don't tell."

"Is your semester about over?" Ben asked, as they stood up to leave.

"Next week," Melissa said.

"At least you'll get a break," Ben offered.

"Hardly." Melissa rolled her eyes. "I have to teach summer school. We're so short on instructors." She fixed her gaze on Ben. "You interested in teaching? We could really use you."

Ben shook his head and replied, "I've been offered a job in Boston."

"You sign that contract yet?" This time, Melissa was looking at Mylie.

Again, Ben shook his head. "Not yet. It's a verbal offer, but I've accepted."

"But it's not set in stone."

"I guess not," Ben replied, shifting uncomfortably on his feet.

"Well, just keep us in mind," Melissa said. "Just in case."

They waved to Melissa as they left, with a noticeably happier Cassie. And although Mylie couldn't be entirely sure, she could have sworn she saw Melissa wink at her.

Chapter 25

Ben rounded the corner to their houses. The first thing they noticed were the blue and red flashing lights and two patrol cars in the front yard of Mylie's house. Granny was standing in the front yard in her house coat, with Stanly leashed in front of her, barking his head off.

"Can you guys hear Stanley barking?" Cassie asked. "I swear I hear him barking."

"What is going on?" Mylie breathed.

Ben stopped the car just beyond the patrol cars.

Cassie got out and ran toward Granny. "Oh my God!" she yelled. "The front window is busted out!"

"What?" Mylie asked, sliding out of the front seat and hurrying around to where Cassie stood. "What the hell happened?"

There was glass everywhere.

"Did Stanley break through the window?" Mylie asked. "How would he even do that?"

"Maybe someone broke in?" Cassie asked.

"Someone threw a damn brick through the window!" Granny called from where she stood. Sheriff Oakes was inside the house. In one hand, he held up a red brick.

"Stay out there," the sheriff said, sensing Mylie was about to make her way inside. "I'll let you know when I have the all clear."

"Are you okay?" Mylie asked Granny. "You're not hurt, are you?"

"What about Stanley?" Cassie asked.

"We're both fine," Granny replied. "I was in the bathroom taking off my face, and I heard this god-awful racket from the living room. I went out to check, and there was a damn brick lying on the carpet."

The sheriff held the brick out to Mylie. "Don't touch it," he said. The front was smooth, it just looked like a brick. But on the backside, written in bold black paint was one word—*bitch*.

"What is that?" Ben asked.

Mylie didn't answer him.

"What an asshole," Cassie said.

"Do you know who would want to do this?" Sheriff Oakes asked.

Mylie knew. She knew exactly who it was.

"It was Robbie Price," Ben said when Mylie didn't answer. "It has to be him."

"We don't know for sure it was him," Mylie offered, even though she knew it was a lie. She knew he was a mean son-of-a-bitch, but she still had a hard time grasping the fact that he would do something like this. But he'd known they were gone. He probably hadn't anticipated that Granny would be there, since she went to the dance every year.

"I ought to get my wooden spoon and whoop his hind end for this," Granny said through clenched teeth.

"I'm surprised he even knows how to spell bitch," Cassie said.

They all laughed, but Granny said, "That's quite enough cursing out of you tonight, Cassandra."

Cassie rolled her eyes. "Can I go inside, Sheriff?" She asked. "I just want to go to my room."

Sheriff Oakes nodded. "Just don't step on any glass on your way."

"Am I allowed to curse, Granny?" Ben asked once Cassie disappeared up the stairs.

Granny nodded. "I reckon."

"You ever get those cameras up and running?" the sheriff asked. "From a couple of summers ago when we had that Peeping Tom?"

Mylie shook her head. "We just have cameras at the warehouse, not here."

"You know there won't be a whole lot I can do about it then," the sheriff said. "Even if you, me, and this whole town knows it's Robbie."

"I know," Mylie replied. "I'd appreciate it if you didn't make this an issue."

"What do you mean?" the sheriff wanted to know.

"We need the report for insurance," Mylie continued. "But I don't want this investigated. There's no point. All he wants to do is upset me, and I'd rather not give him the satisfaction."

Ben stared at her incredulously, but to Mylie's relief, he didn't say anything.

"I'll make a report," Sheriff Oakes replied. "I'll take a few pictures for the file. I'll keep it quiet."

"Thank you," Mylie said, reaching out to shake his hand.

"Mylie," Granny said. "Why don't you go ahead and walk Ben home. The sheriff and I can take it from here."

"Okay," Mylie replied. She walked out to meet Ben, who was now standing near the edge of the yard with his arms crossed over his chest.

"Granny sent me to walk you home," Mylie said to him. "I guess she thinks you can't make it the eighty feet to your front door."

Ben didn't smile. "Why are you letting him get away with this?" he asked quietly.

"Robbie?"

"Who else?"

Mylie sighed. "What do you want me to do? There's no proof he did it."

"But we know he did."

"And what good would accusing him do?" Mylie asked.

"At least people would know," Ben said.

"No," Mylie replied. "No, they'd know I accused him. And he'd go around saying he didn't do it. It would only make things worse."

"That's why he keeps getting away with shit like this," Ben protested. "That's why nothing ever changes."

Mylie glared at him. "You've been here all of ten minutes. You don't get to have an opinion about whether things change or not."

"I've been here all of ten minutes, and I can already tell that nothing has changed," Ben replied.

"Well, *you* certainly haven't changed," Mylie spat back.

"I guess that makes two of us," Ben said.

Mylie stood there staring at Ben as he went inside and slammed his door.

She had a headache.

"Are you coming inside, or are you going to stand there all night looking confused?" Granny called from inside the huge hole in the front window.

"It's weird that I can hear you," Mylie said.

Granny flipped her off.

"Okay, okay," Mylie called. "I'm coming. Let's get this cleaned up."

Chapter 26

Ben was trying to figure out what in the actual hell he'd been think-ing, kissing Mylie like that. He stood at his front window, watching the tarp they'd put up where the glass was shattered.

He shook his head. He'd lost control. That's all it was. They'd have to talk about it, of course, but it wasn't going to happen again. Nothing good could come of it. But holy fuck, it had been hot. More than hot. It had been . . . well, everything he thought it would be. He shuddered to think about what might have happened if Jodi hadn't interrupted them. Ben knew he'd been mere moments away from throwing her over his shoulder and finding a place to lay her down, right there out in the open.

And then they'd come home to a hole in Mylie's house, and he'd been so blinded by rage that he temporarily forgot himself. He was angry at Robbie, and he'd taken it out on Mylie. He knew damn well Mylie could handle herself—would handle herself. He wasn't some knight in shining armor here to defend her honor. But that didn't stop him from being pissed off and wanting to smash some-thing, even though he knew it was childish. He shouldn't have left their conversation like that.

It was too late to talk to her now. Besides, she had Cassie to deal with as well as the window. He hoped the teen was okay. He'd gotten bits and pieces of what happened on the way home. He'd forgotten how awful high school could be. He thought that being back in Clay

Creek would dredge up some of those old feelings, but so far, that hadn't been the case. Nearly everyone, with the exception of Robbie Price, had been nothing but welcoming, friendly even. He liked the way Melissa stayed open for them just to make Cassie feel better. He liked the way Mylie *knew* Melissa would stay open just for them. These were the little things he hadn't known he missed.

Ben stepped closer to the window when he saw a shape moving toward his house from across the street. At first, it was a blur, headed toward him, but by the time the shape got to his porch, he realized it was Mylie. She was poised at the bottom step, staring up at his house, shifting from one bare foot to the other, seemingly trying to decide what to do.

She wasn't wearing anything but a nightgown.

Instinctively, Ben went to the door to unlock it. He wanted to pull her inside. He wanted to kiss her again. He wanted . . . well, he just wanted. But he pulled his hand away from the lock at the last moment and stood there. He could still feel her lingering on his mouth, and he was desperate to be near her again.

If he let her inside, he knew what would happen.

He waited for her to knock and leaned his head against the door, knowing that if she did, he wouldn't be able to ignore her, wouldn't be able to stop himself.

When she didn't, relief and disappointment swirled around him. She knew then, just like he did, what would happen in the morning when they realized what they'd done, when they realized their mistake.

Because that's what it would have been—a mistake.

Ben stood at the door until the light across the street flickered off for good, and he was bathed in darkness once again.

Chapter 27

Ben watched Mylie standing on her front porch, dressed and ready for the dance. She'd asked someone—an upperclassman whose name he couldn't remember. It wasn't like Mylie hadn't gone on dates before. She had, and Ben hated it every time. Still, something about tonight felt different. Maybe it was because she was wearing a dress, something she rarely, if ever, did. Maybe it was because she looked nervous, waiting out there like that, fumbling with her purse and her phone and then her hair.

He'd thought she would ask him. He realized later that, of course, she wouldn't. He'd been so adamant he wasn't *ever* going to a dance. In fact, when she'd asked him if he'd changed his mind a few weeks ago, Ben *laughed* at her. He hadn't forgotten the hurt in her eyes that flashed for just a moment before she stomped off to ask someone else. But asking if he was going and asking if he'd go with her were two different things, weren't they?

He didn't know.

"What are you doing standing at the window?" Emily Lawrence put her hand on her son's shoulder and peered outside. "Oh, I see."

Ben didn't say anything.

"Why don't you tell her how you feel?" his mother asked.

"We're just friends, Mom," Ben replied, glad she couldn't see his face. "That's all."

"You know," his mother began. "I wasn't her biggest fan when we moved here. I thought she and that woman who insists on being called Granny were a little . . ."

"Trashy?" Ben asked, turning and quirking a smile.

"No," his mother replied. "No, I would never use that word. You know that. But I thought maybe they wouldn't be such a good influence on you."

"I know," Ben said.

His mother wouldn't have used that word, but she certainly implied it—with her looks, her actions. It wasn't exactly that his mother thought she was better than everyone else, it was just that she *expected decorum*. She expected people to act a certain way, and Ben had always complied with that expectation. He'd nearly always done what was asked, what was expected. He'd always assumed his close friendship with Mylie, based on those expectations from his mother, was an issue. But, for Mylie, he was willing to risk disappointing Emily.

"But I was wrong," Emily Lawrence replied. "Mylie is a lovely girl. And she's so good to you. I couldn't ask for a better friend for you than her, and if you liked her as more than that, well, I don't think I could ask for a better girlfriend for you, either."

His mother wandered off into the kitchen, leaving Ben to himself. Ben sighed and turned back around. What's His Name was late. The dance started half an hour ago. He watched Mylie sit down on the front steps, careful not to mess up her dress. She was texting someone—probably Jodi to complain that her date was late.

Ben hoped she wasn't being stood up. The thought made him furious. Mylie didn't deserve that. He didn't want her to be humiliated. He didn't want her to have to go alone, even though he knew that she had plenty of friends who would likely find that upperclassman at school the next week and make him regret what he'd done. That still didn't fix what was happening right now.

Ben backed away from the window and ran upstairs to his room. He could do this for her. He could go to the dance with her, even if the thought of dancing in public made him want to throw up.

He prowled through his closet to find something presentable—a pair of black slacks and a dress shirt he reserved for special occasions. He couldn't remember the last time he wore it, but luckily, it still fit, including the loafers he found thrown haphazardly into an old shoebox. There wasn't much he could do about his hair. It pretty much always stuck out somewhere, but he gave himself a good spritz of his grandfather's cologne before rushing downstairs to head out the front door. Maybe it was meant to be, what happened tonight. Maybe he was being given the chance to show her he cared, more than he was willing to admit to himself, to her, to his mother.

Maybe.

Ben made it down the first step of the porch before he heard the crunch of tires on gravel, and a rusted Ford F-150 sputtered to a stop in front of Mylie's house, What's His Name leaning out the window and honking his horn.

Ben watched as Mylie threw back her head and laughed, any anger or disappointment melting away. She hiked up her dress and jumped into the truck. Neither of them noticed Ben standing there as they peeled off into the muggy May evening, leaving Ben alone on his porch in shoes that suddenly felt entirely too small.

Chapter 28

The glass company came out to fix the window the next day. Some-how, Granny had sweet-talked them into coming out on a Sunday. Mylie watched from the kitchen table, a glass of orange juice in one hand and a blueberry muffin in the other.

"Could you at least attempt to make yourself look decent?" Granny asked, coming down the hallway dressed and wearing full makeup.

"It's Sunday," Mylie said, her mouth half full of muffin.

"And we have guests," Granny replied.

"Fine," Mylie said. "I'll go put on some pants."

She took her orange juice and her muffin and went back up to her room. She set the orange juice on her nightstand and flopped down on the bed. She tried to think of something, anything, to keep from wondering why Ben had seen her last night and not come outside. She knew he'd seen her. She hadn't knocked, second-guessing her-self at the last minute, but she saw the curtains ruffle. She knew he was there.

Maybe he thought their kiss was a mistake. She still hadn't decided. That was part of the reason she'd gone over last night after their fight about Robbie. She'd wanted to . . . well, she didn't know exactly. She'd just wanted to kiss him again. She wanted to see if it was as mind-blowing the second time as it had been the first time.

Mylie hadn't known a kiss could be like that. It scrambled her brain. It made her question every kiss she'd ever had before.

She hadn't wanted to fight with him last night. She'd been glad he stood up for her at the dance, and she knew he was upset about the brick through the window. She was upset about it, too. She knew Robbie was trying to get to her. He wanted her to say something, do something that would allow him to blame her for his own behavior, and she wasn't going to give him the satisfaction.

"Mylie!" Granny called from downstairs. "You have a gentleman caller!"

"I'll be right down," Mylie called back, giggling at her Granny's antiquated phrase. She'd been doing that since Mylie was old enough to date.

Mylie threw on a pair of jean shorts and a T-shirt and hustled down the stairs to find Ben waiting for her. Actually, what he was doing was consulting with the glass repairmen about their methods of installation. He didn't even notice Mylie standing there, watching him.

Finally, she said, "Do economists fix windows?"

Ben turned to her and grinned. "Not usually," he said.

"Not ever" one of the repair men muttered, and Ben's face reddened.

"It was nice meeting you gentlemen," Ben said, making his way over to Mylie.

"Nice guys," Ben said.

"They are," Mylie said, angling her head toward him. "Look, about last night . . ."

"What about last night?" Ben asked.

"I'm sorry," Mylie replied.

"What exactly are you apologizing for?" Ben asked.

"Not *that*," Mylie said. "The other stuff."

"Good," Ben replied. "I'm sorry for the other stuff, too. Do you, uh, want to go for a walk?"

Mylie shrugged. "Sure."

"Take Stanley with you!" Granny called from the kitchen.

She slid her feet into a pair of Cassie's Crocs and headed outside with Stanley and Ben. They walked down the road a ways without saying anything, Stanley tugging them forward. Finally, Ben looked over at her and said, "I'm sorry . . . about last night."

"Which part?" Mylie asked.

"The argument," he said. "I shouldn't have taken it out on you. I was just so furious. What kind of a person does that?"

"I think Cassie said it best," Mylie replied. "An asshole."

"I didn't mean to tell you how to handle it," Ben continued.

"Look," Mylie said. "If the sheriff can link it to him, that's one thing. But unless someone saw him do it, this is just a way for him to play the victim. He's already bad-mouthing me all over town. It'll make him madder if we ignore it, anyway."

"Are you sure you want him madder?" Ben asked.

"What, you don't want to protect me?" Mylie replied with a smirk.

Ben grabbed her hand. "I'll protect you. But I also know you can protect yourself."

Mylie looked at him. She willed herself to ask him about the kiss, but she just couldn't. She couldn't bring herself to ask. She wasn't sure, regardless of what the answer was, if she would like it. So instead, she just kept her free hand inside of his and continued to walk.

They reached the stop sign at the end of the road and turned around. Stanley paused, sniffing the air, a low growl emanating from his throat.

"Oh, stop it," Mylie said to him. "Let's go."

But Stanley refused to budge, and his ears pricked at the slight rustling in the bushes.

"It's probably a squirrel or something," Mylie said to Ben, attempting to drag Stanley from his spot. "He sounds mean, but he doesn't have a prey drive. He just wants to play."

"The squirrels don't want to play?" Ben asked with a smirk.

"They absolutely do not," Mylie said. "Stanley, come ON!"

"I don't think that's a squirrel," Ben said, pointing to the bush.

Sure enough, there was a flash of a blue collar, and Mylie realized too late that it was Fat Tony, probably heading back to wherever he went after his nighttime prowling to sleep. Before she could stop him, Stanley broke free of her grip and gave chase, Fat Tony fleeing.

"What is happening?" Ben called after Mylie as she scrambled to regain control of Stanley. "Aren't raccoons supposed to be nocturnal?"

"Don't worry," Mylie huffed. "He's not rabid. He's just an asshole."

"How do you know?" Ben replied.

"We . . . had . . . him . . . vaccinated," Mylie said, her words coming out in short bursts. "Distemper . . . and . . . rabies."

"Well, I'll be damned," Ben said.

Fat Tony had found a tree to climb, and he stayed there, halfway up the tree, just out of Stanley's reach, taunting him. Stanley barked and growled and scratched, but try as he might, he couldn't reach the raccoon.

Mylie got ahold of Stanley's leash, cursing. "Come. On. You. Damn. Dog."

Stanley didn't budge, keeping his vigil at the tree.

Ben stared up at Fat Tony, who Mylie could have sworn was grinning down at Stanley. Without saying anything, he reached down and picked up the massive pit bull and began carrying him like a baby toward the house.

"You're really a ridiculous animal," Ben said to him.

Mylie burst out laughing. "I cannot believe you just picked him up," she said.

"Well, I wasn't going to stand there and watch you two fight all day," Ben replied. "Besides, I think he likes it."

"He'll never live this down with Fat Tony," Mylie said. "Now the raccoon has the upper hand."

Ben patted Stanley's rump and cooed, "Don't listen to her Stan the Man."

Mylie couldn't help but grin all the way back to her house.

Chapter 29

Ben sat down at his computer, exhausted from carrying Mylie's damn dog all the way to her house. Still, he laughed at the image of Stanley chasing Fat Tony. By the time Ben had been ready to put Stanley down, the big lug hadn't wanted to stop being carried and, in fact, tried to jump up in Ben's arms as he was leaving.

He was still thinking about that as he checked his email. Then his eyes caught on a message that had been sent on Friday from the department head at the university where he'd been going through the rounds of interviews. His heart nearly stopped when he read it.

Good afternoon, Dr. Lawrence. We'd like to formally invite you to join us on campus to discuss the terms of employment. At this time, we do not have a date, but if you are amenable to a visit, please let us know, and the committee will provide me with an acceptable time. Looking forward to hearing from you,

Dr. Thomas Baker, department head, Economics

Ben's fingers hovered over his keyboard. He was excited, thrilled. It was the email he'd been hoping for. But there was also another emotion just below the elation that he couldn't quite name. He shoved it to the side and replied.

Dr. Baker, I would love to visit your campus and discuss employment. I apologize for the delay in my reply—I am currently at my grandfather's country house and do not have the best service. I will make any date proposed work for my schedule.

Sincerely,
Dr. Ben Lawrence

It wasn't quite a lie. He *was* at his grandfather's country house, technically. And the town didn't have the best reception. Ben didn't need to mention that he hadn't checked his email because he'd been so wrapped up in other things, other people, that he'd completely forgotten to check it. In fact, he'd nearly forgotten about the university altogether. Dr. Baker didn't need to know any of that. He didn't need to know about Mylie or the raccoon or the hefty pit bull. He doubted very much that Dr. Baker or any of the hiring committee he'd spoken with several times via videoconference would find the story amusing.

Ben closed his laptop and sat there for a while, just thinking about how excited he should be about very nearly being offered the job of his dreams. He wished his mother were alive to hear it. She'd be so proud of him. What he felt right now was sadness, grief, mixed with . . . what exactly? Regret? Apprehension? He didn't know. It was hard for him to have feelings that weren't sorted. Under most circumstances, he could put his feelings into boxes and pack them away, but right now, he was having trouble. Nothing felt settled, and there were few things Ben Lawrence hated more.

Chapter 30

"We've got two weeks before the tournament, and I don't know how we're going to get everything finished on time," Jodi said on Monday. "We've got online orders coming out of our ears, and we're already having to delay several orders because we're out of materials."

Mylie sat staring at the calendar on her desk. She was trying to concentrate on work. She had an entire warehouse full of people working furiously to keep up.

"Mylie?" Jodi was saying. "Mylie, hello? Mylie?"

"What?" Mylie looked up. "Oh, yeah, sorry. Okay, how can we figure this out?"

Jodi shrugged. "Offer discounts for delayed orders," she said. "Maybe send some free stuff. I don't know. If we can get a shipment of supplies overnighted, we might be able to make it work, but that'll cost."

"Do it," Mylie said, nodding. "I don't see that we have another choice, unless we want to go and raid the gift bags we have for the tournament."

"We can't do that," Jodi replied.

"Mylie?" There was a knock at the office door.

"Come in, Joe," Mylie said, waving the man inside. "What's up?"

Joe stepped in, taking off his faded St. Louis Cardinals cap. "Robbie's here. He says to pick up his last check?"

"I thought we put that in the mail?" Mylie asked, looking to Jodi.

"I did," Jodi replied. "On Friday."

Mylie sighed. "Send him in."

"Want me to stay?" Joe asked.

"I can handle him," Mylie replied, not entirely sure she was telling the truth. "Thanks, though."

Joe grunted a reply and stepped out in time for Robbie to step in, eyeing both Mylie and Jodi with suspicion.

"I mailed your check on Friday," Jodi said before Robbie had a chance to say anything. "I'm sure it's already siting in your mailbox."

"I said I'd be by to pick it up," Robbie replied, his eyes narrowing.

"And I said I'd mail it." Jodi crossed her arms over her chest.

"That's stupid," Robbie said. "It's easier for me to come get it."

"I'm sorry for the misunderstanding," Mylie replied. "But you were asked not to come back to the warehouse. That's why we mailed the check."

Robbie scowled. "It's illegal to withhold my check."

"It's illegal to throw a brick through someone's window, too," Mylie replied. "Yet here we are."

"I heard about that," Robbie said, scratching the scruff on his chin. "That's too bad about your window."

"It's too bad about your check."

"You can't keep my check," Robbie repeated.

"Nobody is withholding your check," Mylie said. "Jodi mailed it on Friday. You'll have it today."

"I reckon it won't matter in a couple of weeks, anyway," Robbie replied. "Once I win the tournament, I'll have more money than I could make in a year here."

Jodi rolled her eyes. "Okay, Robbie."

"Gonna be pretty sweet to beat you."

"We aren't on the team," Mylie said, wishing the conversation, and the fact that she was still looking at Robbie, was done. "But good luck."

"You sponsor that team," Robbie continued. "Everybody in town knows you're a bunch of cheats, but I aim to win."

"And everybody in town knows you're a . . ."

Mylie stood up, interrupting Jodi before she could say something they'd all regret. "Please just go," she said.

"Fine," Robbie said, his lips curling up into his gums so that the decay in his front two teeth was visible. "But that check better be in my mailbox, or I'll be back."

"You come back and the only thing waiting for you is going to be a sheriff's deputy," Mylie said, keeping her tone even.

"Come on, now," Joe said, appearing from just beyond the office door. "You heard the ladies."

Joe was every bit seventy years old, but he had the build of a man who'd spent his life working outside. He lived down the road from Robbie just outside of town, and Mylie figured the older man had to put up with Robbie once or twice over the years.

Robbie gave Jodi and Mylie one last look and then spit a wad of Copenhagen on the tiled floor before turning around and striding out of the office.

Mylie collapsed back down into her chair. "God, I hate him," she said.

"You never should have hired him," Jodi replied. "You knew better."

"I know," Mylie said. "I know I did, but I thought maybe . . . I don't know what I thought. I just thought maybe he needed a chance, and his granny is so nice. I thought it would help her."

"His granny knows better than to be asking favors for him," Jodi said.

"Granny never stopped asking favors for my mama," Mylie countered. "Never, ever."

"And look where that got her," Jodi said.

"Raising two kids," Mylie agreed.

Jodi put her hand on Mylie's and said, "You know Granny thinks you and Cassie are the best two people in the whole world. That's not what I meant."

"I know," Mylie replied. "Too bad Robbie's granny can't say the same."

Chapter 31

Ben was growing to dread Courtney the Realtor's phone calls. It wasn't that he didn't want to hear from her when someone wanted to view his house. He absolutely did. But it seemed like she called all the time for various reasons—Had he had a chance to clean the garage? Could she come by and take better pictures for the website? Did he want to know how many views the house, with all the new pictures, was getting per hour?

Today, however, she'd called to tell him that there was a very motivated couple who'd stopped by the realty office that afternoon. Did he mind if she showed the house ASAP? He didn't mind, he guessed, and he watched the couple walk around his living room, staring at the crown molding and commenting on the apparent draft on the far left-hand side of the room. Next to them, Courtney rattled on about the low property taxes and river access. He'd offered to leave, but the couple insisted he stay, just in case they had any questions Courtney couldn't answer.

They seemed to like the house, which pleased him. Ben's grandfather had loved the house. When he'd bought it in the early 90s as a vacation home, it needed quite a lot of work. Ben remembered his grandfather talking about it with his mother, excited about the place he liked to call his "retirement villa." His mother had come down to Clay Creek once to see it, and she'd come back suggesting the old house ought to be condemned. But Ben's grandfather had restored it with such love that by the time Ben and his mother moved there years later, it was more than a retirement villa—it was a home.

His throat bobbed with an emotion he couldn't quite put his finger on—pride? Regret?

Ben didn't have time to dwell on it, because Courtney approached him with the couple, all three smiling.

"This is a great place," the woman breathed.

The man, who seemed less inclined to be impressed, crossed his arms. "It needs a bit of work, though."

"Not really," Ben replied. Courtney gave him a sharp look, but he ignored it. The house didn't need a "a bit" of work. It needed next to nothing, save for maybe some paint and maybe the attic fan could use a replacement. Other than that—the roof was less than five years old and so was the guttering. He'd had it independently inspected and appraised before putting it on the market, so he knew that the house was listed well under what it was actually worth. He wasn't going to let some random man looking for a deal insult the house that his grandfather had dedicated the twilight of his life to.

"Well, I like it," the woman said. "Thank you for showing it to us, Courtney."

"Let me walk you out," Courtney replied, leaving Ben alone.

He sat down at the kitchen table, annoyed with himself. He should have kept his mouth closed. He wanted someone to buy the house. What if he'd just screwed it up with his comment?

Courtney came back inside a few minutes later with a huge grin on her face. "Give them a week or two, and I think they'll be sending us an offer," she said. "Maybe less."

"You think?" Ben asked.

Courtney nodded. "They love it. But they need help to buy, and it's going to take some convincing to one side of the parents."

"So, I didn't screw it up?"

"No," Courtney said. "The wife loves it. She's been talking about it nonstop since they got here, and she was still talking about it when they left. She won't let it rest until she has what she wants."

Ben let out a breath, and Courtney eyed him.

"Having second thoughts, Lawrence?" Courtney asked. "I thought you said you wanted to sell as quickly as possible."

"I did," Ben said. "I mean, I do. This is great news, Courtney. Thank you."

"I'll let you know when I know," Courtney said, heading toward the door. "Oh, and by the way?"

"Yeah?"

"I told them the neighbors were nice, respectable people. Don't tell them any different."

"Well, since they *are* nice, respectable people, that won't be a problem," Ben replied.

Courtney snorted. "I figured your time in the big city might have changed you, but I guess not."

"What is that supposed to mean?" Ben wanted to know.

"You're still just as in love with Mylie as you ever were."

"That's not true," Ben said, but his reply was half-hearted.

Courtney wiggled her fingers at him. She got to the door and said, "One more thing."

"What?" Ben asked. What *else* could she possibly have to say?

"There were some weird noises coming from that vent in the hallway," Courtney said. "You might want to check that out."

Ben knew what she was talking about. He thought he'd heard something earlier, but he'd convinced himself it was just in his head. This time, as he got up from the kitchen table, he heard the loudest scraping noise he'd ever heard in his entire life, and just as Courtney said, it was coming from the hallway.

Chapter 32

"If this gives me a rash, I'm going to kill you," Mylie said from underneath the clay mask Cassie was slapping onto her face. She'd come home from work to Cassie waiting to pounce. Even though all Mylie wanted to do was collapse in front of the television and speak to no one, she couldn't ignore the hopeful look in Cassie's eyes. Besides, all the preparation for the tournament was doing a number on her skin. Jodi was always telling her to drink more water, but Mylie simply said she'd die without a daily Dr Pepper.

"Calm down," Cassie replied. "You're fine."

"It's burning!"

Cassie sighed. "And they say teenagers are dramatic."

"Where did you get this, anyway?" Mylie asked, resisting the urge to claw at her skin.

"The ninety-nine-cent rack at the Gas 'n Go," Cassie replied.

"What?" Mylie sat up, batting her sister's hands away from her face.

"I'm kidding," Cassie replied. "I ordered them online."

"Where?"

"Would you just let me do this?"

"Fine," Mylie grumbled.

Downstairs, the doorbell rang.

"Granny!" Cassie yelled.

"She's not home," Mylie said.

The doorbell rang again.

"I'm not answering it!" Cassie exclaimed, backing away from Mylie. "I have this mask on my face!"

"So do I," Mylie replied.

"Yeah, but what if it's Ryan?"

Mylie tried and failed to raise her eyebrows, the clay on her skin crackling. "I thought you were done with him."

"I am," Cassie said. "But I still want him to come over and beg for me to come back to him."

Mylie stood up and replied, "You watch too many romantic comedies."

"Just go see who it is!" Cassie pleaded.

"Okay, okay. I'm going." Mylie made her way downstairs, determined to tell whoever was at the door to go away, *especially* if that person was Ryan.

When she pulled open the door, Ben stood there, his hands shoved down into his pockets and an amused smile playing on his lips.

Mylie tried not to look at his lips.

"Hello, ma'am," Ben said. "I'm looking for Mylie. Do I have the right house?"

Mylie's hands flew up to her face. Goddamnit. She stepped aside to let him in. "This is Cassie's fault," she said.

"No," Ben said. "I think it looks good. Really brings out your eyes."

"Be careful," Mylie warned. "Or I'll wipe this shit all over that nice, white shirt of yours."

"You wouldn't," Ben said, his eyes going wide.

"Try me." Mylie lunged at him.

Ben leapt out of the way, laughing as he rounded the couch and stood there, hands outstretched to stop her from wiping the cracking mask all over him. "Don't even try it."

"Or what?" Mylie taunted, attempting to climb over the couch and failing to catch his arm.

"Or," he huffed. "You're going to . . . regret it!"

Ben grabbed at Mylie, catching her around the waist and pulling her down onto the couch on top of him.

"Let me go!" Mylie screeched, wriggling as he held her there.

Ben loosened his grip around her waist, his hands wandering down past the small of her back toward her ass.

Mylie went still. "So far, I'm not regretting it," she whispered.

"It's hard to take you seriously with that shit all over your face," Ben said, grinning. He didn't move his hands.

Mylie didn't hesitate. She leaned down and rubbed her cheek against his. "Ha!"

"What are you two doing?" Cassie stood at the bottom of the stairs, glaring at them.

Mylie jumped off of Ben and glanced over at her sister guiltily. "He started it."

"I did not," Ben protested.

Cassie only shrugged. "Don't let Granny catch you two on that couch together."

Mylie felt her face grow hot beneath the mask, and she anxiously reached up to scratch at it. "I'm going to wash this off," she said.

"Good!" Ben called after her as she hurried upstairs. "Because I need your help with something."

FIFTEEN MINUTES LATER, Mylie stood inside Ben's house, staring down into one of the hallway air vents.

"I don't understand what I'm supposed to be looking at," Mylie said, peering down into the vent as a blast of chilly air hit her face. "It's not that hot out. Why do you have the air on?"

"I haven't acclimated to the heat yet," Ben replied. "But that's not my issue. Are you telling me you don't see anything . . . *down there*?"

"No?"

"I swear I heard something earlier," Ben replied. "And then, just before I came over to your house, I saw a face."

"A face?" Mylie asked, twisting around to look up at him. "Like a human face?"

"No," Ben replied. "It looked like an animal, but the hallway light was off, and by the time I turned it on and came back to the vent, it was gone."

"I think you're losing it," Mylie said.

"I swear I saw something," Ben said, leaning his head down next to Mylie's.

Mylie looked over at him and laughed. "You look terrified."

"I'm not," Ben said. "But there *is* something down there."

Mylie stared at him, and he stared back, her smile fading to match his own, serious expression. No, it wasn't serious. It was something else. The kind of expression she'd seen every time they got this close to each other.

"It's a bad idea, you know," he said to her.

"What's a bad idea?" she asked, her breath hitching in her throat.

"This," Ben said, but even as he said it, he inched close to her until their breath met.

"Because you're leaving," Mylie replied.

Ben scooted so his forehead was resting against hers and then replied, "I don't want you to hate me again."

Mylie considered his words. She knew if she let it go further, today or any other day, everything would eventually fall apart. It had to. There was no way around it. Still, she couldn't bring herself to move, to get up and leave like she knew she should.

"What are you thinking?" Ben asked her when she didn't answer.

"I think," Mylie said, "that if you don't kiss me right now, I'll hate you even more."

Ben obliged. It was soft at first, sweet and calm, given their positioning on the floor. But it didn't take long of her nipping at his bottom lip before they were tangled in a heap on the hardwood.

Mylie let out a groan as he traced her jaw and dipped down to her throat, his hands roaming freely on her body. She was about to ask him if they could move to the couch when she heard it.

A noise coming from the vent.

"Did you hear that?" she asked Ben.

"Hmm?" Ben replied, his mouth busy at her collarbone.

Mylie pushed him back. "Listen!"

Another noise, this time closer, almost as if whatever was in the vent was trying to get *out* and into the house.

"See!" Ben hissed, pointing. "I told you!"

Mylie sat up and crawled over to the vent, peering down into it. At first, she didn't see anything but a flash of fur. Then it turned to face her.

"Oh my God," Mylie said. "Oh my God, it's Fat Tony."

Chapter 33

Ben was having trouble digesting the news that the neighborhood raccoon was trapped in his vent. As soon as Mylie realized what happened, she'd dragged him outside and walked around to the back of the house, where sure enough, the door to the crawl space underneath the house was standing wide open.

"I didn't even know that was there," Ben admitted.

"It looks like the lock broke," Mylie replied. "I bet he pulled a duct down and crawled into it and doesn't know how to get back out."

"Why would he do that?" Ben asked.

Mylie stared at him. "He's a raccoon," she said. "I'm not sure that he really stopped to think about it."

Ben sighed. "So do we need to call someone?"

Mylie shook her head. "I don't think Animal Control will do anything. But let me call Morris and ask him if he still has that live trap. If we can scare him out of the duct, maybe we can trap him under the house."

"What if we can't?"

"Then your house is going to smell like dead raccoon soon."

"Call Morris," Ben said, wasting no time.

Ben was both relieved that he was not, in fact, losing his mind. He was, however, slightly annoyed that the stupid animal had messed up whatever might have happened with Mylie. He'd been seconds away from dragging her to the couch when the varmint started clawing at the vent again. Now, he was standing outside waiting for Morris to show up and wishing that he wasn't.

He wanted, *needed,* to touch her again. Ben didn't know how much more of this back and forth he could take. She seemed to feel the same way, and despite the anxiety of it all, despite the alarm bells in his head, he already knew what would happen if he managed to get her alone again. Mylie was standing close to him but not close enough to touch, as if she, too, had the same thoughts.

MORRIS ARRIVED IN short order carrying the live trap. He spent a good ten minutes arguing with Ben about who was going to go under the house to place it, but in the end, Ben lost. Morris cited the fact that he had a bad hip and a case of gout in his big toe.

It was disgusting under the house, but he managed to find the downed duct and place the live trap at the opening. He could hear Fat Tony scurrying around up there and scooted himself out as quickly as he possibly could. He wanted to avoid a trip to the ER and a rabies shot, something he reminded himself he would absolutely *not* have to worry about in Chicago.

"Do you think this will work?" he asked Morris as he heaved himself up from the ground.

"I reckon it will or it won't," Morris replied, shrugging.

"That's comforting."

"I'm sure it will be fine," Mylie said, giving him a reassuring smile. "Fat Tony does stuff like this all the time. He got up in someone's attic last summer and snuck into their kitchen at night to steal food. This is pretty minor."

"Do you want Fat Tony in your vents?" Ben asked her.

"No," Mylie admitted. "But I don't want anything in my vents."

"Well," Morris said, shoving his hands down into his pockets. "I'll let you two kids get back to it. Let me know if this works."

"Thanks, Morris," Mylie said. "See you later."

"I hope nobody tells Courtney about this," Ben said, motioning for Mylie to follow him back around to the front of the house. "She'll lose her mind if a raccoon dies under my house before it sells."

"I'm going to post signs all over town," Mylie joked. "That way you can never sell your house and Fat Tony and I can live in peace."

Ben laughed and sat down on the front porch. "I need a nap."

"You and me both," Mylie replied.

"But first," Ben began, shifting his body toward her. "I think we need to talk . . . about . . . whatever it is that's going on here."

"Okay," Mylie said, sitting down beside him. "What *is* going on here?"

"I don't know," Ben said. "But I know that the last time we came anywhere close to this it was ruined by me leaving. I don't want to ruin anything, Mylie. I don't think I have it in me to do that again."

"We're adults now," Mylie said.

"But I'm still leaving."

Mylie loosed a breath. "Do we have to think about you leaving right now?" she asked. "Can't we just . . . enjoy whatever this is while we can?"

Ben looked at her, surprised. "Is that really what you want?"

"Yes," Mylie replied. "I don't want to wonder anymore about . . . us. I want to know."

"I want to know, too," Ben admitted. "I've always wanted to know."

"Then let's do it," Mylie replied.

Ben raised an eyebrow.

"That's not what I meant!" Mylie smacked him on his arm. "I

meant, let's try this. See where it goes for now, while you're here. But I also think we need to be honest with each other . . . even if it hurts."

Ben knew this was a bad idea. He could tell from Mylie's face that she knew it, too. They were lying to themselves, but at that moment, it felt too good, too right. So, he said, "I'm in."

Mylie stood up. "I'm taking you on a date tonight," she said.

"You are?" Ben stood up beside her, taking a step closer to her so that his hand brushed against hers.

"Yes," Mylie replied. "Meet me on the dock at seven. I'll bring the food and fishing poles. You bring the beer."

"We're going fishing?" Ben asked.

"You and me!" she called, breaking away from him and heading across the street toward her house. "Fishin' in the dark!"

Chapter 34

"Are you sure you know what you're doing?" Jodi asked Mylie later that day as Mylie picked up fishing supplies from the warehouse for her date with Ben.

"No," Mylie replied. "I have no idea what I'm doing, actually."

"And you don't think this is a bad idea?" Jodi continued. "Don't get me wrong, I'm happy for you, I am, but I can't see how this will end any other way but in heartbreak."

"I've spent the last ten years wondering what this might be like," Mylie replied. "I'm not going to spend another second wondering."

"But he's leaving."

"Then he leaves," Mylie said. "But at least I'll know."

Jodi sighed. "So, you're taking him fishing?"

Mylie nodded. "I bet he hasn't been since the last time I took him," she said.

"And you think taking him fishing is romantic?"

"We'll be alone on a boat together in the dark," Mylie said.

"With fish," Jodi said.

"And alcohol," Mylie countered.

"Alcohol does help," Jodi mused. "But still, Mylie, I don't want you to get hurt again. You were a wreck last time."

"I was eighteen last time," Mylie said. "I've grown up."

Jodi narrowed her eyes at her friend.

After Ben left ten years ago, Mylie felt loss. It wasn't just the fact that he wasn't there to talk to, it was the fact that he was physically gone from her—that steadying presence he'd always been. Sure, at first, they'd talked on the phone quite a bit. They'd texted some. But it wasn't the same. He wasn't *there*. They weren't there for each other, and after a while, as their discussions became further and further apart, it was harder to update each other on their lives. Eventually, there were more awkward silences than there was talking.

Mylie sighed. "I just need to know, Jo," she said. "I just need to know what it's like."

"What sleeping with him is like?" Jodi asked.

"No," Mylie said. "I mean, *yes*, but it's not just that. I need to know if this can work."

"But you already know it can't."

"That's not what I mean." Mylie pushed the pads of her fingers into her forehead. "God, can you just let me make a mistake?"

Jodi threw up her hands. "Fine, but you better call me and tell me how it goes."

"I will," Mylie promised. "Don't tell anyone, okay? The last thing we need is for the whole town to be involved."

"So don't tell Granny?" Jodi asked with a grin.

"Absolutely don't tell Granny."

MAKING SURE GRANNY didn't find out that hanging out with Ben meant being on a date proved to be more difficult than Mylie had imagined.

"So, you're taking the boat out for some night fishing?" Granny asked. "With Ben?"

"He said he hasn't been in years, so I offered," Mylie replied as casually as she could muster. "It's no big deal."

Granny narrowed her eyes at Mylie. "Uh-huh."

"It's not," Mylie said. "We used to go out all the time on the boat when we were kids."

"When you were kids," Granny repeated.

"Please don't make a big deal out of this, Granny," Mylie said, packing the last sandwich into the cooler. "We're just going fishing."

"Fine," Granny replied, waving a hand in the air. "I won't make a big deal out of it, but be careful out there on that boat."

"We will," Mylie said, trying to keep her giddy excitement from bubbling over. "I'll be back later tonight. Tell Cassie, will you?"

"She's over at Allie's," Granny replied. "But as soon as she's back, I'll let her know."

"I guess they got things worked out?" Mylie asked.

"Yes," Granny said. "Apparently. But you know how those kids are. I'm sure they'll be feuding again in a couple of days over something else."

"Just enjoy the peace tonight," Mylie said. "You have the whole house to yourself."

"I'm going to take a long bath," Granny replied. "And have a glass of wine and read one of my sexy books."

Mylie laughed. "Enjoy it."

MYLIE HAD THE little boat ready to go by the time Ben arrived, right at dusk, carrying a six-pack of beer in one hand and a bottle of wine in the other. "I wasn't sure what to get," he said. "So, I just got both."

"Perfect," Mylie said with a grin. "We'll have plenty to drink."

Mylie loaded the boat with the fishing poles and tackle, while Ben heaved the cooler and drinks inside. There were two seats inside the little boat, one on each end, and Mylie sat down by the one nearest the motor and started it up. The light was just beginning to fade as they made their way out onto the lake.

She found a cove not far from the house and anchored there, grinning at Ben in the moonlight. "How does this work?"

Ben glanced around. "Well, I guess we could swim to shore if we're attacked by some kind of lake monster, so it works."

"What is it with you and lake monsters?" Mylie asked, remembering the last time they'd been out on a boat and Ben's near refusal to get into the water for a swim.

"I can't see the bottom," Ben replied. "I don't like that."

"You can barely see the top right now," Mylie joked, handing him one of the fishing poles she'd brought. "You still remember how to bait a hook?"

"Barely," Ben admitted. "But I think I can do it."

Mylie squinted in the darkness to make sure he was doing it correctly. She was impressed to see that he expertly baited the hook without any hesitation. She turned to the lake to cast her line.

She sat back in the boat and breathed. She took note of the gentle breeze and the smell of the lake around her. It was here, on the water, that she felt the most at home. She stole a glance over at Ben and had to laugh because his look of concentration on his fishing pole was so intense.

"Are you laughing at me?" Ben asked. He set his pole down and reached into the cooler for a beer. "You want something?"

Mylie picked up the bottle of wine, glad Ben had chosen something cheap with a screw top. "I'm good," she said. She took a drink right from the bottle.

"Reminds me of high school," Ben said.

"Yeah, except back then it was Boone's Farm."

"Like I could forget that red vomit on the floorboard of Jodi's car," Ben replied.

"She won't let me forget it, that's for sure," Mylie mumbled.

Ben took a swig of his beer and said, "Do you do this a lot? Come out here fishing?"

"No," Mylie replied. "Not as much as I used to."

"How come?"

Mylie shrugged even though she knew Ben probably couldn't see the motion. "I don't know," she said. "I guess I've just been busy."

"With work?"

Again, Mylie shrugged. "It does take up a lot of time. I love it, though."

"You always did want to start a business," Ben replied. "It seems like it's doing well."

"I just wanted to take care of myself, you know?" Mylie said. "I like knowing that I'm building something for Cassie, even if she doesn't want to work there. I like knowing I'm doing something good for the community."

"Even if they don't always appreciate it," Ben acknowledged.

Mylie knew what, rather *who* he was talking about. "Robbie Price is just one person," she replied. "Yeah, he sucks, and I never should have hired him, but for the most part, everyone is supportive. It's been good for the town, to have a business like this here."

"I can't believe he's still acting the same as he did in high school," Ben said. "How is it that he hasn't grown up?"

"Some people don't change," Mylie replied.

"That's sad."

"Have you?" Mylie asked Ben. "Changed all that much?"

"Since high school?" Ben asked. "Yeah, I like to think I have."

Mylie thought about it. "Well, you certainly look different."

Even in the dark, even from across the boat, Mylie felt Ben stiffen. "I sometimes wonder if things would have been different if I'd been more confident in high school."

Mylie set her fishing pole down and picked up the wine bottle again, putting it to her lips. After a few moments, she replied, "Ben, it wasn't right the way Robbie and some of the others treated you. But you could have had more friends than just me and a few others. You were so closed off back then. It was like you didn't *want* people to like you."

"I didn't know how to get people to like me," Ben said. "I've never been good at that like you are."

Mylie laughed. It was a rough, sarcastic sound. "I'm not good at it," she said. "I had to learn. Because I couldn't stand for people to feel sorry for me. The girl without parents. The girl whose mother couldn't be bothered to stay home for more than a few days at a time. I *had* to make people like me."

"My dad was good at it," Ben said, his voice barely above a whisper. "Everyone loved him."

Mylie wanted to scoot over and take his hand. "I'm sure he was wonderful," she said. Ben never talked about his father. At least, he hadn't before. She'd tried, unsuccessfully, a few times to get him to talk about the man he'd lost so long ago, but every time, Ben shut down and refused. She understood. She didn't like to talk about the people she'd lost, either.

"He was," Ben replied. "Sometimes I'm afraid I'm forgetting him—how he smiled, what his voice sounded like." He turned himself toward Mylie. "It's always been easier to shut myself off than get to know people. My dad helped me with that, and then when he was gone . . . I don't know."

"I get it," Mylie said.

"This place," Ben continued. "It reminds me of how sad I was. I just missed my dad so much. I missed Chicago. I didn't know who I was without those two things."

"And now?" Mylie asked.

Mylie couldn't see Ben, and he didn't respond. She knew it was complicated. Life was complicated, which seemed like such a cliché thing to think, but it was *true*. There were wounds that didn't always heal, they mostly just scabbed over, and Mylie wondered if Ben's scabs were bleeding now that he was back here confronting his past.

"Hey! I think I've got something!" Ben said suddenly, reeling in his line. "I've got something!"

Mylie scooted over to him and turned on the flashlight she kept between the seats of the boat. She flicked it on in time to see a fish splash up and out of the water, wiggling on the hook.

"You do!" Mylie exclaimed. "Look at that!"

In the glow of the flashlight Ben grinned at her, and Mylie thought to herself that as far as memories go, this was bound to be a good one.

Chapter 35

Ben helped Mylie tie up the boat, and they dumped their fishing supplies on the dock. It was nearly midnight, but Ben got the sense that Mylie wasn't quite ready to call it a night as they walked back toward their respective houses.

"Do you want to come over?" Ben asked, catching her hand as they walked.

Mylie nodded. "Yeah," she said. "I do."

They walked wordlessly back to his house, and he let them inside. He wondered whether he should offer her something to drink, or at least find something to say that would make this less awkward, but before he had time to say anything, Mylie pulled him down to her level and kissed him.

It had the same fire their other kisses had, but this time, there was an urgency, a need, behind it that he was eager to meet.

"Take me to your bedroom," Mylie said.

"Are you sure?" Ben asked her.

She kissed him again. "Yes."

Ben pulled her up the stairs, hardly able to control his hands and mouth that desperately wanted to explore every part of her. When she sat down on his bed and looked up at him through her lashes, he let go of any doubt, any waning control he had, and pressed himself down onto her.

She moaned and grazed Ben's bottom lip with her teeth, and the growl that escaped him startled them both. As Mylie reached up and tugged at his shirt, he allowed her to pull it off, and they began undressing each other between heated explorations.

Ben trailed his tongue down her chin and into the hollow of her collarbone. She arched her back when he encircled her nipple, cool in the warmth of his mouth. Jesus, everything about her was perfect. He wished that his mouth wasn't so preoccupied so he could tell her.

Mylie writhed beneath him, and he couldn't help but laugh into her skin.

"Be patient," he murmured.

But Mylie wouldn't be patient. She put her hands flush across his chest and shoved him up until he was lying on his elbow beside her.

"What are you doing?" Ben asked.

"I want to be on top," Mylie said. "Lie down."

"Yes, ma'am."

Now it was Mylie's turn to work her way down his body, her hands and mouth wasting no time, and he had to admit to himself that it wasn't as easy to stay still when he was on the receiving end. He idly wrapped a hand around her ponytail and then tugged at the cloth band holding it in place, her hair cascading all around her.

He inhaled sharply when she gripped his thighs and took him, *all of him*, into her mouth. Mylie stopped for a moment to look up at him, her eyes glinting with something feral, and it sent Ben's senses soaring.

Just when Ben didn't know how much longer he could control himself, Mylie paused, sitting up and settling herself on top of him. She looked into his eyes.

"I need to feel you inside of me," she breathed.

She grasped her hand around his cock, guiding him into her, and it was all Ben could do to grasp her hips as she rode him, back and forth, until he had to close his eyes with the pleasure of it all.

By the time he flipped her over onto her back, they were both glistening with sweat. Mylie wrapped her legs around him and clawed at his back as he crashed into her, until they both cried out and he collapsed, his mouth finding hers.

"I didn't know it could be like that," she said later as he held her in bed. "I didn't know *I* could be like that."

Ben grinned. "I think there were a lot of things neither of us knew until recently," he said.

"I should probably go home," Mylie replied. "What time is it, anyway?"

"It's too late to go home," Ben replied, squeezing her tighter. "Stay."

Mylie wiggled around so that she could face him. "Do you want me to stay, or is that just something you're saying to be polite?"

"When was the last time I was polite to you?" Ben asked, kissing her.

"Okay," Mylie agreed. "I'll stay. But I've got to be up early so I can sneak in the house and get ready for work."

Ben laughed. "Like we're back in high school."

"This never happened in high school," Mylie reminded him.

"I guess that means we have some lost time to make up for," Ben said, pulling the covers over his head. "We better get to work."

Chapter 36

It was the screaming that woke Mylie. At least, she thought it was screaming. She sat up in bed and rubbed at her eyes, temporarily forgetting where she was. It wasn't until she realized the solid lump sleeping next to her was Ben that she remembered.

"Ben," Mylie whispered, gently shaking him. "Ben, wake up."

"Phlumpumph," Ben murmured, rolling over.

"Ben!" Mylie tried again. "Wake up!"

"What is it?" Ben asked, opening one eye.

"Do you hear that?" she asked. "It sounds like someone is out-side screaming."

Ben sat up and got out of bed, pulling on a pair of pants in the process. "Holy shit," he said, looking out the window. "You've got to come see this."

Mylie felt dread coil in her stomach. "What's going on?"

"Just come look."

Mylie got up and joined Ben at the window. There, on his lawn, were at least six people, all chasing a furry blur and yelling at each other. Mylie could pick out Cassie, Granny, and Morris. Stanley was barking furiously. Farther down, closer to the road, it looked like Courtney and . . . "Oh my God," she said. "Are those the people who want to buy your house?"

"I've got to get down there," Ben said. "I'll meet you downstairs."

Mylie stood there for a few seconds, contemplating what to do.

She hadn't meant to sleep this late. Not only was she going to be late to work but everyone was going to see her coming out of Ben's house. Slowly, she scrounged around for her clothes and tried to collect her thoughts. She shoved her legs through her shorts and found her bra under Ben's bed. Everything had been discarded in the heat of the moment. Mylie wished she'd thought to go home last night, because now everyone would see her.

Instead, she'd fallen asleep next to Ben, curled in the crook of his arm, listening to his steady breathing. She'd woken once in the night and had kissed his chest until he, too, was awake. What they'd done—twice—was nearly enough to make Mylie forget any potential embarrassment. The way he'd looked at her, touched her, gave her goose bumps to think about.

Outside, it was chaos.

Morris was crouched in the bushes off to the side of the house, while Granny and Cassie stood on each side of the bush, shouting instructions that Mylie couldn't quite hear. At the front of the house, Courtney stood, lips pursed and arms across her chest, staring at Ben as if she might murder him. Stanley, unleashed and free, was running back and forth between Morris and Granny.

"What's going on?" Mylie asked, hurrying down the front steps.

Courtney looked Mylie up and down, understanding sparking in her eyes. In fact, there seemed to be understanding in everyone's eyes, and Mylie wasn't sure if she wanted to grin like a cat with a canary or disappear into the bushes.

"Well," Courtney said. "Apparently, Fat Tony stole Morris's cell phone."

"What?" Mylie asked, looking to Ben for clarification. He only shrugged at her.

"How did that happen?" Mylie called over to where Morris stood his ground against the raccoon.

"Well," Morris huffed. "I came over this mornin' to check the trap. And sure enough, he was in there. When I leaned over to open it up so old Tony could come on out, my dang phone fell out of my shirt pocket."

"And Fat Tony stole it!" Cassie finished. She gave Mylie and Ben a look that told them she was enjoying herself way more than she should have been.

The woman in the couple peered around Courtney and said, "Does this neighborhood often have rabid raccoons on the loose?"

"Fat Tony isn't rabid," Mylie said. "He's just . . . well, he's just mischievous."

"Why doesn't someone just shoot him if he's such a nuisance?" the man in the couple asked.

Mylie looked over at Courtney, silently telling her that she better handle her clients before Mylie did it for her. Nobody was going to be shooting Fat Tony. That raccoon was an institution in Clay Creek, and she didn't take kindly to anyone suggesting it—especially random people who didn't even live there, even if he was, in fact, a nuisance and the bane of Stanley's existence.

"You can't shoot Fat Tony!" Cassie said. "He's practically a pet."

"You can't have raccoons as a pet," the man said matter-of-factly. "They're wild animals."

"Nobody is shooting Fat Tony," Mylie said, catching Stanley by the collar. She glared at the man who at least had the good sense to look guilty.

"So, is this really an issue?" the woman asked. "*Pet* raccoons on the loose?"

Before Courtney could say anything, Fat Tony shot out from the bushes, running as fast as his little raccoon hands could carry him. Sure enough, between his teeth was Morris's cell phone.

"Get him!" Morris yelled, chasing after Fat Tony. "Don't let him escape!"

Mylie held tight to Stanley as he writhed and barked. "Not today, Stan," she said to him. "You'd only make this situation worse."

Granny and Cassie took off at a run, and Mylie couldn't help but laugh at Fat Tony zagging left when Morris, Granny, and Cassie zigged left. She watched for a few more seconds before she pulled her phone from her back pocket and called Morris's number.

Everyone watched as the raccoon paused, the phone vibrating and ringing in his mouth. Fat Tony dropped it onto the gravel and then shot like lightning toward the lake.

"I've got it!" Morris hollered, gleeful. "I've got it!"

"Thank the Lord and stars above," Granny muttered. "Morris, you need something to wipe off that raccoon slobber?"

"Jesus Christ," Courtney muttered, sliding her eyes over to the couple, whose eyes were as wide as saucers as Morris gripped his phone and wiped it on his shirt.

"It still works!" he said, holding the phone up triumphantly.

Beside Courtney, Ben was doing his best to control his laughter, but one look at Mylie, and it was all over. The dam broke, and they were laughing so hard that they didn't even notice Courtney herding the couple away in a huff.

"I . . . can't . . . breathe," Mylie said, tears rolling down her face.

"It looks like you've scared off your buyers," Granny said, holding her side. "I feel like I just ran a marathon."

"You practically did," Mylie replied. "But I am sorry about those people. I think they were really interested."

"They'll be back," Ben replied. "I didn't even know they were stopping by. I bet Courtney didn't even bother to call."

Granny arched an eyebrow and glanced from Ben to Mylie

and then said, "Well, if she did, I doubt either of you would have noticed."

"Granny!" Mylie hissed.

"I'm just sayin'."

Mylie ignored her grandmother. She and Ben walked back toward his front porch.

"If you'd told me even a month ago that I'd be spending my time avoiding a raccoon wearing a collar, I would have said you were insane," Ben said.

"That's Clay Creek for ya," Mylie said with a grin.

Ben's glasses were slightly askew in the most adorable way, and she reached up to fix them. He caught her hand and pulled her close to him, drawing her mouth up to his. She let him kiss her, and her knees weakened. She didn't even care who might be watching.

Finally, they broke apart, breathless.

"I could get used to this," Ben said.

"I better get ready for work," Mylie said. The truth was, she could get used to it, too. She *wanted* to get used to it.

"How about I bring lunch over to the warehouse?" Ben asked.

Mylie paused. "Sure," she said, trying to hide her surprise. "That sounds great. I usually take lunch about noon, but since I'm late, better make it closer to one."

"I'll see you then," Ben said.

"Watch yourself, boy," Granny called from across the street. "That girl right there is half my heart."

Mylie didn't wait for Ben's response as she hurried into the house to shower, praying that whatever happened, whatever they got used to, nobody's heart would end up broken.

Chapter 37

The walk of shame into work was noticed only by Jodi, who was waiting in Mylie's office for the tea.

"You have to tell me everything," Jodi said before Mylie could even set down her bag and laptop.

"I need you to tell me where we are on production," Mylie replied, ignoring her best friend's request. "Are we going to have enough supplies to fulfill all the orders and be ready for the tournament next week?"

Jodi nodded. "Yes, and you already know that," she said. "Don't pretend you don't know what's going on here so you don't have to answer me."

"I don't have to answer you," Mylie replied, knowing full well she would. "It's not your business."

"Like hell it's not!" Jodi said. "I've been covering for you all morning!"

"That wasn't my fault," Mylie countered. "Fat Tony stole Morris's phone."

"I heard," Jodi replied. "Which is also how I know that half the town saw you come out of Ben's house looking like you'd slept there."

"It wasn't half the town," Mylie said. "It was Morris and Granny and Cassie and . . . oh, shit."

"Courtney," Jodi finished. "Courtney told everyone you ruined a major sale and spent the night with Ben."

"I didn't ruin her sale," Mylie said, sitting down in her chair. "I'm not the one who gave Fat Tony the phone."

Jodi laughed. "All right, she didn't say you *ruined* it. But she did say that she had to spend half an hour convincing that couple that there isn't a vermin problem in town."

"But there *is* a vermin problem in town," Mylie said.

"Yeah, if you consider Robbie Price vermin."

"I do," Mylie replied.

"So does everyone else," Jodi replied.

Mylie closed her eyes. She didn't want to think about Robbie Price. She wanted to stay warm and happy inside her own little world.

"Okay, never mind. Besides, I have something more interesting I need to know about," Jodi said. "*Spill. About. Ben.*"

Mylie did. She told her *nearly* everything, keeping some of the more intimate bits to herself. She told Jodi about how she and Ben had decided they were just going to go along for the ride of whatever this was, even if they both knew how it would end—with Ben selling the house and leaving. She tried to sound nonchalant about it, but the thought of it made her heart constrict.

"And you're okay with this?" Jodi asked. "Like, really okay with this?"

Mylie shrugged. "I needed to know what it was like," she said. "Being with him in that way, even if it isn't going to last."

"Do you want it to last?"

Again, Mylie shrugged. "I like what we have right now."

Jodi didn't say anything for a long moment, and then she replied, "Well, if you're happy, I'm happy, I guess."

"You don't sound happy," Mylie retorted.

"Look, I like Ben," Jodi said. "You know that. I've always liked him. But he's always been . . . well, you know. Unavailable. I just don't want you to get hurt again."

"I'm okay."

"Then I'm okay," Jodi said, giving Mylie a genuine smile. "But you have to keep me in the loop. Being basically married is boring."

"I doubt that," Mylie replied. "You're basically married to a guy who injures himself on a tractor every single day of the week."

"Yeah, but that's just stressful, not sexy."

Both women began to laugh. They spent the rest of the morning working and talking. It was a welcome change from the chaos of the last few days. She'd nearly forgotten what it was like to just sit and work with her friend as they chattered on about nothing important.

It wasn't until Mylie heard her stomach grumble that she realized so much time had passed. As if on cue, there was a knock on the office door and Ben appeared.

"You ready?" he asked.

Mylie smiled and nodded. "Yep."

Jodi watched them warily as Mylie gathered her things to leave. "I'll keep everything running while you're gone," she said. "But I want to remind you that I haven't even had lunch yet."

"I won't be gone long," Mylie replied. "Thank you."

"Mmmhmm" was all Jodi said.

Mylie and Ben walked down the expansive driveway of the warehouse to the lakefront, where there was a picnic area. It was mostly abandoned, left to decay for more prime spots on the water. Nobody used it now except for the people who worked at Hook, Line, & Sinker.

"This place has seen better days," Ben said.

"Yeah, nobody really goes here anymore," Mylie agreed. "But we replaced the picnic table last year, so it's sturdy enough."

"We?"

"I say we, but it was mostly a couple of the guys who work at the shop," Mylie replied. "Jodi and I pretty much sat around and gave orders."

Ben set the plastic bags from the Cracked Egg down on the table and said, "Was it just me, or was Jodi glaring at me when we left?"

"She was glaring at both of us," Mylie said.

"Why?"

Mylie swung a leg over the bench of the picnic table. "Because she thinks you're going to hurt me and that I'm stupid for getting involved with you when you're just going to leave."

"Ah," Ben said, sitting down opposite her. "So, you told her."

"I had to," Mylie replied. "She's like a bloodhound. She would have sniffed us out sooner or later."

"I remember," Ben said with a laugh. "She was convinced her boyfriend was cheating on her and made us stake out his house for three nights in a row."

"And we thought she was nuts," Mylie said.

"Yeah, and who turned out to be right?"

"Jodi," they said in unison.

"I hope you don't think I would hurt you," Ben said. "Because I wouldn't. Not intentionally."

"I know that," Mylie replied. "Not on purpose."

"Do you think this is a mistake?" Ben asked.

Mylie looked down into the Styrofoam container at her food. "You mean this burger? No, it's perfect. I'm starving."

"That's not what I mean," Ben said. "But this burger does look delicious."

"I think we're adults," Mylie replied. "I think that we're old enough to make our own decisions. I wanted . . . I wanted this."

"Me, too," Ben said quietly. He reached across the table to take her hand.

"In the spirit of being honest," Mylie said. "I want to tell you something."

"What is it?" Ben asked, his brow furrowing.

Mylie shifted on the bench. "You have to promise me you're not going to get all upset and tell me what I should do."

"I can't make any promises."

Mylie rolled her eyes. "Robbie showed up at the warehouse a couple of days ago."

"He did what?" Ben straightened. "After he threw a brick through your window?"

"Yes," Mylie replied. "He said it was because he hadn't received his check, but I looked over our accounts, and he'd cashed it."

"What the fuck is his problem?" Ben's hands balled into fists.

"Jodi called the sheriff after he left, once we'd discovered he'd cashed the check, so at this point, it's just harassment," Mylie continued. "He told her this morning that he'd spoken with Robbie and told him that in no uncertain terms was he supposed to come anywhere near the warehouse *or* my house."

"Will he listen?"

Mylie shrugged. "I hope so. I'll have to see him during the tournament, but that can't be avoided. Besides, he'll be out on the boat all day."

Ben shoved his lunch away from him. "Is there anything I can do?"

"No," Mylie said. "I don't think so."

"Want me to beat him up?" Ben's eyes twinkled with secret amusement.

Mylie barked out a laugh, feeling the knot of anxiety that had settled in her stomach loosen. "Yes, please."

"You were supposed to say no," Ben replied. "Now I have to beat him up to defend your honor."

Mylie rolled her eyes. "Of course, you aren't going to beat him up," she said. "He'd likely put you into a coma, if he didn't kill you first."

Ben stuffed a bit of cheeseburger into his mouth. "I did nearly shove him down at the dance."

"And I got a brick through my window."

"I'm sorry about that," Ben said.

"I'm kidding." Mylie laughed. "But I bet if you waited until he was *really* drunk, you'd be okay."

Ben stood up, leaning across the picnic table to Mylie, brushing her lips with his.

"What was that for?" Mylie asked.

"I just thought our *friend* Robbie out there might like a show," Ben replied.

"In that case," Mylie said, her eyes gleaming with mischief. "Give me another."

Mylie went back to work, albeit reluctantly. She'd wanted to stay out there with Ben, laughing and kissing. It was strange to her, how someone could be such a good friend and also . . . something so much more. She'd never had that before. Usually, the men she dated weren't her friends before they started dating and certainly weren't her friends after. But with Ben, it just felt easy. Well, some of it at least. If she thought too hard about it, she knew she could make a whole list of doubts, but when she was *with* him, it felt good. It felt right.

Jodi didn't say anything when Mylie reappeared, her hair falling out of her ponytail and her lips swollen. She simply smirked and pointed to a pile of paperwork.

Mylie was happy to oblige.

Chapter 38

Ben was not prepared for the level of insanity that the fishing tournament had on the community of Clay Creek. There was still almost a week to go before the festivities, but the town was in full decoration mode, with Mylie at the helm. She'd disappeared from his bed that Monday morning before he woke, the only indication that she'd ever been there was the smell of her perfume lingering on his sheets.

Ben sat down to check his email, but before he could even power on his laptop, his phone rang. A rush of anxiety ran through him when he saw the caller ID.

"Hello, Dr. Baker," he said.

"Dr. Lawrence!" A jovial voice came through the other end. "Good afternoon. I hope I'm not interrupting."

"No," Ben said. "No, not at all."

"Wonderful," Dr. Baker replied. "Well, the committee has met, and we've decided that the first week in June would really work best for us to determine the parameters of our potential relationship."

Ben did the mental calculation. "In one week?"

"Yes," Dr. Baker said. "Of course, if the notice is too short, we can reconvene and pick another date." There was a pause. "That said, we are quite pressed for time. We'd like to have the matter of instructor settled before the second summer session begins in July."

"No," Ben said, swallowing. "That time frame is perfectly acceptable."

"Glad to hear it," Dr. Baker replied. "I'll have my secretary email you with the itinerary and accommodation information."

"I'm looking forward to it, sir," Ben said. "I appreciate this opportunity."

"You're the best man for the job," Dr. Baker said. "We'll talk soon, Dr. Lawrence."

"Yes," Ben said. "Have a good rest of the day, sir."

Ben clicked the end call button and stood there in the kitchen for a few minutes, trying to figure out what just happened. He hadn't expected to schedule this meeting so soon. Universities usually took forever to decide on a candidate. It wasn't an official offer, but the request for a meeting would likely result in one. Foolishly, he'd assumed that he'd have weeks.

Weeks with Mylie.

Weeks to sort it out.

Ben looked around the house. So far, there were no offers to buy it. If he left in a week, he could always come back. Even then, if he officially accepted the position, he'd be moving. There would be no getting around that. Which is what he *wanted*, he reminded himself.

He again wished he could call his mother, and at the same time, he felt angry with her—both that he couldn't work through his feelings with her *and* that what he was feeling right now was because of her, because of her demand that he come here just *one more time* before he sold the house. If he'd stayed in Chicago, if he'd simply told Courtney to sell without thinking twice, he'd already be packing for the coast. Instead, he was here, reconsidering all of his life choices.

No, he told himself. *No, I'm not reconsidering anything.* This was just a temporary moment of doubt. He'd respond to the email. He'd tell the department head he was thrilled and thank him for the offer. He didn't have to tell Mylie right away. In fact, she already knew about the job. He'd led her to believe it was already guaranteed. This didn't change anything.

The phone rang again. He expected it to be Dr. Baker calling back with a piece of information he'd forgotten, but instead, he saw that it was Courtney.

"Ben!" Courtney chirped his name before he could even say hello. "Great news!"

"Oh yeah?" Ben asked, his stomach bottoming out. "What is it?"

"We've got an offer!" Courtney said, her voice rising an octave in excitement. "And I think you're going to want to accept."

This couldn't be happening. He barely listened as Courtney rattled through the details. How could this all be happening in one day? He'd woken up this morning with his only plans being figuring out a way to spend more time with Mylie, and now he'd sold the house and essentially been offered a job.

"Ben?" Courtney asked. "Are you there?"

"Yes," Ben said. "I'm here."

"You don't sound excited," she said. "Don't you like the offer? It's incredibly close to the ask. I thought you'd accept."

"I'm just in shock," Ben replied.

"So," Courtney pushed. "Do you want to accept?"

Deep breaths, he told himself. This was the whole reason he was here. With any luck, the house would be sold in time for him to rent a place in a new city. It would allow him the freedom to do so many things while he established himself at the university. So why couldn't he bring himself to say it? Why couldn't he muster any excitement? He inwardly kicked himself.

"Ben?"

"Yes," he said finally, his voice hoarse. "Yes, I accept."

Chapter 39

Mylie sipped a glass of wine while she watched Ben standing over the stove. He was cooking her dinner. He'd called her at the warehouse, said he'd been craving lasagna, and told her to be at his house by seven p.m. She'd tried to tell him she didn't have time—it was too close to the tournament, but he hadn't been able to take no for an answer. Finally, she'd relented, locking up long after everyone else left and heading straight over to Ben's.

The first thing she'd done when she got there was take a shower. She'd thought about going home first, but she saw Morris's truck in the driveway and decided against it. She'd never get out the door in time. After the shower, she'd rummaged through Ben's clothes and found an oversized T-shirt she could wear, then she sauntered back down the stairs wearing nothing else.

Ben had stopped, stared at her.

"That's not fair," he said.

Mylie looked down at herself and then back up at him, grinning. "I don't know what you're talking about."

"Do you know how hard it was for me not to go upstairs with you the second you said you were going to use my shower?" he asked. "And now you come down here looking . . . like this . . . you're torturing me."

"It's not too late to head back up," Mylie replied.

Ben sighed, tearing his eyes away from her and concentrating on the stove. "Pour yourself a glass of wine."

"It smells good," she said to his back. God, his butt was cute in those jeans.

"It'll be done in a few minutes," Ben said, turning and making his way to the table. He sat down across from her. "How's the wine?"

"Very good," Mylie said.

"Good," Ben replied.

"Ben?"

"Yeah?"

Mylie shifted in her seat, her bare legs sticking slightly. "Are you okay?"

"I'm fine," he said. "Why?"

"You're acting weird," Mylie said. "Like, really weird."

"Why?" Ben asked. "Because I want to cook you dinner?"

"Because you're acting like you're on *Iron Chef*," Mylie replied.

Ben poured himself a glass of wine and refilled Mylie's glass. "I just don't want to mess it up."

"I don't care," Mylie said. She took a drink.

"Well, I do," Ben said, getting up once again to check the oven.

"Okay," Mylie replied. "I wasn't trying to be a jerk. I was just telling you that it wouldn't matter if you burned the lasagna. I just want to be here with you."

Ben loosed a breath. "Do you want a salad?" he asked.

Mylie got up and went to him. She wrapped her arms around his waist and pulled him to her. "Slow down," she said.

"Mylie, we . . . I . . . need to talk . . ."

Mylie cut him off, standing on her tiptoes to reach his mouth. "Come on," she whispered. "Just one kiss."

"I'm trying to . . ." Ben trailed off as she brushed her mouth against his.

Ben kissed her back, ferociously. His hands reached down to cup her ass, riding up the already short T-shirt.

She knew it wasn't fair, to tease him this way. To kiss him when he was trying to be so serious, but she couldn't help herself.

"Can't you just be patient?" he asked, brushing his lips against her neck.

"I've spent years being patient," Mylie replied. "I'm tired of it."

Ben groaned, pressing himself up against her.

"Do you want to go upstairs?" he half-growled.

"Yes," Mylie managed to say.

In one swift motion, Ben scooped her up and began to head toward the bedroom. Mylie shrieked in delight, nuzzling his neck.

She was impressed that he managed to carry her all the way up the stairs. He kicked the bedroom door open and laid her down on the bed.

Mylie sat up on her elbows and watched him undress. First, his marinara sauce–covered shirt and then his pants. When he sprang free before her, Mylie's eyes widened, and Ben gave her a smirk of satisfaction before she pulled him down to her.

Ben's hands grazed her thighs and felt their way up to her breasts, and when Mylie let out a soft groan, Ben replaced his hands with his mouth.

Mylie began to writhe beneath him, and Ben huffed a laugh. He took his free hand and parted her legs, settling between them, and Mylie lifted her hips to greet him.

"I want you," she whispered.

That was all the invitation Ben needed.

Mylie left Ben's house before the sun was up. There hadn't been any conversation after going upstairs. They'd both been too exhausted. Instead, Ben had gone downstairs to turn off the stove, and by the time he was back, Mylie was sound asleep. She attributed it to the great sex, yes, but the week before the tournament was always hectic, and this time it was no different. She'd gone home and showered, dressed, and was back out of the house before either Granny or Cassie woke up. She was glad for that. This week, she *had* to concentrate on the task at hand, and unfortunately, the task was the tournament and not Dr. Benjamin Lawrence.

The warehouse was dark and cool when she arrived, hours before anyone else would be there. It felt almost illegal to be there so early. It reminded her of the first time she'd been there, years before, when it was an abandoned shoe factory.

The Realtor—Courtney, of course, fresh from her real estate courses—was excited to show Mylie something she "could afford." Mylie had been less than thrilled to see the place. For one, it had been too big. Although her fledgling lure business was now too big for Granny's house, too big for the bait and tackle truck, it certainly wasn't big enough for *this*.

There had been wires hanging down, holes in the roofing, and the floor was an absolute mess of leftover parts. It was going to take weeks, and lots of work, to clean the place up.

Mylie had stayed at the warehouse after Courtney left, promising to consider making an offer and to lock up afterward. She'd sat down on the floor and looked around—at the abandoned husk—and wondered if she could make something of it. After all, it was just about the only thing she could afford. All of the other available buildings were too expensive, and she hadn't wanted to rent, hadn't wanted the added stress of a landlord to deal with.

It was then that she'd made a deal with the warehouse. She'd bring it back to life if it would agree to work with her—if it would become a space where she could grow her business. She knew how silly she probably sounded, speaking to a building as if it were a living, breathing entity with a soul, but for some reason, she felt like it was important to make this offering. After all, she knew what it was like to be abandoned, to feel like she was alone. Maybe if she loved this place, if she cared for it, then it would return that love in kind.

And it had.

Year after year, she and this building worked together. Grew the business, hired employees, and became the Hook, Line, & Sinker everyone knew today. In fact, she'd often thought about living there, since it was really the only thing she owned herself. Once Cassie graduated from high school, she considered using the loft upstairs that was reserved for overstock as an apartment. When she'd told Jodi, she'd thought Mylie was nuts, but more and more, Mylie yearned for a place of her own. Or maybe it was a life of her own. She couldn't quite tell. Either way, she wanted to get Cassie through high school first. Granny had never lived alone, but Mylie didn't anticipate Granny having any issue with it. Not when she refused to ask Morris to stay over while "the girls" lived with her. Maybe Granny wanted a life of her own as well. Although her grandmother rarely mentioned the grandfather Mylie and Cassie had never known, Mylie knew that Granny still thought about him, still missed him. What would it be like, Mylie wondered, to love someone that much?

She thought about Ben. He was hers. For now, at least. They hadn't discussed what would happen when the house eventually sold. Selfishly, she hoped it took a while. They were both being selfish, she guessed. It was easier not to think about it, even if she secretly hoped there might be some way they could make this work. At the very least, Mylie wanted the summer, even if she knew at the end of it, he'd go back off to his life somewhere else. Maybe this time, they would keep in touch. Maybe they could work it out. She didn't know.

It was too early for these thoughts, that was all she knew. Soon enough, this place would be buzzing with activity. The whole town would be. In fact, as she'd driven through town this morning, there were already business owners, up early like her, hanging banners and putting up signs, readying for the influx of people in the coming days.

It made her smile. This time of year, Mylie was in her element.

Let the games begin.

Chapter 40

"Our jerseys came!" One of the twins came rushing into Mylie's office.

"Well, open it!" Louise said, motioning to the hefty box that Nevaeh carried.

"Oh my *God*," Angel said. It was not an exclamation of excitement. There was pure horror written on her face.

"What is it?" Louise asked.

"These aren't the right color!" Angel gasped. "They're . . . they're . . ."

Mylie stepped over to Angel and peered down into the box. "Puke green," she finished.

"They were supposed to be moss green!" Louise replied. "I have the order slip right here." She fished around in her purse. "See! Moss green!"

"Well, they messed them up," Angel said. "These are awful. We can't wear them."

"I don't see that you have any choice," Mylie replied. "You and your sister weren't on the team last year. Even if everyone else wears their shirts from last year, you'll still be stuck with these."

"Jessica is gonna flip," Angel breathed.

"We don't have to tell her yet," Louise said cringing, no doubt at the thought of Jessica's reaction to the shirts.

"The tournament is in four days," Mylie replied. "We've got to tell her sooner rather than later."

"There's no time to fix this, right?" Angel asked.

"I don't think the printer can fix it before Saturday," Louise said. "I can ask, but I doubt it."

"Go ahead and check," Mylie said to Louise. "And nobody says anything to Jessica in the meantime."

"Got it," Angel and Nevaeh said in unison.

"I'm going to take these back to the shop right now," Louise said.

"I'll go with you," Angel said.

DOWNTOWN CLAY CREEK was bustling with preparation as Mylie made her way to the Cracked Egg to meet Ben for lunch. The businesses were decorated to the hilt, advertising their wares for the tourists and offering discounts to those who participated in the tournament. The sheriff and the mayor were directing two poor city workers who were trying to hang a banner on Main Street. Mylie wondered how long it would be until the city workers threatened to quit under duress.

At least three harried city employees quit and were rehired during this week. Mylie couldn't believe they didn't all quit before the tournament just to send the mayor into a fit.

"You're late," Ben said, smiling at her.

"It's a nightmare out here," Mylie said, pointing to the street. "Haven't you noticed?"

"The mayor mistook me for one of his underlings a few minutes ago," Ben replied, shoving his hands down into the pockets of his pants. "When I told him I didn't work for him, he proceeded to fire me."

Mylie laughed.

"He wanted me to climb up a very sketchy-looking ladder."

"I'm glad you refused," Mylie replied. "That would have been a one-way ticket to the hospital in Rockbridge."

"I have no interest in that," Ben said, holding the door to the Cracked Egg open for her. "Which I guess is lucky since I lost my health insurance when the mayor fired me."

From the counter, Melissa waved at them.

"I thought you were just working the weekend?" Ben asked her.

"I'm here all this week," Melissa replied. "To help out on account of the tournament."

"You'd think this tournament was the Super Bowl," Ben grumbled.

"It is for Clay Creek," Melissa countered. "Sit down, I'll grab you some coffee."

"None for me," Mylie replied, and Ben and Melissa turned to stare at her.

"I've already had about five cups," she said. "I need some water."

"Suit yourself." Melissa shrugged and headed off.

"I'm going to pretend you didn't just ask for water over coffee," Ben said, sitting down at the counter.

"I'm dehydrated," Mylie replied.

"Our late-night activities take it out of you?" Ben said with a wink.

Mylie shoved her shoulder into his. "Shut up."

"You're coming over tonight, right?" he asked.

"I'll try," Mylie replied. "But I've got to work late. This week is going to be really intense."

"Can I help with anything?"

"Really?"

"Yeah, I'm at your disposal."

Mylie gave him a wicked grin. "Well, I already know that."

"C'mon," Ben said, angling his head toward her. "I want to help."

"Okay," Mylie replied. "Do you think you could come to the warehouse tomorrow? We've got to get our tent set up downtown, and I think the guys could use your help, especially if that means I can leave a couple people to work so we don't get behind on orders."

"Sure," Ben said. "I can do that."

Mylie was about to respond when the doorbell chimed and Courtney sauntered in, her eyes immediately resting on Ben. She lifted her hand into an overexaggerated wave and headed toward them.

Beside her, Ben stiffened, a look of what Mylie could only describe as panic flashed in his eyes before he got up and said to her, "I forgot an appointment with Courtney. I'll be right back."

Mylie watched him dash away, catching Courtney by the elbow and leading her outside the restaurant.

"What was that about?" Melissa asked.

"Beats me," Mylie said with a shrug. "He said he forgot an appointment with Courtney, but I don't know why he all of a sudden had to take it outside."

"Whatever keeps her outside is fine with me," Melissa joked. "She is the pickiest woman alive. Do you know last week she asked me to make her an egg white omelet . . . without the egg?"

"That doesn't even make sense," Mylie murmured, her attention still at the door.

"Nothin' about her makes sense," Melissa replied.

Mylie tried to smile at Melissa, tried to refocus on the menu, to do anything to stop the cold dread now coiling in her stomach. She tried to shake it loose. There was too much to do this week, and she didn't have time for this right now. If it was important, Ben would tell her.

Wouldn't he?

Chapter 41

Ben had barely managed to get Courtney outside before she started blabbing about the fantastic offer he'd accepted. He'd told her in no uncertain terms that she was to keep this news as quiet as possible so he could tell people on his own terms. What he really meant, and what Courtney knew he really meant, was that he wanted to tell Mylie on his own terms.

He did plan to tell her, of course, but he wanted to wait until after the tournament—it was only a few days away—once everything settled down, once he'd had time to think of something, anything, to say. Right now wasn't the time, that's what he told himself. Besides, the deal could always fall through, and what good would it do to tell Mylie before he knew *for sure* that the sale would happen? No good, that's what.

He'd managed to go back inside and enjoy lunch, and Mylie seemed to accept his excuse about the forgotten meeting. They'd had a nice time together, but Melissa had given him a knowing look that had him squirming in his seat. He couldn't get out of the Cracked Egg fast enough. He loved being with Mylie, but he couldn't sit still, thinking about what he needed to say to her and wondering how she might interpret it.

Morris was waiting on his front porch when he got back. The older man stood with his hands in his pockets, staring up at the roof.

"You're gonna need a new roof before winter," he said by way of greeting.

"Oh?" Ben asked.

Morris nodded. "I know a guy, in case you're interested."

"Thank you," Ben replied, unlocking the door and motioning for him to come inside. "That's probably something I'll leave to the new owners . . . whoever they might be."

"Hmmm," Morris said.

Ben studied Morris's face and then replied, "You've heard."

"Might've heard something."

"Please don't say anything to Granny," Ben said. "I want to tell Mylie myself, and something tells me that Granny wouldn't keep that from her."

"I'm not in the habit of keeping secrets from Granny," Morris replied. "But this ain't rightly my business, is it?"

Ben cautioned a smile. "No, sir. I guess not."

Morris sniffed. "My sister works over at that Realtor's. Courtney. She wasn't much of a history student."

"Do you think your sister has told anyone else?"

Morris shook his head. "I told her not to be tellin' other people's business. But you should tell her, son, before word gets out. You know how small towns are."

"I do," Ben replied. "Thank you for the warning."

"That's not my warning," Morris said, angling his head to one side. "Did I ever tell you that I moved off from here back in my twenties, must've been a hundred years ago by now."

"You didn't tell me that." Ben shifted on his feet, wondering how he'd managed to talk himself into a lecture in his own living room.

"I was gone for a time. Left my girl here, my first wife. She passed on some years back, but I loved her," Morris continued. "I thought life was too small here, thought *I* was too big. It was important, you know, to get out and see things."

"I know what you mean," Ben said.

Morris eyed him. "But nothing ever felt quite right out there. I'd look around at the end of the day and find that I had no one to celebrate the good things with and no one to commiserate the bad days with. It felt empty. It didn't matter, you see, if I didn't have the people I loved beside me."

"I understand" was all Ben could think of to say.

"Do you, son?" Morris asked.

"I don't know," Ben admitted. "But I'd like to."

"Good," Morris said, clapping Ben on the back. "Now, I need to crawl under your house and grab that live trap. I left it during the, uh, cell phone debacle."

Ben grinned. "I have it," he said. "I brought it in. I'll grab it."

"Oh, good," Morris replied, relief written all over his face. "I was afraid I was gonna have to fight Fat Tony for it!"

Chapter 42

Cassie Mason was annoyed. She'd woken up in a perfectly fine mood, but that afternoon, she'd learned from Allie that Ryan was dating someone else. Allie had promised not to keep any more secrets from her after the debacle at the dance, but Cassie wasn't sure that she *wanted* to know everything. Sometimes she wished fourteen wasn't so hard. Life had seemed so much simpler when she was twelve, even thirteen, before she'd cared much about boys and being popular at school. High school hadn't been what she'd expected it to be. Her sister made it sound fun, like the best time, but more and more Cassie felt like she was a step behind everyone else—like there was a joke she didn't get.

When she stalked downstairs looking disheveled, Mylie looked up from her orange juice and said, "Are you okay?"

Cassie only grunted.

"Want to talk about it?"

"No," Cassie replied, even though she did. Talking to Mylie was tricky. She was her sister, but not, at the same time. When she'd been little, Mylie acted more like a sister. She could run to Mylie with anything, any little problem, and Mylie would defend her honor to Granny. She'd gotten out of trouble that way time and time again.

Now that Cassie was older, Mylie was still her sister, yes, and acted like her sister a lot of the time, but once in a while, Mylie acted like their mother. Of course, Cassie didn't really have any idea of what their mother actually acted like, but Mylie acted in a way that Cassie assumed a mother would act—more like Granny.

Cassie tried to think about what it would be like to be Mylie and have a sister so much younger than her. Mylie had been the age Cassie was right now when Cassie was born, and she shuddered at the thought of caring for a baby. Once, when Cassie had been very young, seven or eight, she'd gone to a day camp in Rockbridge. It was a science camp, and Cassie was so excited. But when she got there, she'd overheard a couple of the camp counselors discussing the "sad fact" that Cassie didn't have a mother. She wasn't sure how they found out or why that was supposed to be a sad thing, but when she'd gone home that evening and cried about it to Mylie, she'd hugged Cassie and said, "Tomorrow, when I pick you up, you can call me Mom."

"But you're not my mom," Cassie had wailed.

"I know that," Mylie said patiently. "But nobody else knows that except those counselors, and trust me, they won't mention it."

So that's exactly what Cassie had done. That whole week, Cassie called Mylie her mother. It was only later, years later, that Cassie found out that Mylie had marched herself into that camp and threatened those counselors within an inch of their lives. More than that, Cassie hadn't noticed the stares the other parents gave Mylie at pickup time, whispering among themselves that Mylie must've been a *very young* teen mom.

"Hello?" Mylie said, sliding her orange juice class over to Cassie. "Are you *sure* you don't want to talk about it?"

Cassie sighed. "Allie told me that Ryan was dating someone else."

"Dating?" Mylie asked. "Where is he taking her on all that money he makes as an unemployed fourteen-year-old?"

"You know what I mean."

Mylie nodded. "I do, and I'm sorry. I know you really liked Ryan, but if he cheated on you, he'll cheat on this girl, too."

"Maybe," Cassie replied. "Or maybe I just wasn't . . ."

"Nope," Mylie said, cutting her off. "Don't even say what you were going to say. It's not true. It has nothing to do with you and everything to do with Ryan. Besides, you're just a freshman. There are plenty of boys out there. You don't have to settle for the first one you meet."

"You did," Cassie said.

Mylie didn't say anything for a long moment.

"Well?" Cassie asked. "Didn't you?"

"It's complicated," Mylie said finally.

Cassie rolled her eyes. "That's what adults always say when they don't want to talk about something."

"I didn't *settle* for Ben," Mylie replied. "I was sad when he left, which I know you probably don't remember because you were so young."

Again, Cassie rolled her eyes.

"I'm not done," Mylie said. "I missed him, but I didn't wait for him. I still dated other people."

"But you didn't marry any of those people," Cassie pointed out.

"Well, I'm not marrying Ben, either," Mylie replied.

"Why not?"

"Well, we're only just getting to know each other again," Mylie said. "And that is also complicated. I know you hate it when I talk about you being too young to understand some things, but I promise, I'm not trying to make you feel like a little kid. It's just that things are different for us now than when we were your age. That's all."

Cassie thought about it. She liked Ben. She wouldn't hate it too terribly if Mylie *did* marry him. And she understood more than

Mylie thought. She knew that Ben was trying to sell that house. She knew he didn't plan to stay. Did that mean Mylie would leave with him?

"I'm not going anywhere," Mylie said, as if reading the question on Cassie's face. "Don't worry about that."

"I'm not worried," Cassie lied. "But I wouldn't be mad at you if you did . . . you know, go with him."

"First of all, he hasn't asked me to go with him," Mylie said, "Second of all, I don't *want* to go with him."

"Why not?" Cassie asked. "If you love him."

"Because I love you more," Mylie said. "And I love my life here. Ben has always known that."

"Maybe he'll stay," Cassie said.

Mylie gave her a small smile. "Maybe he will."

But Cassie didn't believe her.

Chapter 43

It rained for two solid days. By Friday, the rain let up, but it left the lake swollen and the ground muddy and soggy. There was talk about postponing the tournament, but everyone on the tournament committee agreed that the festivities would go on as planned, mud or not.

"This is ridiculous," Jodi said, attempting and failing to pull her muck boot out of a puddle. "I feel like we're just one rain away from a mudslide situation."

"It'll be fine," Mylie replied. "It's tournament week!"

Jodi rolled her eyes. "We've got twelve food trucks coming this morning. Is the area ready for setup?"

Mylie avoided looking at Jodi. "Sure. Yes."

"Mylie."

"It's almost ready."

"What do you mean *almost?*" Jodi asked.

"I mean, we're working on it," Mylie said. "Sheriff Oakes and Morris are working with the city to put down some gravel so that the tires of the trucks don't get stuck in the mud. But the gravel truck is coming from Rockbridge, and it's running behind because of . . ."

"Because of the rain," Jodi finished. "This is a disaster."

"It's just a minor setback," Mylie said. "We've used all the gravel we can get in town to set up for the fish fry tonight, so that's good, right?"

"Yeah, as long as nobody sets themselves on fire like last year."

"Granny's eyebrows grew back just fine," Mylie replied. "In fact, they look better than ever."

"Have you noticed that one is a little higher than the other?" Jodi asked, quirking a smile.

"Shhhh," Mylie said, trying to control her giggle. "She's very sensitive about that."

"I heard that!" Granny yelled from across the parking lot where she stood with Ben, desperately trying to erect a canopy for Hook, Line, & Sinker.

"Looks great!" Jodi yelled back before she and Mylie dissolved into a fit of laughter.

"Hey, Mylie," Joe said, hurrying over to her. He was carrying a clipboard and had a pencil shoved behind one ear.

"What is it, Joe?" Mylie asked, giving him her full attention. Joe took his duties as foreman at the warehouse very seriously, which is why she'd made him essentially the foreman of the tournament. Nothing got by Joe.

"We're missing two teams," Joe said. "This time last year, they were all checked in."

Mylie studied the list on the clipboard. "Well, those two teams *are* the farthest away," she said, frowning. "Besides, official check-in isn't until tomorrow morning."

"Do you think I should call and check, just to be sure?" Joe asked.

"Would it make you feel better?"

Joe nodded. "It would."

"Then do it," Mylie said, giving Joe a pat on the arm. "Let me know what you find out."

"Uh, Mylie?" Jodi's voice was one octave below panic. "Mylie?"

Mylie tried not to scream. If she had to answer one more question. "What is it now?"

"I think your boyfriend is drowning in mud."

"My . . ." Mylie looked over to the canopy. It took her a minute to realize what she was seeing. Granny was holding on to one of the canopy ties for dear life, but Ben had seemingly disappeared. Then she saw him, face down on the ground, absolutely covered head to toe in red clay mud. "Oh my God."

It was hard not to laugh, even though she felt terrible for him. Once she composed herself, she hurried over to where Ben lay prone in the mud.

"Are you okay?" Mylie asked, standing over Ben. "Come on, let me help you up."

Ben rolled over and tried to sit up. Mylie leaned down to grab his hand, but she couldn't get a firm grasp, her fingers slipping through the muck. She stumbled back and landed flat on her back.

Ben tried to mumble something, but there was too much mud in his mouth . . . and everywhere.

Mylie stayed on her back staring up at the blue, cloudless sky. For a moment, she thought she might just stay there. The mud was squishy and warm. She could probably sleep. Maybe if she just closed her eyes.

"We don't have time for you to take a nap!" Joe yelled.

Mylie groaned and pulled herself into a sitting position. Then she looked at Ben and burst out laughing.

Chapter 44

Ben could taste the mud. It was in his mouth. In his nose. In his ears . . . in his eyeballs. For a moment, he wondered if he was going to suffocate. Then he felt hands on his back pulling him up.

Joe and Morris loomed over him.

"He looks like he's been to one of them spas," Joe said.

"Can ya hear us, son?" Morris asked.

Ben nodded in their general direction.

Mylie was in a similar state, mud coating her entire backside. He wanted to laugh, but the mud.

"Come on," he heard Mylie say. "Let's go get cleaned up." She reached out and took his hand. "We can take the truck. It's already filthy."

He used a handkerchief Morris gave him to wipe his face mostly clean as they bumped along toward the house. Ben couldn't understand how it could be such a beautiful day and so completely disgusting at the same time.

"That's Arkansas for you," Mylie said as if reading his mind.

"I'd forgotten about the mud," he managed to say.

"You know," Mylie continued. "If you don't want to help with setup, you don't have to. I know it's a . . . lot."

"It's fine," Ben replied. "I like it. I like being with you."

Mylie pulled into his driveway. "Ugh, I feel disgusting."

"We better get you cleaned up," Ben said. He got out of the truck.

"We?" Mylie asked.

Ben grabbed her muddy hand and pulled her toward him. "What if we cleaned up . . . together?"

Mylie grinned. "I don't think we have time."

A sly smile crept over Ben's mouth, flecking bits of dried clay onto his shirt. "Won't it be faster if we wash each other off?"

"You're ridiculous," Mylie replied, but she allowed herself to be tugged toward the house and up the stairs into Ben's bathroom.

He turned on the shower and then watched Mylie as she took off her clothes, sighing with relief when the filthy clothes crumpled to a heap on the tiled floor.

God, he loved looking at her. All he could think about was getting her into the shower and lathering her up. She sidled past him and hissed when the hot water kissed her skin. Ben couldn't get out of his own clothes fast enough.

Ben got in behind her, allowing the majority of the water to fall onto her as he squeezed out a bit of his shower gel and rubbed it onto her back.

"Smells like a man," Mylie said, twisting around to look at him. She pulled her damp hair away from her shoulders, revealing her breasts, and Ben took the invitation.

"Well," Ben said, making soapy circles. "I am a man, you know."

She reached up on her tiptoes to nip his neck with her teeth. "I know."

Ben could hardly think. He'd gone from muddy and miserable to . . . this. He felt a pang of guilt for keeping secrets from her. In this moment, she was everything. He couldn't stand the thought of being away from her.

"Are you okay?" Mylie asked him.

"I'm more than okay," Ben murmured into her ear, forcing himself back to reality, back to her.

"I need you closer to me."

Ben kissed her, pushing her into the back of the shower, running a wet hand down her stomach and between her legs. She moaned, parting for him, her breath becoming pants when he got to his knees and let his tongue go to work. Her hands caught in his hair, and he felt her nails rake his scalp when he flicked his tongue over her most sensitive spot.

"Right there," she gasped.

He dug one hand into her hip, lifting her leg over his shoulder, moving faster against her clit until she cried out.

Slowly, he stood, taking the time to kiss her navel, her nipples, and finally the heat of her mouth. He didn't know how he'd lived without her for so long. He didn't know how he could miss something he'd never had until now, but he had. Fuck, he had.

"Turn around," he growled.

She obeyed, placing her palms on the back wall of the shower, pushing her plump ass out, inviting him to do with her what he will, and it drove him wild.

Slowly, so slowly, he slid himself into her. Ben wrapped one arm around her waist until he was so deep inside of her that he could scarcely breathe. They stayed like that for a few exquisite moments until Mylie began to move on him, sliding up and down onto his cock.

Ben closed his eyes and concentrated on her back, on the little dip above her buttocks where water collected, running down to her . . . he couldn't take it. He pressed into her until her breasts were flush against the wall, driving into her with such force that she cried out.

He paused, realizing that maybe he'd hurt her, but she managed to let out a strangled, "Don't stop," and that was all the invitation he needed.

He didn't stop. Not until they were both breathless and gasping for air. Not until his legs felt like jelly, and they slid to the floor, tangled in each other, flushed from the steam.

Finally, after what felt like forever, Ben said, "We're going to be late if we don't hurry."

Mylie rested her head against his shoulder and pressed her fingers into his palm. "I don't care," she said. "Stay with me just a few more minutes."

Ben did. He wished, right then, that he could stay with her forever. He wished it could *be like this* forever. There was nothing he wanted more than to feel her weight against him, feel her breathing beside him, knowing that it was because of him, *for him*, that she gave herself.

He'd tried to tell her the night he cooked her dinner. He'd wanted to. The longer he waited the worse he felt, but it never seemed like it was a good time. He'd tell her later, about the house. After the tournament. After he'd had time to decide what to say and how to fix it. Right now, he was going to hold her close. He was going to let himself pretend that this was the beginning and not the beginning of the end.

Chapter 45

"What took you so long?" Jodi asked later that afternoon as they directed food trucks into the newly graveled area. "I thought you'd fallen asleep or something."

Mylie gave her friend a guilty look. "I'm sorry," she said. "We just lost track of time."

"Sure you did," Jodi said, pursing her lips. "Sure you did."

"Where are we on the fish fry?" Mylie asked, changing the subject. "All of the trucks have agreed to shut down at three p.m., so that the VFW makes a maximum profit on this fundraiser."

"We'll be ready by then," Melissa said, ambling over to them.

"I'm so glad you're here," Mylie said. "I was worried that maybe Bernice and Granny might end up in a fight again."

"I've got old Bernie on a tight leash," Melissa said with a grin.

"The last two teams are here!" Joe said, clipboard in hand. "They're checking in at the hotel."

Melissa turned her attention to Ben. "Hey, you know how I told you about the community college looking for adjunct instructors?"

Ben nodded. "Yeah."

"Well, the dean for arts and sciences called me yesterday to ask if I know anyone who might be able to teach full-time this fall," Melissa continued. "She needs someone to teach Microeconomics, Macroeconomics, and Statistics."

Mylie kept her eyes on Joe, but she was listening for Ben's response.

Ben didn't immediately reply.

"Anyway," Melissa said. "I gave her your name."

"Wow," Ben said. "Uh, thanks, Melissa."

"So, do you think you might be interested?"

"I really appreciate it," Ben said. "But I just don't think that's something I can do right now."

"Okay," Melissa said, giving his arm a pat. "Let me know if you change your mind."

Mylie felt herself deflate.

"Are you pleased, boss?" Joe asked.

"What?" Mylie blinked. "With what?"

"With the way things are coming together!" Joe replied. "I think it's all pretty good, considering."

Mylie nodded, trying to shake the knot in her stomach. Joe was right. Despite the rain and the mud and the gravel and the food trucks, everything was going off as planned. Nothing was going to go wrong. She wouldn't let it.

She left Ben with Melissa and headed over to check on the Hook, Line, & Sinker tent. Luckily, the white on the top of the tent hadn't gotten muddy in all the fuss to put it up. There was an impressive display of different lures and fishing tackle, and their raffle for a full tackle box of goodies was filling up nicely.

Mylie was surprised to see Granny sitting behind the booth, behaving herself.

"What are you doing back here?" Mylie asked her.

Granny shrugged, but there was a mischievous gleam in her eye. "I gave one of those girls you've got volunteering a break."

"Why?"

"I may or may not be hiding," Granny admitted.

"From who?" Mylie wanted to know. "What have you done now?"

"I haven't done *anything*," Granny said.

"I don't believe you," Mylie said.

Granny reached into the pocket of her Bermuda shorts and pulled out her flask, dropping it onto the table. "I might've filled this with shine this morning," she said.

"Okay," Mylie said. "You always fill your flask with moonshine during the tournament."

"Well," Granny said. "I might've poured a bit into Morris's sweet tea."

"Granny!" Mylie gasped. "Why would you do that?"

"He was gettin' on my nerves," Granny replied. "Trying to tell me how to put up this tent, what the display should look like; you know how he gets sometimes."

Mylie shook her head.

"You should have seen the look on his face when he took a big swig," Granny said, clasping her hands over the giggle that threatened to escape past her lips.

"Anyway, he went home to brush his teeth just in case he gets too close to anyone from the Assembly of God."

Mylie pressed her mouth into a tight line, but it was only to keep herself from laughing along with Granny. "He's never going to forgive you," she said.

Granny waved her off. "Oh, child, he'll be fine. You think he's never had a nip or two? He pretends to be a teetotaler, but I know different."

"Mylie?" Jodi said, appearing behind Mylie.

Mylie was too busy trying not to laugh to answer.

"Mylie!" Jodi said, her voice rising an octave. "Hey, Mylie!"

"Huh?" Mylie turned to Jodi. "What? What's going on?"

"It's the twins," she replied. "They got into an accident just outside of Rockbridge."

"Oh, my God, are they okay?"

Jodi nodded. "They're okay, but Angel has a concussion and Nevaeh broke her wrist."

"Have you talked to Louise?" Mylie asked. "Is she with them? I should call her."

"She's on her way," Jodi said. "She said to tell you not to worry. They're both going to be fine, but there is no way they can compete."

"No, no that doesn't matter," Mylie said. "As long as they're okay."

"Jessica and Louise still want to go on with the tournament," Jodi said. "We just need to find two more people."

"I guess I can do it," Mylie said, thinking.

"I can't," Jodi said. "I'm a judge, remember?"

"Right," Mylie said.

"You should ask Ben," Jodi continued. "I'm sure he'd be happy to help."

"We'll lose for sure," Mylie said, laughing. "But I guess I could ask him."

"Seems like he'd do just about anything for you," Jodi said, wiggling her eyebrows.

Mylie thought about their shower activities earlier and felt the heat rising up her neck. "I'll talk to him, okay?"

THE REST OF the day went along smoothly, and Louise kept Mylie up-to-date on the twins. Aside from the fact that Nevaeh might need surgery, they were doing fine. The food trucks shut down at three p.m. as promised, and by the evening, just as the fish fry was getting going, the entire downtown area was packed with locals and tourists alike.

Ben had been more than happy to be added to the team, but he'd balked at wearing the T-shirt, which was admittedly three sizes too small for him.

"I'm not wearing that," Ben said.

Mylie laughed. "You can just wear any green shirt. And thank you. You're a lifesaver."

"Hey, after this is all over, can we talk?" he asked. "There are some things I want to discuss with you, but I know it's too hectic right now."

"Sure," Mylie replied. "What is it?"

"It's not a big deal," Ben said, but something in his voice told Mylie it was a lie—something about the way he looked at her. She didn't have time to think about it, though, as people streamed in and out and Joe and Jodi kept running to her to tell her they were out of supplies. She'd already made several trips back to the warehouse.

"Have you seen Cassie?" Granny asked an hour later, balancing a plate of fish in her lap.

All around them people were smiling and laughing, having a good time. A local band had decided to set up at the last minute, and people were streaming in and out of the main group, where Granny, Morris, and a few other people had set up lawn chairs to listen.

"I haven't," Mylie admitted. "I thought she was with Allie somewhere?"

"I'm sure she is," Granny replied. "But I heard a rumor some of the kids were stealing beer from the beer garden."

"I'll go check on her," Mylie said.

She waded through the sea of people, narrowly avoiding Robbie and his family as they piled their plates high with fish and joked about the tournament tomorrow. With the twins out, Mylie wasn't sure if they stood a chance at winning, but there was nothing to be done about it now. Maybe if Robbie won, he'd stop being such an asshole.

There was a group of teens on the edge of the library parking lot just off the square. Mylie squinted into the oncoming darkness to see if Cassie was one of them. She saw Ryan with a few boys and, sure enough, off to the other side, were Cassie and Allie.

"Cassie!" Mylie called, heading over to them. "Hey, Cassie!"

The look of surprise and guilt on Cassie's face was enough to tell Mylie that something was up. The group closed in around each other as she approached.

"Cassie," Mylie said. "Granny's been looking for you. Are you not answering your phone?"

Mylie stepped close to the group of girls and peered in just in time to see Cassie and Allie kicking two empty beer cans away from them and into the grass.

"What are you doing?" Mylie asked, grabbing Cassie's arm and pulling her away from her friends.

"I didn't take them!" Cassie said, trying and failing to wrench herself free from her sister. "It wasn't us."

"Did you drink them?" Mylie demanded. "Because looking at your face, it sure seems like you drank them."

"Don't tell Granny," Cassie said, tears welling up in her eyes.

"Cassie," Mylie hissed. "You've got bigger problems than telling Granny. You're fourteen years old. What do you think is going to happen when someone tells the sheriff a bunch of *high school freshmen* are drinking in the library parking lot?"

Cassie only shrugged.

"You're going home," Mylie said. "Come on."

"Come on, Mylie!" Cassie protested. "Please, you're embarrassing me."

"I have not even begun to embarrass you," Mylie hissed. She turned her gaze to the other teenagers in the parking lot. "Hey!"

They all turned to stare at her.

"You all better go find your parents right now," Mylie yelled. "Do it now, before I do it for you!"

The group scattered, and Mylie stomped off toward her truck, pulling Cassie along with her. They waded through the crowd of people, stopping long enough for Mylie to whisper to Jodi that she was taking Cassie home and to let Granny know everything was fine. She'd talk to Granny later.

They rode in the truck silently for a few minutes before Mylie said, "Are you okay?"

Cassie looked green. "I don't feel great."

"How much did you have to drink?"

"I don't know," Cassie replied. "Not much, but it tasted awful."

"Yeah, that was cheap beer," Mylie said. "Honestly, what were you thinking?"

"We were just trying to have fun," Cassie said, her voice sullen. "This town is so boring."

"Yeah, and puking all over the library parking lot is going to make it better," Mylie muttered.

"Like you never did anything like this," Cassie shot back.

"I'm not saying I didn't," Mylie replied. "But at least I had the good sense to do it in the woods without an audience."

"I'll remember that for next time," Cassie said. "Mylie, I think I'm going to be sick."

Mylie steered the truck over to the side of the road and cut off the engine just in time for Cassie to jump out and vomit.

Mylie walked around to the other side of the truck and held

back Cassie's hair as she heaved, rubbing her back in small and soothing circles.

"I'm okay," Cassie said finally, sitting down on the grass away from the mess. "I'm okay."

"This feels like punishment enough," Mylie said, sitting beside her.

"You can't punish me anyway," Cassie said, sniffing. "You're not my mom."

The words stung more than Mylie wanted to admit. She knew she wasn't Cassie's mother. They were sisters, but their relationship had never been like regular sisters. Mylie helped raise Cassie. Things were different.

"I know," Mylie said carefully. "But right now, you've got me, and I'm telling you that barfing on the side of the road is punishment enough."

"So, you won't tell Granny?"

"You and I both know Granny is going to find out," Mylie said, helping Cassie up and back into the truck. "It's in your best interest to tell her before she finds out from someone else."

"I just want to go home and go to bed," Cassie groaned.

"Can I trust you to stay by yourself?" Mylie asked. "How many beers did you have? Tell me the truth."

"Just a couple," Cassie admitted. "And Allie and I shared them."

"Okay, then you'll be fine," Mylie replied. "I'm going to drop you off, run back to the fish fry, and then I'll come home. I just need to make sure our tent is shut down for the night, okay?"

Allie nodded. "I don't see why this is such a big deal," she said.

"Because you're fourteen," Mylie replied.

"Like you and Granny never drink."

"That's not the point," Mylie said. "We're both adults."

Cassie was turning greener by the second, but she said, "I just wanted to see what it was like."

When they pulled into the driveway, the truck's headlights caught on the FOR SALE sign in Ben's yard. It was so quick that Mylie had nearly missed the gleaming white UNDER CONTRACT that had been added to the top part of the Realtor's advertisement.

"What does that mean?" Allie asked. "Under contract?"

"It means," Mylie said, "that the house has sold."

"Did you know?"

"No," Mylie replied. "I didn't."

Chapter 46

Ben was having a blast. He couldn't remember the last time he'd had this much fun at a party, if that's what anybody would call the fish fry. The band was playing, people were eating and drinking, and all around him the laughter and merriment made him feel light and free. If he could only find Mylie. Aside from the incident with the mud, the day had been perfect.

He was helping take down the Hook, Line, & Sinker tent and listening to Jessica and Jodi give him instructions about the tournament in the morning when Mylie arrived, looking flushed and irritated.

"Everything okay?" he whispered to her when she wordlessly got to work breaking down the canopy and packing up the leftover lures and tackle.

"It's fine," Mylie said, refusing to look at him.

Ben touched her shoulder. "Seriously, what's wrong?"

Finally, Mylie turned to face him. "I don't want to talk about it here. It's been a long night."

"Is it about Cassie?" Ben asked. "Jodi mentioned you had to take her home."

"Let's just talk about it later."

"Okay," Ben replied. They worked in silence for a while before he continued, "I just hate that you aren't having a good time. Tonight has been so much fun."

"Well, I'm glad *you're* having a good time," Mylie said, stuffing a few bags of tackle into a duffle. "Ow, shit. Goddamnit."

"What? What is it?"

Mylie held out her hand. There was part of a hook sticking out of her thumb. "I forgot some of these bags are open. Shit."

"Mylie!" Granny called, seeing the hook sticking out of her thumb. "What did you do?"

"Nothing," Mylie muttered.

"You know better than to grab a bunch of bags with hooks in them," she said. "Let me see." Granny inspected the wound. "I don't think I can get it out. It looks like it's really in there."

"It's fine," Mylie said, attempting and failing to pull the hook out.

"Now it's bleeding," Ben said, taking her hand.

Mylie stiffened. "Go see if Morris has a pair of plyers."

"Absolutely not," Granny said. "You're going to have to go to the urgent care in Rockbridge."

"No," Mylie replied. "It's fine. I . . . ouch!"

"If you don't go get it taken care of tonight, you won't be able to fish tomorrow," Granny said.

"I'll take her," Ben offered.

"I can drive myself," Mylie offered, and Granny and Ben turned to stare at her. "What? I can."

"I'll drive," Ben repeated.

"I promised Cassie I'd get home," Mylie protested. "She's not feeling great."

"Well, nobody feels great after drinking cheap beer," Granny replied.

"You know about that?" Mylie asked.

"Of course," Granny said. "Don't worry. I'll leave here in a couple of minutes. I won't say a word to her until tomorrow morning."

"She threw up on the way home," Mylie said. "I told her I think that's punishment enough."

"I'll offer her a beer in the morning," Granny replied. "*That* will be punishment enough."

Ben grinned. That was just exactly something Granny would do. In fact, he remembered her doing that to him and Mylie when they got caught drinking down at the dock their sophomore year in high school. To her credit, she hadn't told his mother, who would have given him a lecture and cried for a week, wondering where she'd go wrong to turn her child into such a delinquent.

"Come on," he said to Mylie. "Let's get that hook out of your thumb."

Mylie followed him silently to his car and didn't say anything as they drove, her hand resting on the console, the hook jiggling with every bump.

"Does it hurt?" he asked her.

Mylie shrugged. "It's going to hurt more coming out."

"Do you remember when Granny threw a hook at that guy at the lake?" Ben asked. "It stuck right in his forehead."

Mylie gave him a half smile but didn't say anything.

"Okay," Ben finally said. "What's wrong, aside from the hook in your thumb?"

"Were you going to tell me you sold the house?" Mylie stared straight ahead at the road in front of them.

Ben gripped the steering wheel. "Who told you?"

"Nobody," Mylie said. "I saw the UNDER CONTRACT sign in your front yard."

"Courtney," Ben mumbled.

"You could have told me," Mylie said.

"I tried," Ben said. "I swear, I did."

"When?" Mylie asked. "When did you try to tell me?"

"Monday night! And then you were all over me, and I . . ."

"Oh, so it's my fault now?" Mylie asked.

"No," Ben said. "I'm not saying that."

"It sure seems like you're saying that."

"I'm just saying, I wanted to tell you."

"And you didn't."

Ben sighed. "There's something else I need to say."

Mylie didn't respond.

"I'm going to Boston next week," he continued. "There's a job at a university there . . ."

"Great," Mylie said, cutting him off.

"I'm sorry," Ben said. "Mylie, I'm sorry."

"Take a left up here," Mylie said in response, pointing to the little strip mall. "You can just sit in the car. I'm sure this won't take long."

"I'll go in with you," Ben said, parking the car.

"Do what you want," Mylie replied. She didn't wait for him.

Chapter 47

Ben sat in the waiting room with Mylie, silently weighing his options. He couldn't talk to her here, not if he wanted to keep his tongue intact, but he hated the way she was staring straight ahead, not looking at him.

The nurse behind the counter simply looked at Mylie's hand, asked for her information, and shouted to someone in the back, "We've got another hook situation!"

Ben knew from his grandfather's practice that it wasn't uncommon for people, especially in the summertime when there were tourists about, to end up with a waiting room full of fishing-related injuries. One summer, he'd even had the displeasure of seeing a boy with a snapping turtle attached to his bottom lip.

He smiled at the memory, although it had been pretty traumatizing at the time. He'd stayed away from all turtles after that.

A door in the clinic swung open and a woman with a clipboard said, "Mylie Mason?"

Mylie stood up. "You can wait out here," she said to Ben.

Ben got up and trudged behind her, waiting for a reprimand, but she said nothing. When the nurse gave him a questioning look, he said, "I'm with her."

"It's fine," Mylie said, rolling her eyes.

They were led back to a hallway where Mylie stood on a scale and had her blood pressure taken. "Too high," the nurse said, tutting about it.

"Well, I do have a fishing hook in my thumb," Mylie replied. "And," she continued, "it's been a long night."

Ben winced. He certainly hadn't made it any easier on her. Part of him wanted to return her anger. It was true that he'd kept a secret from her, but it was also true that she knew he was going to sell the house, that he was taking a job far away. None of this was new information. She'd known and still chosen to be with him while he was here. The fault didn't lie solely with him, did it?

The nurse left them alone in one of the sterile rooms and closed the door behind her, and Mylie resumed her thousand-yard stare.

"Is this how it's going to be?" Ben asked finally.

"I don't know what you mean," Mylie said.

"Fine," Ben replied, crossing his arms over his chest.

"What do you want me to say, Ben?" Mylie asked. "Congratulations?"

"No," Ben said. "No, I just want to talk about it."

Mylie sighed. "What is talking about it going to change? Are you still selling the house?"

"Yes."

"Are you still leaving next week for the East Coast?"

"Yes."

"Then what?" Mylie asked. "What is there to say?" She raised both of her hands up, banging her thumb on the side of the table next to her chair. "Ow! Shit!"

"Is that Mylie Mason I hear?" came a deep, rumbling voice from the opening door. "Well, hello! It is you!"

"Dr. Burton!" Mylie said, grinning. "I didn't know you were working tonight."

"Well, I usually try to take off for the tournament weekend, but our other doctor is on maternity leave," Dr. Burton said. "Now, what do we have here?"

Mylie held out her thumb.

"How did this happen?" Dr. Burton asked.

"I was packing up some tackle, and one of the packages was open," Mylie said. "I guess I wasn't paying attention."

"You know better than that," Dr. Burton replied. He checked over her thumb with a gloved hand. "I'm pretty sure I can get this out, but I'm going to apply a local anesthetic. You may need a stitch or two."

Mylie grimaced. "Okay, do whatever you have to do, but I have to be able to fish tomorrow."

"Well, I can't say it'll be comfortable," Dr. Burton replied. Then, as if he was just noticing Ben for the first time, he turned to him and said, "Are you her ride?"

Ben nodded. "Uh, yes. Yes, sir."

"Great," Dr. Burton replied. "Her hand is going to be numb for a couple of hours."

Mylie didn't so much as squirm through the entire process of having the hook removed from her thumb, even though Ben thought he might have to look away a few times. It wasn't so much that it was bloody as it was painful to look at. Only once did she reach out for his hand and squeeze. Even then, she didn't look at him.

"It'll be sore tomorrow," Dr. Burton said when he'd finished. "Be careful out there on the boat. Don't get it wet when you shower, and please don't get it in that lake water."

"I'll try not to," Mylie replied.

"Here." Dr. Burton pushed himself across the room on his rolling stool and opened up one of the drawers of the cabinet. "Take a few of these rubber gloves. Cover it for a few days, but especially tomorrow."

Mylie nodded. "Okay," she said. "Thank you."

"How's your granny?" Dr. Burton asked, a twinkle in his eye.

"Still dating Morris," Mylie replied, giving the doctor her first genuine smile in hours. "But I'll let her know you asked after her."

"You do that," Dr. Burton said. "Remind her that I'm a doctor."

Ben coughed. Dr. Burton had to be nearly twenty years younger than Granny.

"She's a beautiful woman," Dr. Burton continued, looking over at Ben. "Those Mason women, I don't know what it is about them, but they'll hook ya."

"Hilarious," Mylie said dryly.

Dr. Burton only winked.

Chapter 48

Mylie tried to think of something to say to Ben as they drove home. She knew he wanted to talk, knew that he felt awful about not telling her about the house or his trip. Still, she couldn't help but feel betrayed. They'd agreed to be honest, and while he hadn't outright lied, this was still a lie by omission.

"If you don't want me to be on the team anymore after today, I understand," Ben said, finally breaking the contentious silence between them.

"I need you on the team," Mylie replied. "Without you, I'd have to find someone else, and it's nearly eleven p.m. It's too late."

"Okay," Ben said.

Mylie sighed. "I just wish you'd told me. I didn't mean to react that way, but I really thought we'd promised to be honest with each other. Knowing you knew, even for a little while without telling me, really hurts."

"I'm sorry," Ben replied. "I was afraid if I told you that you'd be angry and it would ruin whatever this is between us. I never meant to hurt you."

"I would have been sad," Mylie said simply.

"The East Coast isn't another planet," Ben continued. "I've been thinking about it. We can make this work, even if I'm not here."

"It might as well be another planet," Mylie said. "How often do you plan to come back?"

Ben was silent, and then he said, "I don't know. I thought you could come visit me."

"So, I have to do all the visiting?" Mylie asked. "I'd have to be the one to rearrange my schedule and get on a plane to visit you?"

"It's just that I'll be starting a new job," Ben said. "Finding a place to live, starting a life in a new place. It would make sense, at least at first."

"I have a life, too," Mylie replied. "It's just as important as yours."

"That's not what I'm saying." Ben gripped the steering wheel so tightly that Mylie could see the bone white of his knuckles glinting in the moonlight.

"Okay," Mylie said. "Okay, so after you're settled, you'd start coming back here, to Clay Creek?"

"After a while," Ben replied, his tone noncommittal.

Mylie shook her head. "For how long?"

"What do you mean?"

"What I mean is," Mylie began, angling herself toward him, careful to keep her injured hand on her lap. "How long would we do this?"

Ben shrugged. "I don't know."

"Are you ever planning to leave the East Coast?" Mylie asked. "Move back here?"

Ben was silent.

"That's what I thought," Mylie continued. "You want me to come visit you, to see you, to be with you, all on your schedule. You want me to give up my life, maybe entirely, to be with you without making any sacrifices of your own."

"You don't have to live here!" Ben said, the anger that had been building inside of him finally erupting. "You act like you're chained to this place. Like you can't leave."

"I don't *want* to leave," Mylie said.

Ben slowed down as they neared their houses, his car idling between them, unable to choose a driveway. "How do you know?" he asked her. "How do you know, when you've never even been anywhere? You don't know what life is like anywhere else but here, in this town, full of *nothing!*"

Mylie sat back. "This town isn't nothing," she said, her voice steady. "The people here aren't nothing. *I* am not nothing."

"That's not what I mean," Ben replied.

"Yes, it is." Mylie pushed open the passenger's side door. "It's what you've always meant, Ben. I'm just glad you've finally said it out loud."

Mylie got out of the car before Ben could reply. "I'll see you in the morning," she said.

She walked the rest of the way to her house, cradling her hand to her chest, and when the door was safely shut behind her, she finally allowed those old wounds to crack open and spill out.

Granny was sitting on the couch waiting up for her, her reading glasses shoved down onto her nose. Mylie went to her and nestled herself in the crook of the older woman's neck and cried, letting the tears stream down her face while her grandmother comforted her.

"Shhh," Granny said, stroking her hair. "It's going to be all right, child. It's going to be all right."

Mylie let the words wash over her, let her grandmother's voice calm the ache inside of her chest, but she knew that for the first time in a long time, it wasn't going to be okay.

Chapter 49

Twelfth grade

Ben didn't want to be at the party. He'd only gone because of the fight he'd had with Mylie. He wanted to fix it if he could. All around him people were laughing and having a good time, most of them drunk with a mixture of alcohol and the relief of being done with high school. They were finally adults.

"If you're looking for Mylie, she's not here."

Ben turned to find Jodi standing in front of him. She was still wearing her graduation cap, although by now it was slightly askew on top of her head.

"Is she coming?" Ben asked.

Jodi shrugged and shoved a red cup into his hand. "You might as well stay to find out."

Ben watched Jodi shimmy away from him, and he looked around for a place to sit. The music was unbearably loud. He almost wished he'd agreed to go back to Chicago right after graduation, like his mother wanted, instead of in the morning. But he'd insisted on staying, on going to this party, just so he'd have more time with Mylie.

And now she wanted nothing to do with him.

He needed to forget about it. Forget about her. He was leaving for Chicago in the morning, and after that, to college. He had plans. They both did, he guessed. She wanted to open her own business modeled after her grandmother's bait and tackle truck, and he . . . well, he wanted to leave Clay Creek. He wanted to live his life outside of this place. At least, that's what he told himself the minute he'd moved here in the sixth grade.

Then he'd met . . . there she was. Ben saw Mylie from across the room, leaning against a door frame with a drink in her hand, looking impossibly bored. He knew she wasn't—it was just the face she wore when she didn't want anyone to talk to her.

"I found her!" he heard Jodi call from somewhere in the throng.

Ben made his way over to where she stood. She wouldn't look at him, but he knew she saw him.

"Hey," he said.

Mylie crossed her arms over her chest. "Hi."

"I thought you'd change your mind and not come."

"I thought *you* would change your mind and not come."

Ben sighed. "Could we not argue tonight?" he asked. "It's my last night in town. I don't want to leave things like this."

"Then don't leave," Mylie said.

Ben took a drink from his cup. It tasted awful, vaguely like gasoline. He downed the rest of it. "Can we talk? Somewhere not here?"

"Fine." Mylie led him outside to the back porch. It overlooked the lake, and she turned her back to him to stare at the moonlit water.

Ben stood next to her. "You know," he said. "I am going to miss the lake."

"You hate the lake," Mylie said.

"No," Ben replied. "I hate what's in the lake."

"You screamed like a girl the last time we went swimming," Mylie said, cracking a smile. "I thought you were going to hyperventilate."

"Jodi grabbed my leg underwater," Ben protested.

"Come on, Ben," Mylie said. "What are you doing here?"

"I wanted to see you," Ben replied. "I didn't get to say goodbye."

"Bye," Mylie said, taking a step away from him.

Ben felt slightly dizzy. He wished he knew what had been in that cup. "No," he said, his voice a bit hoarse. "I'm not leaving it like this."

Finally, Mylie faced him. "But you *are* leaving."

"I have to," Ben said.

"I know." Mylie tried and failed to smile. "I know you do, but I don't have to like it."

Ben grabbed her hand and tugged her closer. "I'm going to miss you more than the lake," he said.

Mylie leaned into him, and for the first time in years, Ben decided he didn't want to fight the urge to kiss her, to hold her, to know what it was like to be more than friends, so he leaned in as well.

Mylie parted her lips, and Ben instinctively reached a hand around her waist to pull her closer. He leaned farther into her and was so close he could smell her strawberry-scented lip gloss when she pulled away from him.

"This isn't a good idea," she said. Mylie was looking up at him, and what she was saying with her eyes didn't entirely match the words coming out of her mouth.

"I thought . . ." Ben replied, trailing off.

"I don't want to start something we can't finish," Mylie said. "I mean, what happens if I let you kiss me?"

Ben let go of her. "I don't know."

"You're still leaving."

"I am."

"Then what's the point?" Mylie asked.

Ben shrugged. He didn't know. For the first time, he hadn't thought it through. And now, now that he'd come so close only to fail, he knew why he'd never let his impulses get the better of him before.

"I'm sorry," he said finally. "I thought that this was what you wanted."

"What *I* wanted?" Mylie asked.

This was all coming out so wrong. "That's not what I meant," Ben said. "Look, can we just forget this ever happened? You're right. This was a mistake."

The hurt on her face was palpable, but she nodded, and Ben was caught somewhere between feeling both guilty and angry. What *did* she want? "Yeah," she said. "Let's forget it."

"I'll call you tomorrow morning before I leave?" Ben asked.

"And then again once you get there?"

Ben forced his face into a smile and said, "Yes. Then again once I get there."

Chapter 50

Mylie woke up the next morning with both Cassie and Stanley in her bed. The dog was at the foot of the bed, snoring, and Cassie was asleep beside her, one arm thrown around Mylie's middle.

"Orumph," Cassie sighed when Mylie attempted to slither out from underneath her.

"I'm sorry," Mylie replied to her sleeping sister. "I have to get ready for the tournament."

"Mylie?" Cassie cracked one eye open.

"Yeah?"

Cassie sat up, holding her hand to her head. "Oh, God. I feel awful."

"Good," Mylie replied. She held out her bandaged thumb. "That makes two of us."

"Wait," Cassie said as Mylie turned to leave.

"What is it?" Mylie asked. She walked back over to the bed and sat down. "Are you seriously not okay?"

"No, it's not that," Cassie said. "I just wanted to say . . . well, I just wanted to say I'm sorry. About last night."

Mylie smiled. "It's fine, kiddo," she said. "I'm not saying I love what you did, but I also can't say I haven't done it myself."

"It's what I said," Cassie continued. "About you not being my mom."

"Well, I'm not your mom."

"You kind of are," Cassie replied. "I mean, I know you're not, but you are, you know? And I shouldn't have said that."

"It's okay," Mylie said, wrapping her arms around Cassie. "Besides, Granny is going to make you throw up the second you go downstairs, so that's punishment enough."

"I thought you said puking last night was punishment enough!" Cassie called as Mylie got up and walked out of the bedroom. "Mylie! Mylie, come on!"

Mylie laughed to herself all the way to the shower, until she had to put on one of the plastic gloves. That was less than pleasant. Still, this was her favorite day of the year. She wasn't going to let her shredded thumb *or* Dr. Benjamin Lawrence ruin that. She didn't have time to think about any of that right now.

By the time she was out and dressed and headed downstairs, Cassie was up and looking miserable at the kitchen table.

"I couldn't make her feel any worse," Granny whispered to Mylie. "But I am going to make her stay home today. If she can't behave in public, she can stay in this house for a while until she promises that she can."

"Fair enough," Mylie said, leaning in to give Granny a kiss on the cheek. "But I'm glad I won't be here when you tell her."

THE LAKE WAS chaos. Teams were preparing for the tournament; people were milling about, with their coolers full of beer already; and the line to sign in for the competition was a mile long.

"I've already gotten us ready to go," Jessica said, standing next to Louise. "I was here earlier than anyone."

"Great," Mylie replied, giving Jessica a thankful smile. "I slept later than I meant to."

"I stayed at the hospital with the girls last night," Louise said.

"How are they?" Mylie asked.

Louise looked down at Mylie's hand. "About as good as you are, I reckon."

"I'm fine," Mylie said. "I just have to keep it from getting wet. Dr. Burton gave me some gloves to wear."

"Maybe we aren't meant to compete," Jessica mused. "With Nevaeh and Angel, and now you . . . maybe we should just forfeit."

"Absolutely not," Mylie replied. "We've got our team. We're doing this."

"Where is Ben?" Louise asked. "I haven't seen him yet this morning."

Both women looked to Mylie.

"He'll be here," she said. At least, she assumed he'd be there. She didn't think, even after their argument the night before, that he'd bail on them.

Mylie walked down to the docks, where the majority of the boats were tied in, checking over their equipment. With everything she'd had going on over the last few weeks, she'd paid little attention to the fine details of the competition, the way she had before. She'd always made sure her team had everything they needed. She was thankful Jessica and Louise picked up the slack.

Two boats over, Robbie and his team were packing their own boat. She ignored them, concentrating instead on the delicious-looking sandwiches in the cooler. There was no beer in their cooler, thank goodness. They didn't drink when they were in a tournament, although part of her wished they could bend the rule. Spending the day with Ben was going to be an exercise in effort.

"I hope everyone else is ready to get their asses beat," Robbie called to no one in particular.

Mylie popped her head up, and Robbie gave her a feral grin. "Morning, Mylie," he said.

She resisted the urge to flip him off. "Good morning," she said.

"I heard a couple of your teammates got hurt," Robbie continued. "Sure is a shame."

"They'll be okay," Mylie said.

"Heard about your thumb," Robbie said as if he hadn't heard her. "Seems like your team is cursed."

"I'd be more concerned about your own team if I were you" came a voice from behind Mylie. It was Ben, wearing what she could only assume was his grandfather's old fishing gear.

She tried not to laugh.

"Hi," he said to her. "Sorry I'm late."

"It's okay," Mylie said. "You're still here in plenty of time."

"Do you think we could . . ." Ben trailed off.

"I don't want to talk," Mylie said, understanding what he'd left unsaid. "Let's just get through today, okay?"

Ben nodded, a muscle in his jaw feathering.

Jessica and Louise weren't far behind Ben. Melissa, who'd taken over the position of emcee from Morris a few years ago, gave warning that it was time to board the boats.

"You just let us take charge," Louise said to Mylie and Ben. "Especially you, city slicker." She pointed a lure in Ben's direction.

Ben held his hands up. "I'll do whatever you tell me to do."

"Whatever we tell you to do?" Jessica asked, a wicked smile on her lips.

Ben turned beet red and looked to Mylie for help, but she only shrugged as Louise started the motor and they moved out into the lake, looking for the right spot to begin.

"The point," Louise said, shooting Jessica a look, "is to catch fish. You want to catch a lot, for sure, but really quality is what matters. We'll throw the little ones back. The team with the fattest fish wins."

"We need to find us a secluded cove," Jessica said and then

stuck her tongue out at Louise. "Let's idle here and watch the other boats go. It'll be easier to pick a spot after everyone else is concentrating on their catch. I don't put it past Robbie and his gang to find us."

Louise nodded her head in agreement. "I know the perfect spot."

They had six hours to catch the fattest fish they could hook. Mylie wasn't at all confident that they would win. There were teams that had far more experience than hers did. She loved to fish, but her business was making the materials for people to use, not catching fish herself. Jessica and Louise were seasoned, and they barked orders like captains. She and Ben did what they were told, and it seemed to be working well. Still, she was nervous.

The first three hours went by quickly. They caught several fish worth keeping, Ben included. In fact, he'd caught the biggest fish so far, and the smile plastered on his face made Mylie's heart crack open.

"Good job," she said to him as they sat waiting for the next nibble.

"Thanks," Ben said.

Mylie looked down at her phone to see a couple of missed calls from Cassie. The reception out on the boat was terrible, and she couldn't call her back. Cassie knew where she was, and Mylie hoped it wasn't important. She figured if there was something Cassie needed at home, she'd call Granny.

"Everything okay?" Mylie typed into a text, hoping that it would send.

"I wonder how everybody else is doing," Ben said, tugging on his line a bit. "Think they're catching anything?"

"I don't know," Mylie said. "Sometimes the fish will bite anywhere, but maybe we've found a sweet spot."

"Mylie," Ben said. "I need to apologize for last night. What I said . . . I didn't mean it. I didn't mean to say or even imply that you or this town aren't important. I don't believe that. It's just that sometimes I get so caught up in my own bullshit. I'm so sorry."

Mylie closed her eyes. She didn't want to talk about it. Not here, with two other people close enough to hear them. In fact, she didn't want to talk about it at all. It wasn't going to change anything.

"I know you are," she said finally. "I know you're sorry, but you still said it."

"I didn't *mean* to say it."

"It doesn't matter," Mylie said, looking at him. "You still said it, and I don't think you were lying when you said it."

Ben sighed. "I don't want it to be this way," he said. "Can't we just go back to how it was before?"

Mylie wanted to. She wanted to so badly that it hurt. "I don't think we can."

"I got one!" Louise yelled. "Hell, I think it's a big one!"

Mylie and Ben turned their attention to Louise. She was reeling in what looked like a huge bass.

"This is perfect timing," Jessica said, helping Louise put the fish into their container. "We need to start heading back. We've got about half an hour."

"What do you think?" Mylie asked. "Do we stand a chance?"

"As good as any," Louise said, starting the boat motor and heading back toward the shore. "I guess we'll find out at the weighing station."

Mylie looked down at her phone. Her text sent, but she hadn't gotten a reply from Cassie. She guessed she'd ask once they got back in. Surely, she'd be there waiting with Granny.

"Let's go win this shit!" Jessica shouted.

Mylie looked over at Ben, who gave her a tentative smile. She tried, and failed, to smile back.

Chapter 51

The day had been harder than Ben imagined. No amount of talking himself up worked. He still had to face Mylie. He'd tried to apologize, and she'd refused to accept it. That was her right, he knew. There was no excuse for what he'd said, and he guessed it was selfish to try to get her to forgive him just so he could leave with a clear conscious.

And he *was* going to leave.

He was glad that he was leaving in a couple of days. Part of him thought that if he stayed here in Clay Creek until he closed on the house that he might not be able to go through with it. But if he left and got some space from Mylie, from everything, it would make it that much easier.

Once he was established in his new life, maybe the one he'd been thinking about more and more with Mylie wouldn't seem so appealing.

As they exited the boat, the other fishermen were doing the same, hauling in their catches and heading toward the weighing station that was set up near the stage. There would be three winners, and the grand prize winner would be announced shortly after every team's fish was weighed.

Ben looked around. It seemed like all the teams were accounted for, but he didn't see Robbie. He hoped that meant he'd quit.

"How'd it go today?" Granny asked, appearing beside him. Her gaze lingered on Ben. Oh, shit. Granny knew. She knew he'd fucked up.

"I think we stand a chance," Ben replied.

"I'm talking about with Mylie," Granny said.

Of course, that's what she was talking about. She likely knew everything already, and so he said carefully, "I tried to apologize."

"Good," Granny said.

"She didn't accept it."

"Good," Granny repeated.

Ben looked at her. Granny's face was set in a grim line. He'd seen her angry plenty of times, but never at him.

"I wanted this to work," Ben said. "I swear I did."

"She's loved you since you were kids," Granny continued, as if she hadn't heard him. "As smart as you are, Ben, you're just too stupid to see it."

"Granny," Mylie said, hurrying up to where they stood. "Did Cassie call you? She tried to call me a couple of times, and now she isn't answering."

Granny shook her head. "No, I haven't heard from her. She was mad this morning—something about having to break her plans with Allie. But she was moping in her bedroom when I left."

Mylie's eyebrows knitted together. "I hope everything is okay."

"They're weighing now!" Louise called out to them.

"I'll give her a call after they weigh," Granny said. "I'm sure she's fine."

Melissa was announcing each team as they weighed in. The first two teams had mediocre catches that Ben thought they could probably beat. Admittedly, he knew very little about the weight of fish.

"It makes you more competitive than you think, huh?" Louise whispered to him. "I can see your brain working. I agree. Ours weigh more."

Ben couldn't help but laugh. "You're right. That's what I was thinking about."

"Where's Robbie?" Mylie asked from beside Louise. "His team is up there, but he's not."

Louise shrugged. "Those fish look pretty small to me," she said. "Maybe he was embarrassed about it."

"Holy shit," Granny said, pointing to the scale. "Those fish weigh *a lot*."

They all squinted to where Robbie's team stood. It was true—their small fish did weigh quite a bit. Every fish seemed to weigh more than the last.

"That's impossible," Mylie said.

"Maybe they're bigger than they look from here," Louise offered.

Robbie's team continued to dominate as they weighed the rest of the fish caught by the other teams, including theirs. There was some murmuring through the crowd, and the judges looked uncomfortable with the obvious winner. Still, after every team's catch had been weighed, Robbie's team was the clear champion.

Everyone looked more confused than disappointed, including Mylie, who was frowning over at the winning team, sans Robbie.

"Where is he?" she asked more to herself than to Ben.

Mylie pulled her phone out of her pocket when it started to ring, a look of relief washing over her face. "It's Cassie," she said. She turned her back to talk to her sister while everyone else's attention stayed focused on the stage.

Beside him, Ben could hear Mylie's relief turn into something else entirely.

"What?" Mylie asked into the phone. "What are you talking about? I can barely hear you. Where are you? *What*? Hello? HELLO?"

Mylie pulled her phone away from her ear and stared down at it.

"What's going on?" Ben asked.

Mylie looked at him. Rather, she looked past him to the stage where Robbie's team was about to collect the trophy and their check with their winnings.

"They cheated," she whispered.

"They did what?" Granny asked, stepping closer to Mylie.

"We have to find Cassie," Mylie said. "We have to find her now."

She made to break off into a run, but Ben grabbed her arm. "Slow down," he said. "Tell us what's happening."

Mylie's eyes were wild. "I think she and Allie caught Robbie cheating," she said, her breath hitching. "And he saw them. That's all I could gather."

"Where are they?" Granny asked, panic written all over her face. "Did you get a location? She's supposed to be at home!"

Mylie shook her head. "I think she said near the bridge—Cassie's family has a hunting cabin out that way. I couldn't hear her very well, but I think that's what she said."

"We need to find the sheriff," Granny said. "I can't believe that child left after I told her not to."

"That's going to take too long," Mylie said. "Who knows where Sheriff Oakes is."

Granny moved over to where Louise and Jessica were standing and whispered something to them. They nodded and hurried off.

"They're going to find the sheriff," Granny said hurrying back to Mylie. "I told them to tell him to head out to Allie's parents' cabin."

"Where are Allie's parents?" Mylie asked.

"They're out of town," Granny replied. "I'm sure that's why those two hatched this plan. They thought nobody would figure it out."

"I'm going to go find them," Mylie said.

Granny nodded. "It'll be faster if we take the boat."

Granny and Mylie started off toward the boat with Ben trailing after them, his head spinning. Surely, he hadn't heard right.

"I'm coming with you," Ben called after them.

Mylie didn't say anything, but she grabbed his hand and squeezed it. As they made for the boat, Ben heard Jessica call for the judges and then for someone to find Sheriff Oakes. Pandemonium broke loose as people realized something was happening, but Ben didn't have time to watch.

They had to find Cassie.

Chapter 52

Mylie felt like she might vomit. Her stomach roiled as they sailed toward the trail near the bridge over the lake that led to the hunting cabin. It felt so far away. If the girls had run into Robbie, it wouldn't have been good—not after he'd been drinking on that boat all day. Not when he realized Cassie was Mylie's younger sister.

Mylie could kick herself for not being more suspicious when Robbie didn't show up at the weighing station and that she hadn't realized that small fish weighing so much was a clear sign that something wasn't right.

"We'll find them," Ben said to her. He wrapped one arm around her middle as they plowed ahead on the water.

Mylie tried to nod. It was starting to get dark. Maybe Robbie didn't know where they were. Maybe this was all a misunderstanding. That was possible, wasn't it?

"The fish were full of lead pellets," Granny said grimly.

"They checked them?" Mylie asked.

Granny nodded into the fading daylight. "I just got a text from Louise. No sign of Robbie, either. I'm going to lose reception soon."

Granny pointed ahead of them. "It's just up there," she said. She pointed to a shallow embankment ahead of them. "That cabin isn't more than a few hundred yards from there. You can't see it from the shoreline, but it's there."

Mylie took a deep breath. And then another. Ben kept her anchored there to him, and she was grateful for his warmth right then, despite anything else going on between them. Right now, nothing else mattered but finding those girls and finding them before Robbie did.

The boat was barely to shore before Mylie jumped out, her shoes hitting the water. Ben was close behind her.

"I want you to stay here and wait for the sheriff," Mylie instructed Granny.

"Like hell I will."

"Please," Mylie said, reaching out and touching her grandmother's arm.

Granny sighed. "Fine. But if I don't see you coming back with those girls in ten minutes, I'm coming up."

"Okay," Mylie said, knowing that was the best compromise she'd get out of Granny.

Mylie looked down at her cell phone. No reception. She'd never minded that before—being out in the woods or on the lake always meant spotty reception for calls and texts—but right now, it made her furious.

"Take a left at the top of the trail," Granny called after them. "You'll see it."

Mylie headed up the trail. It didn't take long to get to the top. Ben beat her by a few paces, and he waited for her at the fork so they could continue moving left. In the distance, just beyond a cluster of trees was the tiny cabin.

"Just up here," Mylie said, breathless from the hike and anticipation of finding Cassie. They had to be here. They just had to be.

"I can see it," Ben said to her. "I don't see anyone outside."

There weren't any lights on in the cabin, and Mylie scanned the area for Robbie. She didn't see him. Maybe he was gone. Maybe he hadn't found them at all. Maybe.

As they neared, Mylie heard barking.

"That's Stanley," Mylie said. "He won't let anyone get near them, especially someone he doesn't know."

She ran up the steps and tried to open the door before Ben could tell her to stop. It was locked. She shook the handle. When it didn't budge, she put her ear up to the door, straining to hear something, anything.

Mylie could hear muffled voices. She opened her mouth to yell, but Ben grabbed her arm and pulled her back.

"Don't say anything," he breathed. "He's in there with them."

Mylie's heart pounded in her chest. "How do you know?"

Ben motioned to the windows on the left-hand side of the cabin. "I saw him."

He led Mylie around to the side. She could barely see inside, but she could hear Robbie. She could hear his sneering voice, like sandpaper sliding against wood.

"I won't hurt ya," he was saying. "Come out now, girls. Let's chat."

Mylie got up on her tiptoes to get a better look. She didn't see Allie or Cassie anywhere, but she could hear Stanley's continued barking, which meant they had to be hiding in another room.

She also saw the glint of steel in Robbie's hand. It was a fish fillet knife, the kind nearly everyone in Clay Creek had, the kind of knife used to gut a fish. She sucked in air and crouched down, pulling Ben with her.

"I can go in," Ben said to her. "I can distract him while you get the girls out."

Mylie thought about it. They didn't have much time. They couldn't wait for the sheriff. If Robbie had spent all day drinking in his boat, he was at least a hundred times meaner than normal.

And if he thought Cassie and Allie had seen him cheat, that would make it even worse.

"Okay," she said at last. "If you can get in the front door, I can sneak around to the back."

Ben nodded, and Mylie slipped off around the side. There was a small window at the back, and Mylie peered inside to see Cassie and Allie huddled together, Stanley with his nose to the door, blocking where she knew Robbie stood.

She tapped on the glass as quietly as she could.

Cassie turned around and the relief on her face made Mylie all the more desperate to get them out. She motioned to the window, and Cassie hurried over.

"Can you open it?" Mylie mouthed.

Cassie tried. It cracked just enough that Mylie could wiggle her fingers through and grasp Cassie.

"It's okay," Mylie said. "Try again."

This time, both Cassie and Allie tried to open the window. It slid open enough that they could fit through, and Mylie helped them out, both girls sobbing with fear and relief. Even Stanley was able to make it through the window with all three of them helping.

Inside, Mylie could hear Ben's steady voice and the surprise in Robbie's when he realized Ben was there.

"Run around to the front and find Granny," Mylie said to them. "Be quiet. The sheriff is on his way."

Mylie ran around to the front of the house, where the door was now wide open. Granny was farther up, pointing to the cabin, while Sheriff Oakes said something into his walkie. When Granny saw them, she ran toward Cassie and Allie and gathered them into her arms. Stanley danced around them, clearly happy to be out of the cabin.

"Ben's inside," Mylie rasped, pointing toward the cabin door that now stood wide open. None of them could see inside. It was too dark, too far away.

"Stay here," the sheriff ordered. He began to stalk toward the cabin, where the voices coming from inside were getting increasingly heated.

Mylie followed him from a distance, ignoring the pleas from Granny and the girls to stay with them.

"Come on out now, Robbie," Sheriff Oakes called. "It's over."

Mylie could see Ben begin to back out, but he turned in the doorway to face the sheriff, and that's when Robbie pounced. He came at Ben like a semitruck, tackling him to the ground.

Ben writhed against him, and they fought. Robbie still had his knife and angled it toward Ben's neck as the sheriff yelled for Robbie to stop, his gun drawn.

Even from where Mylie stood, she could smell the whisky and anger wafting off Robbie and toward them, stifling them.

Ben had one hand gripped on Robbie's forearm, barely keeping the knife from slicing him. Mylie let out a yelp as it nicked Ben's neck, but Ben was faster than Robbie gave him credit for, punching Robbie in the face with his free hand.

Before any of them could stop him, Stanley had dashed inside, barking. As Robbie lay back on the wooden floor, holding his face, Stanly nipped at him.

Robbie let out a yelp and scrambled to escape, which gave Ben enough time to move away and for the sheriff to have a clean shot.

"Don't move," Sheriff Oakes said in a more authoritative voice than Mylie had ever heard. "I *will* shoot you."

Robbie spat blood onto the floor, but obeyed.

Mylie ran to Ben, kneeling down on the ground to inspect him. "Are you okay?"

Sheriff's deputies surrounded the house, but Mylie couldn't see anything other than Ben splayed out beneath her.

"I'm fine," he grunted, sitting up. There was a small trickle of blood coming from his neck. "It's just a scrape."

Stanley licked Ben's face.

"Thanks for the help, Stan the Man," Ben said.

"You're such a good boy," Mylie said to the dog, rubbing his ears. "Such a good boy."

Together they watched as Robbie was tackled and cuffed, the fillet knife kicked to the side where he lay. Behind them, there were shouts and cries of thanks from Granny and the girls. Mylie stood and helped Ben to his feet.

"I didn't do anything!" Robbie was yelling. "I didn't do anything!"

"They're going to want to check you out once we get back to town," Mylie told Ben. She slipped her hand into his. "Thank you."

Chapter 53

Ben hadn't enjoyed having the EMTs look over him, checking for signs of trauma. He was fine. The cut on his neck was nothing substantial. He wouldn't even need stitches.

Cassie and Allie were fine, too. Scared, but fine. He'd watched as Allie's mother gave Allie a stern lecture about the cabin being off-limits without adults while at the same time crying tears of relief and pulling the teenager into her, keeping her there. Her parents had been out of town near Little Rock, but they'd rushed back, and Ben alternated between watching their reunion and watching Cassie cry and apologize to Granny and Mylie. All the two older women did was wipe Cassie's tears and embrace each other, the relief over finding her and Allie unharmed cooling their anger over Cassie sneaking out.

It hadn't taken much to get the members of Robbie's fishing team to admit that they'd been stuffing their fish with weights to ensure their win over the other teams in the tournament *and* that when Robbie realized Cassie and Allie had seen them from the shore, he'd set off to find them.

Ben didn't want to think about what might have happened if they hadn't gotten there in time. At least now Robbie was being carted off to jail. It wasn't likely that he'd make bail anytime soon.

Mylie hadn't let go of his hand until he'd been pulled away by a reporter, a wiry man with black-rimmed glasses who'd been there to cover the tournament and ended up with, in his words, "something so much better."

Ben had refused an interview and wandered off to find Mylie. She was sitting at the remnants of the stage by herself, her face a mask of calm.

"Hi," he said to her.

"Hi," she replied. She looked at him, and he realized that there were tears staining her cheeks.

"Hey," he said, reaching up to wipe them away. "Don't do that. Everybody's fine."

"I know," Mylie said. "Thanks to you."

"Thanks to *us*," he corrected her.

"Well," Mylie said. "I guess this was an interesting way for you to spend one of your last nights in Clay Creek."

"I think I probably could have come up with something better," Ben replied, nudging her shoulder with his own.

Mylie laid her head on his shoulder. "Thank you," she said. "For today."

Ben folded her hand into his own. "I'm sorry," he said. "About everything."

"I wish things were simple," Mylie replied.

He wished they were, too. He wished he knew exactly what he wanted, wished he could make the right decision right then and there so that nothing ever had to feel the way he felt right now, the way he knew how *she* felt. He always thought his life plan coming together would make him feel accomplished, happy. So, why did it feel so shitty when Mylie removed her hand from his and sat up straight, leaving a space between them?

"We'll be okay, right?" Ben asked. His throat felt tight.

After a long moment, Mylie replied, "I think we have to be."

"I don't regret this," Ben said.

Mylie looked at him—really looked at him before she said, "I need you to know that I'm not scared of leaving. I'm not afraid of finding a life somewhere else. I've never been afraid. This place, all these people, are part of who I am. I like who I am, and it doesn't matter what anyone else thinks, what you think." Mylie pulled her hand away from his. "I love you, Ben. I've always loved you, but that doesn't mean I'm willing to give up the life I've built to be with you."

Ben didn't know what to say. Part of him wanted to tell her he hadn't been asking that, but another part of him knew that was exactly what he'd been asking her to do. Before he could reply or even begin to think of a response that would be enough, the crowd began to fill back in toward the stage, and Melissa waved, rushing toward them with the tournament trophy.

Finally, he said, "I understand."

There was nothing left to say, and she'd been trying to tell him that.

"I've been looking for you two," Melissa said. "We still have to announce the winners of the tournament."

Ben slid off the stage. He'd forgotten about the tournament. Mylie slid off the stage and away from him. She didn't look back.

Melissa hefted herself up onto the stage and tapped the mic. "Attention!" she called to the remaining tournament-goers. "Despite the events of the last few hours, we have to officially present the winning team with the trophy. In this case, it goes to the team with the highest weight *without* lead."

There were murmurs and a few chuckles throughout the crowd.

"That honor," Melissa continued, "goes to Hook, Line, and Sinker!"

This time, everyone cheered, and Ben felt himself being dragged up to the stage along with Mylie, Louise, and Jessica.

Louise accepted the trophy and the award check, and after a few minutes of congratulations and claps on the back, the crowd began to thin out, at last heading for home after the long, and entirely surprising, day.

Ben returned home to darkness. It was still warm out, but the house felt chilly. It was as if it sensed what he was about to do and rebelled against it, but he didn't think he could stay the two more days he was scheduled to stay before leaving for the coast. This house was better suited for a family, people to fill it up with love and happiness—not someone who couldn't even admit to the woman he loved that he loved her. Not someone who couldn't take a risk for the sake of his own fucking heart.

They were friends. They'd always be friends, but it was time to go, to let go. He'd pack up tonight. He'd leave, and he wouldn't spend another day in Clay Creek.

Chapter 54

Ben was gone the next morning. Mylie had expected it. She didn't know why or how she knew he'd be gone, but she did. She stared at the FOR SALE sign in the yard, with the bright white UNDER CONTRACT placed at the top, and refused to cry. She wouldn't think about how she'd told him she loved him and that he hadn't said it back. She wouldn't think about him again.

It was over.

Chapter 55

Clay Creek was quiet again. The tourists and fishermen who'd descended upon the town for the tournament were all but gone, and now the only thing left to do was wait for the next wave of people, who would make this place their home come July.

It had always been Granny's favorite time of year—the quiet just before the storm. It was busy, with everyone working to make it as appealing as they could. The shops downtown repainted their storefronts, they made sure the lights on their signs worked, and everyone was in a good mood.

The older woman looked at her two grandchildren as they ate their breakfasts, a solemn silence filling the space between them. Cassie had mostly recovered from the events of the evening of the tournament, but she'd rotated between Granny's bed and Mylie's for the last two weeks. Granny didn't mind. She never minded, and Cassie had accepted her one-month grounding without complaint. In fact, she'd seemed relieved to be banned from going anywhere. Perhaps she'd had enough adventure for the moment.

But it was Mylie who made Granny worry. Mylie, who seemed as if a spark had dimmed inside of her. Lord, she could kick that Lawrence kid for hurting her.

Mylie looked up at Granny and gave her a small smile. "I'm fine, Granny. Stop worrying."

"I know you are," Granny replied, trying and failing to believe the words. "What do you have planned today?"

Mylie shrugged. "Work," she said. "But I was hoping maybe you two would like to go out to dinner in Rockbridge tonight. We can go to that pizza place Cassie loves so much."

Cassie's eyes lit up. "Yes!"

"Sounds good to me." Granny cleared the breakfast plates. "We'll be ready when you get home from work."

Mylie left the house seemingly lighter, and Cassie took herself up to her room. Granny sat down on her bed, trying to work up the energy to vacuum. She knew she'd slowed down a bit over the years, but she often reminded herself that she was still up and at 'em with the chickens on most days.

She looked over at the picture of her late husband. He'd died before either Mylie or Allie were born. Sometimes she wondered if his death when their daughter had been just five years old was the cause for the brokenness in her, in both of them. Violet Mason had loved that man with her whole heart, and when she'd lost him, it took a long time to wake up in the morning without wanting to join him.

It hadn't always been easy living with him, either. He was temperamental, but then again, so was she. It always made her smile to think of the way he'd proposed to her, late one evening after an argument about a flat tire. She'd changed it herself, instead of allowing him to do it for her, and he'd paced back and forth on the side of the road until he couldn't take it anymore and declared, "Well, Violet, will you ever let me ask you to marry you, or do you plan to propose to your own damn self?"

She'd looked up at him, covered in dust and her red hair flying in all directions, and replied, "I reckon I'll let you do it, Jim, if you're so inclined."

And that had been it. They'd married two months later and eventually settled into this house. She fingered the floral bedspread with a hand that looked older than she felt and missed that man as much as she'd allowed herself to miss him in years.

It was the reason, as much as she enjoyed Morris, that she'd never remarried. Violet had room for only one man in her heart, and he'd been gone nearly as long as he'd been alive. She hoped that Mylie wasn't like her in that respect.

She'd never cared if Mylie got married, and she hadn't asked Mylie to stay here and help raise Cassie, although some part of her always knew she would. That was just Mylie. It was who she was at her core, and although Granny sometimes worried that she and Cassie held Mylie back, she knew it wasn't true. Mylie made her own decisions. Always had if her choice in Ben Lawrence were any indication.

But Granny saw the way Ben looked at Mylie. They'd been looking at each other like that since the sixth grade. It was the way she and Jim had looked at each other, and Violet Mason had always thought that one day, Mylie and Ben would end up together, even as the years went on and it seemed less and less likely.

When Ben came back and she watched the two of them reconnect, it felt right—like it was meant to be. Granny sighed and got up, making for the hallway closet where the vacuum was stored. She'd think on it as she cleaned, and maybe the hurt in her heart would ease a bit. Maybe there was still hope yet.

Chapter 56

The campus was absolutely beautiful. It looked like the kind of place Ben had always thought he'd end up—with lush, full trees and perfectly manicured grass. Although the spring term was over and the summer term had only just begun, students filled the sidewalks and gathered in the common areas.

Ben looked down at his campus map. The economics department was just ahead. It was a solemn-looking building of gray stone. He smiled at a few students as he took the steps two at a time.

There was a secretary sitting at a desk in the front office of the department head, furiously typing on a keybaord. She barely looked up when Ben entered, motioning for him to have a seat.

"Dr. Baker will be with you shortly," she said.

Ben sat, clutching his satchel to his chest. Knowing that the job was his didn't make him any less nervous. The last time he taught a class was when he was a TA, and it had been freshman-level economics.

"Dr. Lawrence." A man with a head of steel-gray hair and a mustache to match stood in the doorway of the office beyond the secretary. "Come on in."

Ben got up, smiled at the secretary who didn't even bother to look up at him, and followed Dr. Baker into his office.

"It's nice to see you again," Dr. Baker said, gesturing to Ben to have a seat. "I'm thrilled you're here."

"Me, too, sir," Ben replied, sitting down. This time, he lay his satchel on the floor next to his seat.

"Everyone on the hiring committee thinks you're the best candidate for the job," Dr. Baker said, opening a blue file folder on his desk. "Your list of publications is impressive, and we've gotten excellent references from your former professors."

"That's good to hear," Ben said.

"And I think you'll love the city," Dr. Baker continued. "I've been an old married man for a long time, but I hear the nightlife is wonderful for a young, single man such as yourself."

"That sounds great," Ben replied, but the words rung hollow in his ears.

There wasn't anything Ben wanted less than to spend his time after work going out and meeting new people. Once, not so long ago, both of those things would have been exciting. He'd spent years envisioning his life this way—in a new job, in a new life. It had been his singular goal for so long, and he was furious that he could no longer make himself rise to the occasion. For the first time in a long time, it felt like he didn't know who he was—who he was supposed to be.

"Dr. Lawrence?"

Ben blinked. He hadn't heard a word of what the other man was saying. "I'm sorry," he said. "I must be more jet-lagged than I thought."

The older man smiled. "That's all right, son. Why don't I show you around the department, introduce you to a few people who weren't on the committee? It just occurred to me that your interview was virtual, and you haven't actually seen the campus."

Ben stood up, grateful for the distraction. "I'd love that," he said.

He spent the next couple of hours parading around the economics department, shaking hands with future colleagues, and learning about a few things he'd need to remember for the fall semester—don't park on the east end of campus. It's nice and shaded, but your car will be covered in bird poop when you leave. Always keep a jacket in your office during the winter because the buildings are freezing. Don't ask IT for anything unless it's an emergency. Buy your own office chair. The words washed over Ben, and by the time he was done, it was nearly time to meet the Realtor he'd hired to help him find an apartment.

An official offer was made, and he was left with a copy of a contract and instructions to return it as soon as he could. It hadn't escaped Ben that Dr. Baker seemed a little disappointed he hadn't signed it right then and there, but Ben had said he wanted to read over it in more detail when he was alone. Dr. Baker had accepted this. After all, economics professors were nothing if not shrewd.

By the end of the day, he was sitting in a café not far from the university with a copy of a contract and a copy of a lease laid out in front of him when a harried waitress brought him coffee.

"Can I get ya anything else?" she asked, pen poised to take an order.

"No, thank you," Ben said. "I'm good."

She nodded and walked away.

Ben nearly laughed. Not because anything was really that funny, but he'd become used to knowing every single person he encountered these last few weeks. He never would have been able to get out of a conversation that easily at the Cracked Egg. But hadn't this been one of the reasons he enjoyed city life? He could go anywhere and be anonymous. There was never anyone in Chicago or a city like this asking about his day or wanting to know about his love life.

So, why did he find himself missing it?

The papers on the table loomed before him, a reminder of the decisions he had to make. There was an apartment less than a block from here, so close to campus that he could walk or bike if he wanted to. It was nice, and incredibly, it was also affordable. He wouldn't have trouble making the rent, not with the salary offered on the contract.

He thought about the house in Clay Creek. Selling it would give him a nest egg. In a few years, he could buy a house of his own once he decided if he wanted to stay here and teach or wander somewhere else, and while he would have traded that money to have his grandfather and his mother back in a heartbeat, he couldn't deny that everything was falling into place.

Still, Ben couldn't bring himself to sign either piece of paper. Every time he began to search his satchel for a pen, he started to feel sick to his stomach. Signing, making any kind of a decision about this life, meant the end of something else, the end of another type of life. Granted, it was a life he hadn't yet started. It was the *idea* of this life that he couldn't shake, couldn't stop thinking about.

For so long, he'd had this idea about what his life should be. He'd spent years planning everything down to the last letter. He'd been unwilling to stop long enough to consider other options, but the weeks he'd spent in Clay Creek had caused those plans to crack. And now he was sitting here wondering if leaving there, leaving Mylie, had been the worst mistake of his life.

Ben took a sip of the coffee that had long since gone cold. He caught the waitress's eye, and she came over.

"Need a refill?" she asked.

"Yes, please," Ben replied.

"Can I get you anything else?"

Ben picked up the menu. "Do you have any recommendations?"

The waitress brought the tip of her pen to her mouth. "Hmm . . . it depends on what you're in the mood for."

"I don't know what I . . ." Ben trailed off as a crash sounded from somewhere behind them. The waitress turned to watch as a busboy scrambled for a pile of dishes that now lay on the floor in pieces.

"I'm sorry," the waitress said, turning back to him. "What did you want?"

The menu blurred in front of him. What *did* he want? Certainly nothing from the menu. There was an emptiness sitting in the pit of his stomach that he didn't think anything in this café could satisfy. It didn't really matter that his coffee was cold, or what he ordered to eat. It didn't matter whether he signed this contract in front of him, or found an apartment, or made friends with the locals. Nothing that he did, nothing he said, nothing at all mattered without the one person he wanted to share it with.

Ben sat back in his chair, the realization of it all washing over him like a tidal wave.

He knew.

He knew what he wanted. It had been in front of him the whole time, and he was so damn stubborn, so stupidly confident that he hadn't allowed himself to see it. How could he have been so blind?

"I think I'll just take the check," Ben said, staring up at the waitress who was looking down at him, confused.

Was it too late? Had he ruined everything? He didn't know, but for once in his life, he was going to take a risk.

Chapter 57

Hook, Line, & Sinker closed for a week in June after the tournament. It was a tradition they'd started the first year in the warehouse, to give everyone time to get ready for the tourist season. The tournament was always one of its major sources of income, and so it seemed only fair after everyone worked so hard to give them some time off.

"What are you going to do next week?" Jodi asked Mylie on the Friday before they closed. "I think Jared and I may spend a couple of days in Little Rock."

"That sounds fun," Mylie said. "I haven't been to Little Rock in forever."

"You should come with us," Jodi offered.

Mylie shook her head. "You and Jared should take some time for yourselves," she said. "I don't want to be the third wheel."

"Jared's the third wheel," Jodi replied, grinning.

Mylie laughed and was surprised how good it felt. Cassie was starting to get restless, and Granny was hovering over both of them like they were broken birds. Mylie hated the thought of Granny worrying about her. It had been a long time since she felt like a burden to her grandmother. She wasn't aching to go back to it.

Besides, Mylie was *fine*. Sure, it was hard to look out at his empty house every morning when she left for work. But soon enough, the new neighbors would move in. She hoped her first impression of them had been wrong. They were probably lovely people. And maybe, when the house was finally occupied by someone else, it would feel less like Ben's house. Maybe the wounds she'd been picking at would finally heal.

"So?" Jodi asked. "Do you want to go with us?"

"It sounds fun," Mylie said. "But I think I'm going to stay here and hang out with Cassie. You know she can't leave the house right now except to go somewhere with me or Granny. She's about to lose her mind."

"I can't believe Granny didn't ground her forever."

"That seemed a bit unreasonable," Mylie replied, a small grin forming in one corner of her mouth. "Allie's grounded, too. She's not even allowed to use her phone. I can't imagine how that would have felt at fourteen."

"Remember when my mom caught us out on the pontoon?" Jodi asked. "What were we, fifteen? God, she still talks about it. I'd never been in so much trouble."

"I remember," Mylie said. "You lost your dad's anchor, and we had to pay for a new one."

"Now the lake owns it," Jodi said wistfully.

"The lake owns everything," Mylie replied.

"Speaking of the lake . . . and the tournament," Jodi began.

"We weren't talking about the tournament," Mylie said.

"Well, anyway," Jodi continued. "Do you want to talk?"

"About what?" Mylie replied, even though she knew exactly what Jodi meant.

"Mylie," Jodi said. "You haven't said anything about Ben since he left. You haven't cried, you haven't screamed, you haven't said a word. It's honestly terrifying."

Mylie placed her hands on her desk, palms down. "There isn't anything to talk about."

"I disagree."

"Nothing will change it," Mylie tried again. "No amount of crying or screaming will change it."

"Sometimes it just feels good to do it," Jodi offered.

"I don't want to," Mylie said simply. "He made his decision."

"Did you think you could change his mind?" Jodi asked.

"No," Mylie said. Honestly, she hadn't thought she could change his mind. She thought he might change his mind on his own, but she never thought *she* would be the one to change it. "I just thought we had more time."

"So, he just left *again* without saying goodbye?" Jodi replied. "He didn't even ask you to go with him?"

"He asked me," Mylie said. "I told him no."

Jodi's brow furrowed. "Why?"

"It wouldn't work," Mylie replied. "I don't want to spend years going back and forth when I know that he's never going to be happy here. He's never going to want the same life that I do."

"Is the life he wants so bad?" Jodi asked.

"It's just not my life."

"I love you," Jodi replied. "And I will always support your decisions. But I don't want you to throw something important away because you're being stubborn."

"I'm not being stubborn."

"Aren't you?"

"Ten years ago, you let Ben go," Jodi said.

"He let me go, too," Mylie said.

"You're both idiots," Jodi replied. "But you don't have to be an idiot now."

Mylie sighed. "I'm not trying to be an idiot," she said. This conversation was making her tired.

"I know," Jodi said. "Listen, please come with us to Little Rock.

It'll give you a chance to clear your head. Get out of town. Maybe you'll get some clarity."

"I'll think about it," Mylie said.

"You've got a lot to think about," Jodi said, standing up and collecting her things to leave. "I'll call you later, and you can let me know what you've decided."

"About Little Rock?"

Jodi shrugged. "About anything."

Emily Lawrence waited for Granny to walk down to the dock that evening. Granny was chaos embodied, but she did have a routine. She often sat on the dock at night and read a book. Emily watched as the older woman exited her house, book in hand and an unlit cigarette in her mouth. She waited a few minutes and then left her own house, making her way down to the lake.

"I saw you watching me from your window," Granny said before Emily had a chance to say anything.

"How do you do that?" Emily asked.

"I have many talents" was all Granny said. She motioned for Emily to sit in the Adirondack chair next to her.

Emily sat down and stared at the lake in front of her. She'd never liked the lake. She didn't like any body of water that she couldn't see the bottom of. She didn't like the way it waited there, dark and cool, lurking in every corner of the town. When she'd told her father that, he'd laughed and called her a worrywart. Maybe she was.

"Did you come out here to chat or glare at the water?" Granny asked.

Emily sighed. "I guess you know we're moving back to Chicago after Benjamin's graduation."

"I've heard," Granny replied.

"I took a teaching job back at my old school," Emily continued.

"Clay Creek's not quite as fancy as the private school," Granny said. She didn't look away from her book, but Emily saw the smirk on the other woman's face.

"You know, Granny . . ." Emily said. Granny looked over at Emily in surprise. She'd always refused to call her Granny and insisted on using her given name, Violet. "I don't think I'm too good for this place."

"Oh, no?" Granny asked.

Emily shook her head. "No. And I don't think my son is too good, either."

This time, Granny looked at Emily. "That's a mighty fine thing to say now that you've ensured he's going to college halfway across the country."

"That's always been his plan," Emily said. "I support him, always, just like I know you support Mylie."

"That I do," Granny replied.

"We both want what's best for them," Emily said, her voice quiet.

"I don't always know what's best for Mylie," Granny admitted. "That girl is so determined to carve her own path."

"She's headstrong," Emily agreed. "But I like that."

"You're alike in some ways," Granny said, giving Emily a smile. "Both of you want your own way all of the time."

Emily huffed a laugh. "I just wanted you to know, before I left, that I am so glad the Mason women are our neighbors. I couldn't have picked a better friend for Benjamin if I tried."

"Mylie is going to miss him," Granny said, reaching out to take Emily's hand. "We'll miss you both."

"We aren't going to sell the house," Emily said, wiping a tear from the corner of one eye. "I've decided to keep it for now . . . just in case."

"In case what?" Granny asked.

"In case," Emily said, giving Granny a knowing smile, "Benjamin ever comes to his senses."

Chapter 59

Ben had never particularly enjoyed driving. He liked driving a U-Haul on two-lane country roads less. He'd called Courtney from that little café and told her he couldn't go through with the house sale. She'd been furious, reminding him how hard she'd worked for him, her commission, blah, blah, blah. He'd placated her only by promising that if he ever did decide to sell, he wouldn't use anyone else, *and* that he'd give her a larger commission.

"I didn't really think you'd go through with it, anyway," Courtney had said before she hung up. Her comment wasn't malicious. She'd said it as a matter of fact. "None of us did."

Ben hadn't asked who "us" was. He wasn't sure he wanted to know. That had been nearly a week ago. Since that time, he'd flown back to Chicago, rented a U-Haul, gone to the storage facility he'd rented after his mother died, and loaded everything up.

He hadn't told Courtney he was coming back home, just that he hadn't wanted to sell. *Home*, Ben thought to himself. That's what the house was. That's what Clay Creek was. More than anything, that's what Mylie was. He'd felt that bond between them stretch thinner and thinner the farther away he got from her. He hadn't been able to feel her in that city, and he realized that if he stayed, he'd never feel her again. He'd severed the invisible string once, and he never wanted to live that way again.

Ben pulled into the gas station just outside of Clay Creek and went inside.

"I need seventy-five dollars on pump eight," he said to the cashier, handing over his credit card.

The cashier eyed him. "I heard you left town," she said.

"Well, I'm back," Ben replied.

"Mmmhmm," the woman said, swiping the card.

Ben signed the receipt she gave him and handed it back to her. "Thanks," he said. "Oh, and Margie?"

The woman stared at him.

"I'd appreciate it if you'd let me get out of the parking lot before you start calling people."

Chapter 60

Mylie stared down at her suitcase, trying to figure out what to pack. If she was going to make it to Little Rock to catch her plane, she was going to have to hurry. She considered calling Ben, talking it out. But she was afraid she'd lose her nerve. It would be too easy to hang up, to not say anything at all. If she was in front of him, though . . . she wouldn't be able to escape it.

Even now, she wasn't sure what she wanted to say. All she knew was that the last couple of weeks had been the most miserable of her life. Maybe once she saw him, she would figure out what to say. All she'd done so far was decide she had to go.

It had been the day Courtney came to the house next door and ripped out the FOR SALE sign in the yard. She figured that meant the new owners were getting ready to move in. Something inside of her pulled taught and snapped.

Jodi promised to take care of the shop while she was gone. Her eyes lit up when Mylie told her the plan. "I hoped you'd go," she'd said.

Telling Granny and Cassie had been more difficult, but to her surprise, they reacted much the same way Jodi had.

"How long will you be gone?" Granny asked.

"I don't know," Mylie replied. "I took two weeks from work. But depending on how things go, it could be less."

"I doubt that," Granny said.

"How do you even know where he is?" Cassie asked.

"I know what city he's in. I know what university he's working for," Mylie said. "But I'm going to call him. I promise I won't show up to his workplace like a stalker."

"Sounds romantic to me," Cassie replied.

Mylie was grateful that her family and friends were so supportive. It was the only reason she had the confidence to do this—to take this leap. For her whole life, she'd known that her life was here, in Clay Creek, and she'd always thought that meant everything about her life should have to exist here, too. But maybe, just maybe, she could have something, someone, who existed outside of that.

Mylie packed the last of her clothes and was starting on her toiletries when she heard a shriek from downstairs.

"What is it?" Mylie yelled.

"Stanley escaped!" Cassie yelled.

Mylie went downstairs and outside onto the porch, where Granny and Cassie were scanning the yard for Stanley.

"He just started running down the road," Granny said, throwing her arms up in the air. "Damn dog."

"I was trying to put his leash on," Cassie explained to Mylie. "But the second I got ready to clip it, he bolted."

"Maybe he saw Fat Tony," Mylie replied.

"If I were Fat Tony," Cassie said. "I'd probably want to be as far away from the new neighbors as possible."

"Don't worry about that," Granny replied. "I think our new neighbors will be just fine with keeping Fat Tony around."

There was a twinkle in Granny's eye that Mylie didn't quite understand.

Down the road, they could hear Stanley barking, his form appearing and disappearing as he ran back and forth from their line of vision.

"Is he chasing something?" Mylie asked.

"I think I hear a car," Cassie replied. "He's going to get run over!"

All three women hurried off the porch, calling to Stanley as they walked. The noise from the vehicle became louder and louder until they could see it—an orange-and-white U-Haul truck beating its way down the street. Stanley was running along beside it.

The U-Haul stopped, idling in the middle of the road. Mylie lurched forward, hoping to catch Stanley and force him back inside so the neighbors could pull into their driveway. This wasn't making for very good neighborly relations if the poor people couldn't even get to their house without Stanley getting in their way.

The driver's side door of the U-Haul swung open, and Mylie prepared herself to apologize.

"I'm so . . ." The words caught in Mylie's throat when she saw the man jump down from the van—not a new neighbor at all, but an old one—Dr. Benjamin Lawrence.

Chapter 61

Mylie stood there, struck dumb. He was *here*. He was right here in front of her, his hands slid casually into his pants pockets, a crooked smile playing at his lips.

"What," she managed to ask, "are you doing here?"

The man before her shrugged. "I live here."

Mylie couldn't breathe. "You what?"

Ben held out his hands. "Let's play a game."

Mylie stared at him. "What?"

Ben kept his hands extended, staring at her until she placed hers under his. "What are you doing here?" she asked.

Ben jerked his head toward his house and said, "I live here."

"No, you don't," Mylie replied. She couldn't make her brain work, couldn't figure out if she was imagining what she was seeing.

"My turn," Ben said. "Did you miss me?"

Mylie didn't take her eyes off of his. "Yes," she said. "What about your job?"

"My job is at Rockbridge Community College," Ben replied. "Which reminds me, I need to call Melissa and thank her."

"I don't understand."

Ben closed the distance between them. "I'm here," he said. "I'm here, and I'm not leaving. Clay Creek is my home . . . *you're* my home, Mylie."

"I was coming to find you," Mylie whispered as he wrapped his arms around her waist.

"You what?" Ben asked.

"I was coming to see you," Mylie repeated. "I bought a plane ticket. I was packing when Stanley . . . I guess he knew it was you."

Ben released Mylie and reached down to pat the panting dog's head. "Thanks for the vote of confidence, Stan the Man."

Mylie grinned. She didn't know if she would ever stop grinning.

"You were coming to find me?" Ben asked her. "You bought a plane ticket?"

Mylie nodded. "I didn't, I don't, want to lose you."

"It'll be pretty hard to lose me in a town this small," Ben quipped.

"You gave it up," Mylie said. "For me? Your job? Your plans?"

"It doesn't make sense without you," Ben said. He leaned down and kissed her, his lips gentle. "Nothing makes sense without you."

Chapter 62

Morris stared down into the grill, concern knitting his eyebrows. "You think these steaks are ready to come off, son?"

Ben put his hand on Morris's back. "I don't think just yet."

Mylie leaned over to Granny and whispered, "How many times is he going to ask that question?"

"Until he's satisfied that he's in charge," Granny replied.

It was the last BBQ of the summer. It wouldn't be long before the balmy evenings would turn cool, and the lake would go back to its natural state without the boats, Jet Skis, and fishing poles. The months since Ben's return had been nothing short of a whirlwind.

Mylie was glad for the slower pace, even if old Morris hadn't changed a bit. She watched Ben and smiled. She almost couldn't believe it. He was here, with her, and everything felt right.

"I'm bored," Cassie said, and leaned back in her chair. "And I'm hot." She reached down and scratched Stanley's ears.

"You're fine," Mylie replied, rolling her eyes. She watched as Cassie fed Stanley a piece of a potato chip.

"How come you get to have your *boyfriend* here, but I don't get to?" Cassie asked.

"Because we're at *my boyfriend's house*," Mylie replied.

"It's your house, now, too," Cassie said.

Mylie grinned. It was true. She'd finally finished moving in the rest of her things that morning. They'd spent most of the summer remodeling the kitchen and master bedroom in preparation for Mylie's inevitable move.

"I tell you what," Mylie said to her sister. "Ben and I will have you and your new boyfriend over for a movie one day next week. Give Granny and Morris some alone time."

Cassie thought it over. "Okay," she said finally. "And then I can spend the night?"

"And then you can spend the night," Mylie agreed.

Cassie got up and herded Stanley off the back porch and into the yard. Ben passed her on his way to Mylie, and Cassie punched his arm.

"I'm letting Morris take control," Ben said to Mylie and Granny.

Granny shot Mylie a knowing look.

"Let's go inside and grab more chips," Mylie said to Ben. "I'm pretty sure Cassie has single-handedly eaten them all."

"Bring me a beer!" Granny called after them.

"I don't think we have any more chips," Ben said, once they got inside.

"I know," Mylie said with a grin. "I just wanted to get you alone."

Ben tugged at the band of her jeans shorts and pulled her into him. "How long do you think we have?"

"I'd say about thirty seconds before Morris needs the meat thermometer," Mylie quipped.

Ben laughed and then leaned down to kiss her. "This has been the best summer of my life," he said.

"Mine, too," Mylie replied, kissing him back. "Mine, too."

Acknowledgments

Priya Doraswamy: For everything. Absolutely everything.

Lucia Macro: For nearly a decade of editing my work, and now, a wonderful friendship.

Ariana Sinclair: For taking this book on and always being so kind.

Matt & Jude: For loving me despite all my mess.

Dad: For feeding the raccoons!

Mom: For letting Dad feed the raccoons!

Annie England Noblin lives with her son, husband, and three dogs in the Missouri Ozarks. She graduated with an MA in creative writing from Missouri State University and currently teaches English and communications at Arkansas State University in Mountain Home, Arkansas. She spends her free time playing make-believe, feeding stray cats, and working with animal shelters across the country to save homeless dogs.

Discover more from
Annie England Noblin

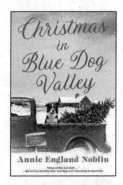
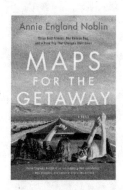

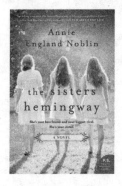